AETHER BOUND

THE RISE OF LILITH - BOOK 1

WonderCon 2023

MEGAN HASKELL

ISBN (Paperback) 978-1-950307-06-7
ISBN (eBook) 978-1-950307-05-0
ISBN (Audiobook) 978-1-950307-15-9

Published by Trabuco Ridge Press
22365 El Toro Road #129
Lake Forest, CA 92630

Edited by Kim Peticolas
Cover Design by MoorBooks Design

CHAPTER I

A tray clattered onto the bar, stacked glasses rattling and crumpled cocktail napkins spilling across the polished wood.

"Hey Lil! Six Blow Jobs, plus a whiskey with whipped cream for me," Virginia grinned as she moved the dirties off her tray and into the dish bucket. "Gotta show 'em how it's done."

I chuckled as I poured the Rum Runner I'd been shaking into a glass and dropped a fruit skewer and parasol on top.

"Another bachelorette party? Isn't this the third one tonight?"

"'Tis the season!"

I pushed the fruity drink across the bar to the frat boy who'd just graduated. If he hadn't already told me his entire life story in a drunken slur, the Greek letters tattooed on his shoulder would have given him away.

"Add it to the tab!" he shouted over the blast of a trumpet. He slid a single across the sticky counter. "But this ish for you." He almost tipped his drink over.

"Thanks!" I forced a smile, but didn't bother pulling the sodden bill from the counter. My hands were already setting out the shot glasses for the ladies with the pink sparkly sashes and sloppy smiles.

"They're always so optimistic, and yet always underperform," Virginia took care of the dollar bill for me, putting it in the tip jar shaped like a grinning skull being swallowed by the Kraken. "Too bad really. He's kinda cute in a puppy dog sorta way."

I poured the Kahlua into the glasses with one hand as I shook the can of whipped cream with the other. "Have fun. Not my type."

"That's right. You prefer the soulful artistic type. Like a certain trombone player, maybe?"

I couldn't help glancing at the bandstand in the corner. Silas was blasting a solo into the noise of tonight's crowd, the brass bell of his horn lifted high into the air.

"Too loud," I replied. "Flashy." I slid the foamy shots toward Virginia and she quickly arranged them on her tray. "And that hat! I mean, really?"

Silas loved this ratty old gray fedora that he wore propped at an angle on his head. It was ugly as sin. It was so ugly, it was kinda cute—not that I'd ever admit it to him or anyone else.

Virginia shot me an incredulous half smile. The vaguely serpent-shaped pink cloud that wrapped her neck shifted and stuck out its tongue as if tasting the air. "Deny it all you want, but he's a hottie and the tension between the two of you is . . ." she waved a hand toward her face and blew a lock of hair out of her eyes. "I mean, I don't know how you sleep at night!"

I wiggled my fingers in the direction of the bachelorettes. "Go show them how to have a good time and stop bugging me. I'm busy." I wasn't sure if I was talking to Virginia, or the demon draped over her shoulder. But since no one else could see it, I was careful to make sure my comments wouldn't raise any eyebrows. Luckily, it turned its attention away from me and toward the ladies she would be serving.

I turned to the next customer at the bar, a middle-aged woman wearing clothes designed for someone half her age. She was trying to get Ty's attention, even though he was halfway down the bar with a crowd of admirers, and I was standing right in front of her.

I leaned forward, making sure she could hear me. "What can I get'cha?"

She hardly glanced at me, her eyes all for Ty's pretty boy looks and flair with the bottles. My partner behind the bar was a performer, entertaining the crowd nearly as well as Silas's band. He was always a favorite with the ladies, and we kept him in the middle station so that his audience could spread out and more people could watch.

"How about one of those?" She pressed her lips into a sultry pout and leaned farther onto the bar, angling her chest toward her target.

I glanced around the crowded bar, looking for a better match for her. "Ty's a bit tied up—"

"I'd like to tie him up myself," the woman interrupted as she rested her chin on the heel of her hand.

Quick. She was a wit. Or thought she was. I may have gagged in the back of my throat a bit, but I made sure to keep it off my expression. She was here for a good time, the yellow demon on her shoulder whispering to her of lost youth and second chances. If I had to guess, I would have pegged her as a recent divorcée who needed a one-night stand and no regrets in the morning. She was good-looking—probably an early trophy wife who'd been dismissed for the latest model. A touch too much Botox, a bit high maintenance, but still young enough to be a tempting conquest for a younger man. I had just the ticket.

I started mixing up another Rum Runner. "Like I said, Ty's working, but I bet if you take this over to the cute guy in the muscle tee over there," I pointed to frat boy's table, "you might find exactly what you're looking for."

Divorcée shifted to check out the frat boy's table. There were four of them, all wearing neon board shorts and tank tops. Frat boy had the best muscles of the group, but the others weren't bad either. One of them had a dimple on his cheek that would have made Zac Efron jealous. I imagined any or all would do for her just fine.

She hummed appreciatively as she surveyed the younger men. "You might be right."

"If I'm wrong, your next drink's on me. If not," I shook the tip jar and lifted an eyebrow to make my point.

The yellow demon took the bait, pulling her toward the boys. "If you're right, I'll double your bet."

Since the fruity drinks we served up weren't cheap, that was a pretty good payout. Especially since I knew I'd win. Frat boy was already opening the table to her. She wiggled her hips in a little two-step to the beat and set the drink down.

I grinned. Frat boy was going to have his hands full with that one. My eyes drifted back to the bandstand again. Silas was singing now, a poppy tune about the rhythm of the beach in the summertime. It was a good night. Busy. Just the way I liked it. Less time to think and make mistakes.

I glanced out the open window toward the ocean waves that could just be heard between sets when traffic wasn't too busy. The moon was out and full, the sky clear. I wiped down the counter in front of me.

A woman slid into a narrow gap between a busty blonde and a heavyset guy wearing a Hawaiian shirt. Her hair was a wild mass of graying curls barely held back with a long flower-patterned scarf that tied around her head and draped over one shoulder. A lifetime of laughter hid behind twinkling blue-gray eyes and deep within the lines of her face. She wasn't our usual clientele, to be sure, but she didn't carry a demon on her shoulder, so she was here by her own choice. And sometimes the older crowd was the most interesting to serve.

"What'll you have?" I asked.

"A storm is coming," she replied. Her voice warbled slightly, but I could still hear her easily enough over the sound of the band starting their next song.

I frowned, wracking my brain as I set a cocktail napkin in front of her. "Afraid I don't know that one. Is it like a Fog Cutter?"

She shook her head. "I know who you are and what you can do. You won't be able to hide much longer."

I sucked in a startled breath, but before I could flinch away, she grabbed the flower-topped pen from the bun in my hair and started doodling on the napkin.

"I don't know what you're talking about." She couldn't possibly know about my little gift. I'd been careful. None of my coworkers knew anything about the demons or my visions. If they found out, I'd be fired—or worse.

My eyes were drawn to the little white square and the old lady's drawing. Two crescent moons mirrored each other on either side of a circle. The center was filled with what looked like a lower-case letter "h" with three crosses attached.

"Your abilities are growing stronger. They'll come for you soon." Her tongue poked out of the corner of her mouth as she retraced the design, making the lines heavy with ink.

Goosebumps prickled across the back of my neck. I glanced toward the bouncer at the door. Carlos was sitting in his chair checking IDs. He'd come running if I called, but the little old lady didn't seem particularly dangerous. A nutter maybe, but not threatening. I hoped.

She gazed at me with clear eyes and pushed the finished drawing toward me. "It's your birthright. A gift that comes with responsibility."

"Listen, lady, I'm happy to make you a drink, and you can doodle all you want, but you don't know anything about me or my *birthright*." My childhood was my business and no one else's. I tugged on the cuffs of my long-sleeved Hawaiian shirt to cover the scar on my forearm.

Her smile was kind, but pitying. "Do not reject who you are, young sister. Your time has come." She pressed the napkin forward again. "You're going to need this."

A male shout and a few female screams drew all eyes to the far side of the bar, near our third bartender and backup bouncer, Bruce. Bruce was part Samoan and looked like a smaller version of The Rock . . . if you squinted your eyes a little. Usually no one wanted to mess with him, which is why he was stationed farthest from the door. The man was a teddy bear, always ready with a smile. That is, until a punch was going to be thrown. Then all bets were off. He could pound heads with the best of them.

Bruce flipped up the gate at the end of the counter and stomped his way out into the crowd. I couldn't see what was going on between the customers, but ephemeral lightning flashed between hulking blue-gray demons that only I could see. The spirits growled and hissed, urging their hosts to violence.

"Carlos!" I shouted, calling in reinforcements from the front door. Bruce could slow things down, but the bouncers would eject the troublemakers in a heartbeat. It's what they were paid to do. I needn't have worried though. He and his partner, James, were already pushing their way through the crowd to Bruce. Within minutes, Bruce was back behind the bar, and the two bouncers were shoving a couple of biker-looking guys in black leather jackets toward the front door. A woman followed behind, mascara smeared beneath her eyes, ruining her other-wise perfectly coiffed rockabilly style.

"Cyclists," I joked as I turned back toward the old lady with the frizzy hair. "Always getting into trouble."

The woman was gone.

I scanned the room, but she was nowhere to be seen. One of

the frat boys stood in her place, the one with the dimple. "Another Rum Runner. And if you've gots another friend hide'n somewhere, shend her my way, wouldja?"

The napkin lay on the counter beneath his hand. I don't know what made me do it, but I surreptitiously slid it away and shoved it in my pocket.

"I'll keep an eye out."

CHAPTER 2

Iwas counting out the tips at the end of the night when a trombone case thumped onto the bar.

"Crazy night, eh?" Silas asked.

The rest of his band was standing around chatting with the servers, Virginia and Gabi, as they packed up the last of the gear. The two women had already wiped down the tables and flipped the chairs on top so the barback, Ferghus, could mop the floor later. They were only waiting for me to divvy up the tips and they'd be out of there.

"Yeah, crazy." I thought of the napkin in my pocket. Ever since that woman had disappeared, I'd had a sense of dark foreboding, like her words were prophetic or something. I could usually identify the crazy and ignore it, even pacify it, but something had been different with this one. Despite her wild hair and bohemian outfit, she hadn't seemed mentally deranged. Her eyes had been unclouded, her words clear. She hadn't even had a demon on her shoulder. Yet something about her niggled at the back of my mind.

Silas rubbed his thumb across the polished wood. "The

band's heading over to the old barn. Gabi and Virginia are coming. Maybe Ty. Feel like joining us?"

My skin heated. I couldn't meet his gaze. I stared down at the money in my hands. Silas was sweet. And Virginia wasn't wrong; he was hot in a nerdy band-geek kind of way, with his battered fedora and awkward smile. It was just . . . I couldn't let myself get close to people. I knew too much, all the time, thanks to my *gift*. I'd learned a long time ago to keep it a secret, but every so often something slipped out, and when it did, the people I cared about ran for the hills. Or tried to lock me up.

It was easier not to care, not to get involved. No matter how much I wanted to.

"Not tonight," I replied. "I'm exhausted."

"One of these nights I'm going to convince you to go out. With us, I mean."

I pressed my lips together to keep from smiling. I still couldn't meet his gaze. "Maybe."

"Well, if you change your mind, you can call me. I'll keep my phone on." Silas slapped his hand down on the wood before grabbing his case. "Have a good night, Lil."

I glanced up as he stepped back from the bar. His gaze met mine. A zing of electricity prickled along my nerves.

"I really do hope you change your mind." An encouraging smile pulled at the corner of his lips as he dipped his chin and turned away. Regret and longing washed through me, but I didn't call him back or change my mind. It was all for the best. Really.

As soon as he was out of earshot, Bruce sidled up, still wiping down the last of the wet but clean glasses. "You know, someday you're going to have to give that boy a chance."

I shrugged, looking up into the six-foot Samoan's face before giving him the same answer I gave Silas. "Maybe." I handed him his own stack of bills, which he shoved into a pocket. "But I noticed you're not going out with them, either."

"I'm an old married man."

"You're thirty. Only two years older than me. And you've been married for what, six months? I bet your wife is still awake and waiting for you."

"And we have better ways of spending our time than paying too much to get into a party." Bruce waggled his eyebrows and grinned. "But I'm not talking about you going out with *them*. I'm talking about you going out with *him*. Silas has had his eye on you for months. Cut him some slack, would you?"

I patted the big man on his muscled shoulder as I passed behind him to exit the bar. "I'll think on it."

Bruce insisted on driving me home. Virginia and Gabi had gone with Ty and the band about half an hour earlier, so it was just the two of us, and I appreciated the gesture. I only lived a couple miles away, and I had my bike, but at three in the morning on a Saturday near the beach, you never knew what could happen. I'd had a few self-defense classes and always carried pepper spray, but Bruce had a truck and I was on his route home.

As we exited the bar, flashing police lights caught our attention. Laguna Beach was usually pretty quiet this time of night. Even the highway was mostly deserted.

"I wonder what happened," I asked, staring out at the red and blue strobes. It was hard to tell from a distance and in the dark, but it looked like whatever it was, was on the rocks at the base of the cliffs that overhung the water. Three ATVs had gathered around the area, and flashlights swept their beams across the craggy boulders.

Without really thinking about it, my feet moved in that direction. I wasn't normally a looky-loo, but something about the scene called to me.

"We're over here," Bruce called. He'd already thrown my bike into the back of the truck and was standing at the driver's side door

I waved him off, my gaze locked on the rocks. A woman's scream echoed off the rock face. A man shouted. The words were lost, but fear and anger vibrated through the night air. There was something else in there. Something that felt old. And wrong.

I took off running. Luckily, the crosswalk light was already flashing. I dashed across the highway and ran out on the sand.

"Lil!" Bruce shouted. I ignored him. He followed anyway.

The woman screamed again. This time, I could hear the water gurgling in her throat before she was silenced.

The cops were moving up the rocks. "Let her go!" one of them shouted.

A hulking shadow leaned over the end of the pile of rocks that bled out into the water. At just after three in the morning, it was nearing low tide, and the rocks were more easily accessible. Still, the cops scrambled to reach the struggling pair.

As I approached the scene, a cop turned, her hands held out wide. "Stay back," she warned. "There's nothing to see here. The beach is closed, so go home."

My gaze never left the rocks. I focused on the scene, adjusting my vision to parse the shadows and take in the details. "I know them. They were in the bar tonight." I replied.

It was the woman with the tear-smudged mascara and the biker guy. One of them anyway.

The cop's expression immediately narrowed into interrogation mode. "What bar?"

"The Trident. I'm a bartender. They were ejected for fighting. I didn't see everything." I looked back over my shoulder. Bruce was walking toward us, his expression wary. He must have stopped to take off his shoes. Smart. I was going to be cleaning sand out of my sneakers for days. "He stopped it," I said, throwing a thumb over my shoulder and the poor guy under the bus.

The cop immediately moved to intercept Bruce, and I was left to sneak a little closer. I wasn't looking to interfere with whatever the cops were doing, but there was still something about the struggle that drove me on. I couldn't leave it be.

The woman was in the water, her head barely breaking the surface. Each time she tried to pull herself up, the biker guy pushed her back down. He'd lost the leather jacket he'd been wearing, but the thick soled black boots must have been enough protection to let him clamber across the rocks that the cops now struggled with.

Oddly, the man's face was almost completely devoid of expression. He didn't make a sound. Only his eyes were pinched around the corners, as if in concentration. Like he was trying to solve a puzzle with no solution.

A shadow twisted through his body. His back spasmed. For a fraction of a second, the biker's expression shifted from nothing to fierce glee, then back.

"Did you see that?" I asked.

The cop speaking with Bruce turned to face me. "See what?"

She hadn't been watching. The man was possessed, and I was the only one who knew it.

My hand drifted to my pocket. It might have been my imagination, but the napkin felt warmer than it should have.

I concentrated on the man's face, willing the demon to show itself again. Ever since that night, the night I got my scar, I'd been able to see the spirits that twisted people to their purpose. Some of them were good, even virtuous. The angel on your shoulder, so to speak. Some were . . . not. Most did no real harm. Like the divorcée in the bar, they were desires made real. Or at least, real to me. No one else could see them.

Never before, however, had I seen a demon *inside* a person's skin. I thought of all the horror movies I'd ever seen—it wasn't many, I really didn't need to add to the nightmares in my head —and shuddered. I was no priest to give an exorcism. I was just a bartender. An average one at that.

Still, if I was the only one who could see what was really going on with this biker dude and his lady, I had to do something to help.

My feet had taken me to the edge of the water. Waves lapped at my toes. Already, my sneakers were soaked. I stared out at the couple on the rocks and the police who had nearly reached them.

The biker guy muttered something. I thought I heard the word "sacrifice" and maybe "depths." If that was his goal, he had very nearly succeeded.

I waded in up to my knees. They were still twenty yards away, maybe more, but I could see him more clearly. And more importantly, I could see her. Her movements were growing weaker, the time between breaths, longer. The cops were almost there, but it wouldn't be enough. She wasn't going to last.

On instinct, I looked up into the night sky. Wind whipped around me, tossing loose strands of hair into my mouth. I gazed at the full moon.

I don't know why, but I'd always thought of the moon as female. Her soft light was gentle and calm. Not the fiery burn of the sun. Not that women couldn't be fiery, of course, but there was just something about the moon that felt soft and feminine.

"Lady," I whispered, feeling silly and a bit too woo-woo for my own taste. Despite my strange skill, I'd never been into tarot or spiritual mumbo-jumbo. "If you're there, your daughter needs you. Don't let her drown. Don't let her fall to that possessed brute. Help her."

It wasn't an elegant speech. I had never been great with words. But hopefully it would be enough. I looked to the design on the napkin, which seemed to glow ever so slightly. It was probably my imagination. But I traced the image with a finger and then sent my thoughts out to the drowning lady in the red polka-dot top. Whatever strength my little gift might have, I willed it into the woman.

Her arm flailed, hitting the biker's shin. She latched on, heaving herself up onto the rock just enough to keep her head above water. The biker kicked his foot out, connecting with her shoulder, but she didn't let go. He kicked again, but his other foot slipped, the rubber of his boot succumbing to the slick seaweed and bird crap that probably covered every inch of the rocks that far out.

The biker landed hard, just as the police came in range. One pinned him to the rocks while the other helped the woman. She sobbed, clutching at the officer's shoulders. Her once-perfect curls hung limp around her shoulders.

"You're going to have to come with me," the female officer with Bruce called from behind me. "We'll need a statement about the assault at the Trident."

With the woman safe, the desire to watch what was happening disappeared. "I didn't really see anything, like I said."

I shuffled my way across the sand to Bruce's side. By this point, my sneakers were completely ruined, which sucked because they were practically brand new.

"All the same, you were there," the officer replied. "It'll be easier to go now, rather than track you down later."

CHAPTER 3

By the time I got home from the police station, it was already long past dawn. I'd told the cop at the beach that I didn't know anything, and I hadn't been lying. Unfortunately, with all the paperwork, it still took hours to process what had happened and why I'd been there in the first place. Luckily, it was Sunday, which meant the bar was closed and I had a full day off. Sweet relief.

I let myself into my tiny studio apartment and locked the door behind me. Beach rents were expensive, and I refused to have a roommate. Between my crazy hours and preference for solitude, it wasn't worth it. Which meant the only thing I could afford within walking or biking distance of the bar was a four hundred square foot room with an attached bathroom and a kitchenette stuffed in one corner. It was a nice kitchenette, though.

With a grimace, I pulled off my destroyed sneakers and still-soggy socks, and carefully set them next to the door to avoid bringing sand inside. Maybe when they dried out I would be able to shake most of it off outside. If I were really lucky, a trip through the washing machine might salvage them. Probably not though.

The blackout curtains were already pulled closed—thanks to my nocturnal employment, I had sprung for the really expensive ones that were so thick not even a pinprick of light shone through. I'd even hung them with special squared off rods so that the curtain pressed up against the wall and the sun couldn't peek in around the edges. The only light that did make it into the apartment came through the small frosted glass window in the bathroom. All I had to do there was shut the door.

My eyelids were drooping, my last reserves of energy nearly depleted, but I couldn't get into bed with dirty feet. It was one of those things. Skirting around my queen-sized bed, I wobbled toward the bathroom, walking on the sides of my feet to keep as much of the sand and dirt from my floor as possible. I stepped into the tub before pulling off my black work pants, knowing the cuffed hems would have hidden pockets of grit that would spill everywhere, then rinsed my feet off. That done, I stumbled back out into the room and fell flat on my face onto the bed. I probably still stank to high heaven with the sweat and alcohol from the bar, but I'd worry about that in the morning. Evening. Whatever.

)◯(

A pounding on the door woke me minutes later. At least, that's what it felt like. Glancing at the clock on the wall that was shaped like the sun—one of the few decorations I'd managed to hang since I'd moved in over a year ago—I realized I'd actually been asleep for four hours, and it was nearly the afternoon. It wasn't long enough.

I groaned and pulled the fluffy comforter over my head. I'd splurged on lightweight down. My apartment was my oasis and

I enjoyed cozy things. Big pillows, fuzzy blankets, and high-end coffee. Everything else was secondary.

The knocking came again. "Hey Lil! You in there? I thought we were going for a jog today!"

It was Ezra, my older brother who had made it his mission to try to improve my health and fitness. Despite the fact he was wheelchair bound, he was far more active than I had ever been. In fact, he was training for his fifth paratriathlon, hoping to place for the first time.

"Go away," I groaned.

"Come on, sis," Ezra shouted. "Wakey wakey."

The yappy dog upstairs started barking at the commotion. Clearly, this building needed better windows. With sound proofing.

Knowing Ezra wouldn't leave me alone until I let him in, I dragged myself over to my dresser to pull on a pair of shorts, then opened the door.

Ezra pushed his way in on two wheels, spinning around in the kitchen nook. I was always impressed that he never knocked anything over.

"You look like hell. Rough night?" Ezra asked with a grin.

"You wouldn't believe it if I told you." Actually, he probably would. We didn't talk about it much, but he knew I fought my mother's affliction. He knew and he didn't judge me for it or think I was insane. It was part of why he was so determined to keep me physically grounded. He thought exercise would prevent the demons from taking hold and twisting my mind, as they'd done to her.

"Hot date?" He peeked meaningfully toward the closed bathroom door. "Should I wheel myself back outside?"

"Ha ha." I rubbed a knuckle in the corner of my eye, trying to get out the sleepy dust and unstick my lids. "A woman almost died on the beach last night. I saw the whole thing and got pulled into the police station to give a report. Goddamn cops

MEGAN HASKELL

wouldn't believe that I didn't know anything. Asked me the same five questions about twenty times."

"What happened?"

"Yeah, that was one of them."

Ezra rolled his eyes. "No, really."

"It was on the beach, near bird rock. A guy was trying to drown his date. They'd been kicked out of the Trident just after midnight, and when Bruce and I were leaving after closing up, we saw the police lights. Thing is . . ."

I paused, hesitating for just a moment. I worked so hard to seem normal that I hated saying anything to anyone, even him, even when it would be a relief to share what I knew with someone who wouldn't judge me for it.

"Thing is," I repeated, "the guy was possessed. Like actually, physically possessed by a demon. I've never seen anything like it before."

"What did you do?" There was no judgment in his voice, no doubt of what I said. I couldn't express how much that meant to me.

"I . . . I think I sent it away. Or maybe I sent something to help her. I don't know. It was . . . I'm still processing it all."

"No wonder you look wrecked."

"Right. So can I go back to sleep now?"

"Nope. I have to be home for dinner. Dad's making steak."

"You still go to Sunday dinners?" I hadn't talked to my father in nearly eight years. Not since I'd been let out of the mental hospital where he'd stashed me as a teenager. As soon as he'd realized I could see the demons like my mother, he'd tried to pawn me off as somebody else's problem.

Ezra had already been out of the house by that point, off to college to study computer science, but he'd visited at every opportunity. He'd been the only one who had believed me. The only one I could trust. In large part because I scared off his own demons, and he could feel the difference. Dad had never let me try. The minute I turned eighteen, I discharged myself from the institute and never looked back.

"Yeah. You know, he'd love it if you came."

"Not a chance."

Ezra shrugged. He knew a lost cause when he saw it. We'd been having this argument for years. "Well, get dressed. I'll take it easy on you today."

"You know I only exercise because you force me to."

"Yep. Which is why you can't skip it. You'd turn into an alcohol-fueled blob in no time."

"I don't drink that much."

"Sure, sure. Let's go."

CHAPTER 4

I would never, ever admit it to Ezra, but it felt good to move. The sun was out, and the trail was crowded, but one look at my brother in his off-road wheelchair had people gawping and moving out of his way. As always, he was a man on a mission, his arms pumping at the levers that pushed his chair across the hard-packed dirt at speed. I was hard pressed to keep up with him, especially on the downhill sections. At least on the uphill, he had to slow down, too. Of course, he never asked for help and I never offered. His endurance was better than mine.

When we paused for a breather at the picnic area, I knew there was something on Ezra's mind. He passed me a bottle of water from the pack on the back of his seat and cleared his throat.

"Next week is the anniversary—"

"I know," I cut him off. I didn't need the reminder of the day when all hell broke loose. When my mother tried to kill me and my brother tried to save me. He *had* saved me and had sacrificed his legs to do it. He'd been sixteen. I'd been twelve.

It was the first day I saw a demon.

"I'm going to visit her grave with Dad."

I swallowed a gulp of water, and the rising anger.

"Why? Why would you do that?"

"She was sick, Lil." Ezra said the words without inflection, without anger or rancor or the edge of betrayal.

"Sick like me, you mean."

"No. You've been able to fight them. She wasn't strong enough."

I shook my head. "She'd fought them for at least twenty-five years. Who's to say I'll even last that long? And what happens when I fail? Who will I try to murder in their sleep?"

A man sitting nearby shot me a wide-eyed glance and I dropped my voice. "I'm too much like her."

My mother had been a vibrant light in our world. She loved to dance in the rare Southern California rain and laughed like an angel. She always had blue paint under her fingernails from whatever seascape she was currently working on, and smelled like the vanilla and lavender essential oils she wore as perfume.

When we were little, she would read to us from a giant book of Greek myths. We each had our favorites and would take turns choosing the story for the night. Hers inevitably involved Poseidon or the ocean, while I preferred the wise and adventurous goddesses Hecate and Athena. Ezra almost always chose one of the labors of Hercules or adventures of Achilles. He said the demigods were more realistic because they were half human. Sometimes we'd mix in the myths of other cultures, too. Trickster gods like Loki and Coyote, even the ancient Babylonian creation myths. They were all fair game for the bedtime adventures.

But as we grew older, she started to disappear. At first, she would forget to pick us up from school. She said she lost track of time. But then her absences grew longer. By the time I turned twelve, she would disappear for days or weeks at a time, leaving my dad scrambling for childcare and us kids wondering what we had done to chase her away.

It wasn't until that night in my room that I understood why she would leave. I'd been asleep. I woke to find her pacing in the dark, muttering something about betrayal and protection. I couldn't really understand her words. That didn't matter. Her eyes were wild and distraught, her movements sharp and staccato. Every so often, she would look at me in my bed and all I saw was despair burning within the golden brown of her iris.

I remember pulling my sheets up to my chin, whispering her name, asking what was wrong. She didn't answer me. That is, until she leaned over the bed with a knife in her hand. The blade glinted in the light from the hallway. Slashed down toward my neck. My arm instinctively came up, getting between the edge and my face. The knife was sharp. It cut deep, to the bone.

I screamed, then. Ezra's room was next to mine. We shared a bathroom. Jack and Jill, that's what they called it. He'd still been awake, studying for an exam or something, and had come running. He'd grabbed mom around the shoulders, but she struggled against him. He was sixteen and already taller than she was, but he was trying not to hurt her and she . . . well, she wanted one thing. My blood.

They'd stumbled backward. I was screaming and sobbing. Dad was working late, on call at the hospital.

Somehow Ezra pulled my mom out of my room and into the hallway. The hallway that overlooked the living room like a loft. There was a banister, but it wasn't enough.

It was like it happened in slow motion. The memories are etched in my brain. I'll never not see it.

Mom threw her head backward. Broke Ezra's nose. He let go. Reached his hands to his face. She slammed an elbow into his gut. He hit the banister. His feet left the ground.

I was still in my bed, blood everywhere from the cut on my arm, but I reached out as if I could catch him.

His arms pinwheeled, trying to catch his balance, but they were covered in blood, too. I remember the red. He couldn't get a grip on the polished wood. He went over, falling spine first onto the carved wooden edge of the antique couch my mother had purchased on a whim.

I'd seen the demon, then. It had wrapped itself so tightly around my mother it might as well have been inside her skin. It was my first encounter, but it wouldn't be my last.

Mom snapped out of it. I could see the change, and yet I couldn't forgive her for it. She ran from the house and never returned.

I don't remember calling nine-one-one, but I must have. I have flashes of riding in the ambulance, of screaming at the doctors when they tried to pull me from Ezra's side so they could stitch up my arm and take him for tests. I refused to leave him. It wasn't until my dad got there that they convinced me to let them do their jobs.

"You're nothing like her," Ezra replied, pulling me out of my dark memories and back into the sunlight of the present day. "They leave you alone. You manipulate them, not the other way around. I've felt it. She couldn't do that. If she could, she wouldn't have attacked you. It wasn't her fault."

I paced away from Ezra, taking another swig from my water bottle and staring out across the ocean. About a week after the incident, lifeguards found an abandoned pile of clothing with my mom's purse on their tower. She'd written a note, begging forgiveness, and had surrendered herself to the sea. Her body was never found.

We buried that pile of clothing, her last remains. I'd never been back. The waves may have claimed her, but they hadn't washed away her sins.

"What kind of mother takes a knife to her own daughter?

Pushes her son over a railing?" I shook my head again, still not looking at Ezra, though I could feel him behind me. "She should have fought harder."

My gut clenched, anger simmering deep within my core. I'd never forgive her. It didn't need to be said.

Ezra sighed.

We stayed at the lookout point for another few minutes before finally heading back to Ezra's van. We didn't talk much, but it wasn't because I was angry or upset. It was just that I had nothing more to say. The past was the past. It couldn't be changed.

"Have fun at dinner," I said as Ezra dropped me off. "I mean it."

"The offer's open. I'm sure Dad would like to see you."

"Tell him I'm okay. That's all he needs to know."

Ezra frowned but didn't disagree. I shut the door and he drove away.

CHAPTER 5

Tuesday night. Slowville. Not that it was a surprise, but Tuesdays were honestly the worst. We had a few regulars, but even though it was summer, the tourists wouldn't come in force until Thursday. And without a live band playing, there wasn't much draw for the locals.

Which was why it was just me and Ty behind the bar, with Gabi working the tables.

She was part-time while she went to nursing school. To look at her, you wouldn't necessarily expect that. She kept her hair short and edgy, with colored highlights scattered throughout. This month, they were purple and blue. With heavy eyeliner and a stud in her nose, she seemed more likely to be on a hip-hop stage than giving people sponge baths, but she was serious about helping people recover from trauma.

With a frown, Gabi leaned across the bar, drawing both me and Ty toward her. "The guy in the corner is giving me the creeps," she whispered. If no-nonsense Gabi was saying that, it was serious.

"What'd he do?" Ty asked while giving the guy a glaring appraisal.

The man was rather nondescript, sitting by himself at a shadowy table out of the way of all the other customers, near the wood-carved bust of a wrathful Poseidon that leered down from the wall above. He was probably in his mid-forties, if I had to guess, and I was usually pretty close. The loose button up tee fit the beach scene, and his hair was tidily combed to one side. A little out of date, but not noteworthy. He wasn't like the bums that occasionally wandered in looking for a freebie or to make trouble.

"Nothing," Gabi replied. "Except, he ordered a glass of wine. Do we even stock wine?"

I turned to search through the bottles. We were a beach bar, not a restaurant. If it didn't require a shake or a stir, it wasn't on the menu. "Not really. I guess . . . sherry might be close enough? But that doesn't explain why he creeps you out." I poured the sherry into the closest thing I had to a wine glass, a Marie Antoinette coupe. I figured, give the guy a legendary glass supposedly molded into shape by the infamous French queen's perfect breast and he might not complain.

"It's that smile. He reminds me of a wax figure at Madame Tussaud's in Hollywood. Have you ever been there? It's creepy. They all look like people, but not quite. He's like that."

"Uncanny valley," Ty chimed in. "I hate that."

"Right? It's like he's not even a real person." Gabi pulled her water bottle from behind the counter and took a swig. "Honestly, I'd try to take his pulse if he hadn't already spoken to me."

As I watched, something seemed to move beneath the man's skin, like a hand inside a puppet. Immediately, my mind flashed back to the biker dude on the beach. My hand drifted to my pocket. For whatever reason, I'd kept that napkin doodle. When I'd seen it on my dresser this afternoon, I'd carefully folded it and shoved it in my black work pants. Maybe it was a good luck charm. Or something.

Gabi's insight might not be too far off. Now that I knew

what I was looking at, I could see the shadows crawling over and around the man's body. Tentacles curled and uncurled around his arms, originating from someplace on his back. When he caught me looking, his smile widened, revealing a flash of pointed shark's teeth within a maw wider than a human should possess before resettling into his human skin.

If the guy had been human, he wasn't anymore. I'd never before come across anyone so thoroughly possessed. Even Mom had still retained her core being at the end. The biker guy might have been a close second, but I hadn't been close enough to really see his influences.

"The cherry on top is that he's been asking about Lil."

"Me?"

"Not by name, but he asked about any female bartenders, and . . . well, you're the only one."

What did Mr. Button-Up want with me? "You didn't tell him anything, did you?"

"Of course not." She paused. "Maybe your name, before I realized how much of a creepster he is, but that's it."

"Should we get Carlos in here?" Ty asked. "Do you think he's a stalker?"

"No, it'll be fine," I replied. The guy wasn't a problem yet, and even though we had a "reserve the right to refuse service" rule, I hated to make a big deal out of nothing. If he tried something, I'd call in the muscle, but until then, I was happy just to stay behind the counter.

A woman at the far end of the bar called for Ty's attention and we all went back to our duties. I kept an eye on the guy in the corner, but he didn't do much of anything but sit there, staring at his glass with that awkward bemused smile. The shadowy tentacles were disconcerting at first, but even that eventually slipped to the back of my mind as work took over.

Ezra came in at about ten with his latest fling. There was something about a hunky dude in a wheelchair that got him all sorts of attention. Of which, he never hesitated to take advantage.

Tonight's woman was a blonde-haired, blue-eyed, sportswear model type. Thin, but not waifish, she wore a tight tank with a short, flouncy skirt that showed off toned arms and legs.

Perfect for the health nut.

Gabi—who was picking up a Mai Tai for another table—cocked an eyebrow. "Bet you ten bucks she orders a Skinny Margarita."

"I'll take that bet," I replied. "It'll be a Paloma."

"No suggestions." Gabi popped the gum she habitually chewed while at work.

I placed a palm across my heart in mock offense. "Have I ever?"

Gabi grinned as she turned and winked at Ezra, passing him on her way to the table.

"Hey sis!" Ezra called as he wheeled himself up to the lower cutout section of the bar designed for accessibility. "Meet Tempest! Tempest, meet my sister, Lil."

I lifted an eyebrow. Odd name for a Southern California girl. Summer, sure. Lily, pretty common. Sierra, not unheard of. But what kind of parent named their daughter after a storm?

"Hi Tempest. Interesting name."

"I have interesting parents." She smiled and held out her hand, clearly not taking my inquisition personally. That was good. I had a tendency to be a little too blunt with people. I blamed it on three years in a social hellhole, but it was probably just me. "Nice to meet you."

I returned her smile and shook her hand after wiping it on a clean towel first. Never good to greet someone with sticky hands. "What are you doing with this ne'er-do-well?" I nodded toward my dark-haired playboy brother, who watched us with a shit-eating grin.

Tempest smiled. "Having a pretty good time, actually. Your brother keeps a girl on her toes."

"Tell me about it." I faked a grimace. "He forces me to *exercise* of all things."

"The nerve." Her grin widened, revealing perfect teeth.

"So what can I get you two tonight?" I asked as I wiped down the low counter before Ezra put his elbows in sticky drink residue. He could never sit still in his chair and preferred to lean on tables or counters whenever possible. He said it made him feel like less of an invalid.

I always told him there was nothing invalid about him, but then, my disability was in my head, not visible on my body.

"Can you do that cucumber thing you made me last time?" Ezra asked.

"Ooh, that sounds good. What's in it?" Tempest's wide-eyed excitement was endearing.

"Oh, a little of this, a little of that, and a few cucumber slices." I replied.

"It's like a spa water, but alcoholic," Ezra added.

"Sugar?"

"Just a dash of agave."

"Sounds delish. I'll have what he's having."

"Damn, lost the bet." Gabi came up beside Ezra and gave him a sideways hug. "Good to see you!"

"Oh?" Tempest asked, non-plussed by Gabi's affectionate greeting. Gabi and Ezra had become friends, but I knew there was nothing going on between them. She was a little too studious for Ezra's taste, and he was too healthy for hers. I'd seen her eat more candy than anyone over the age of twelve.

"I figured you for a Skinny Margarita kinda girl."

"And I had you with a Paloma. So we both lost," I added as I mixed the drinks.

Tempest laughed, not taking the bet personally and gaining a few points in my estimation. She didn't seem like Ezra's usual airhead wannabe fitness instructor. "Tequila's for a taco bar. Without Ezra's suggestion, I probably would have ordered a Mai Tai. So you still would have both been wrong!"

"Full sugar?"

"One's not gonna kill me. Maybe even two. I was more worried you'd put Stevia in this thing." She lifted the glass I handed her in an air-clink. "I can't stand that stuff." She took a sip and I watched her expression relax into satisfied appreciation. "But this is amazing. Summer garden party in a glass."

Another fifteen points to Tempest. "Glad you like it."

Ezra clinked glasses for reals and took his own sip.

I left them to it, moving away to mix up a few more drinks while they laughed and chatted.

Awhile later, I felt a change in the atmosphere. It was like the barometer had dropped, but the moon shone bright through the open windows, not a cloud covering its face.

I scanned the room. A gray mist, like ashy smoke, drifted around the creepster's feet. The smoke spread out, slowly forming into a wriggling mass of serpentine figures. The cloud continued to grow and change, getting larger and more defined with each passing second. The snakes' jaws gaped, revealing a row of needle-thin teeth. The bodies grew taller and narrower, and I realized my first guess had been wrong. They weren't snakes, they were eels.

Gabi, all unknowing, walked toward the cloud. I was stuck behind the bar. I almost yelled at her to stop. But I couldn't do that without seeming like a total nutcase. No one but Ezra knew of my issues, and I didn't want to reveal them now, here, like this. No matter that Mr. Button-Up was suddenly far more dangerous than expected.

One of the eels lunged toward Gabi's free hand. I gasped as it bit her, sucking her fingers into its mouth up to her knuckles. She didn't seem to feel it. Didn't even break stride. She passed

Mr. Button-Up on her way to another table, but the shadow eel went with her, detaching from the rest of the demon cloud.

Mr. Button-Up smiled but didn't look up. He still hadn't taken a sip of his drink, though he'd been sitting there over an hour. To be fair, I wasn't sure sherry was exactly what he wanted, but he could have changed his order.

I watched horrified, as the eel demon began working its way up Gabi's arm, little by little, swallowing her whole. She didn't react. Nothing seemed to be happening. Her hand and arm moved as if nothing was there. Yet the eel climbed higher and higher, until its mouth was at her shoulder.

Could this all be in my head? Was I finally going crazy?

Mr. Button-Up chuckled, eyes trained on his glass. There was no one around him. What could he possibly find funny?

The rest of the shadow eels slithered around the man's feet. They didn't make a move on any of the other customers, but then, none of them were nearby.

When Gabi came back to the counter, I leaned toward her and listened for the influence of the eel demon. It was entirely silent. Odd. Most demons I'd come in contact with were constantly whispering their desires into the host's ear. Most sought immediate influence.

The eel just hung there; its incorporeal teeth latched onto Gabi's arm.

"Are you feeling alright?" Maybe its influence was deeper than I could see. Maybe it was doing something inside her mind instead of speaking with words. As much as I'd been seeing the creatures since I was twelve, I hadn't spent a whole lot of time studying them. I didn't need to add to the crazy.

"I feel great. Why?" Gabi's smile was genuine, though her eyes looked a little glassy. Maybe I was reading too much into things.

"I just wanted to make sure that guy wasn't bothering you."

"He didn't seem interested in me." She glanced over at his table. "He wanted *you.*"

I shuddered. Something about the way she said that felt wrong. I would have sworn her gaze turned more intense, her eyes going bloodshot around the edges.

But was it real? Or was my mind playing tricks on me?

I couldn't be sure.

With a flick of my fingers, I tried to dislodge the eel on her arm. It didn't budge. There had only been a few cases where I'd really tried to get rid of the demons hanging around people. Mostly, they were harmless, encouraging desires that people already had. Appease them, and they calmed. But to get rid of them completely took more effort.

I'd done it once before, for Ezra, when he'd finally accepted that he wouldn't recover from the fall. He would always be bound in a wheelchair. For a guy who'd been a star athlete even as a high school sophomore, that had been a debilitating blow. A demon had latched onto him, a depressive demon, one that had wanted him to wallow in self-loathing. I couldn't let that stand. I had researched everything I could on exorcisms and spiritual influences. Most of it had been utter nonsense, but at last I'd been able to cast it away with a saltwater spray. It had seemed silly at the time, but the demon had left and taken Ezra's depression with it.

I pinched a bit of salt from the margarita bowl and tossed it toward Gabi's shoulder.

"What the hell? What was that for?" She demanded. At least she still sounded like herself.

Rather than letting go, the wisp of cloud that made up the eel's body narrowed around her arm, as if grasping her even tighter.

"Nothing. Sorry," I mumbled. I shouldn't have bothered trying to fix anything. It wasn't as if I had any real ability to affect the demons. Only appease them.

Gabi's gaze traveled back to the man at the table, as if drawn there by a magnet. Or magic.

"Maybe you should go talk to him. He seems important," she whispered.

My eyes narrowed at the sudden change in opinion. "How so?"

Gabi shrugged. "You should go talk to him."

The demon was definitely influencing her, but it didn't seem to be hurting her, so maybe she was right. Maybe, if I just went and talked to Mr. Button-Up I would be able to figure out what he wanted and get him to leave. Appease the master, and the slave might go away.

CHAPTER 6

I approached the table with trepidation, and a towel clenched in my fist. The towel wouldn't do me any good of course, but I liked to keep my hands busy. And maybe I wouldn't hit him.

I wouldn't hit him. I'd never hit anyone in my life. Well, except for the snotty wrist cutter at the institute. She had deserved it.

So would he if he didn't let Gabi go.

"Why are you here," I blurted.

Mr. Button-Up grinned, eyes still turned down to the untouched glass of sherry.

"I find this body desires wine."

"Then why aren't you drinking it?"

"It pleases me to make the body uncomfortable. A test of wills, of sorts." Something moved under the man's skin. "Like the man you interrupted on Saturday. He loves her. Did you know? He tried to fight me and failed. She would have gone to Rán's embrace and he would have followed eventually, both to feast in Aegir's Hall for eternity, enjoying the very same things they love in this mortal world. But you interrupted."

"What are you talking about?"

"I rode him to the law enforcement office, to find out how and why I had been thwarted." The man's gaze turned to face me directly. For a flash of a moment, his eyes shifted from human brown to the solid dead black of an ocean predator. "I saw you."

Shivers cascaded down my spine. If there had been any doubt that this man was dangerous, it was gone now. Years of camping as a young child had ingrained in me that you never backed down from a predator. Never ran. Big noise and wild motions were the only way to escape something more dangerous than man.

I slapped my hand on the table, drawing every eye in the near-empty bar toward our confrontation. "What do you want?" I growled.

"I am minding my own business. Perhaps you should mind yours." He spoke loud enough that the witnesses would hear. I was being the aggressor, even though he was the predator. Damn it.

"I won't let you take her," I replied, keeping my own voice down. "Whatever you want, you can find it somewhere else."

"Listen now and listen well." Mr. Button-Up whispered. I was forced to lean in lest I miss his words. "Do not interfere again or it will go worse for you and yours."

He snapped his teeth at my nose and I jerked back. He laughed.

Then, like water draining through a bucket of sand, the demon slid from the man's skin and disappeared. The eels followed.

Mr. Button-Up blinked a few times, then grasped the stem of his glass. He looked up at me with guileless eyes.

"Can I help you?" he asked.

I straightened from the table and shook my head. "Sorry for bothering you."

What had happened to this man? Where had he gone while the demon possessed him? Did he even know he hadn't been in control? Had the demon done something to his memory?

I had so many questions but didn't know how to ask any of them without sounding like a complete lunatic. I probably looked like one already, hovering over his table. Hopefully no one was paying any attention anymore.

The man frowned but swirled the wine in his hand. "What is this?"

"Sherry. It was the only wine we had."

He frowned, took a quick, loud sip. Grimaced. "This is vile. Why would you serve me this?"

"You ordered it?" I made it a question, then waved my hand around the room. "We're not a wine bar."

"Well, I'm not going to drink it."

"That's fine, sir. But you still owe me ten dollars for the pour."

"Outrageous." The man rolled his eyes and blew out an exasperated sigh but reached into his pocket for his wallet. "I won't be back."

I stepped out of his way and mentally riffled through every diplomatic service statement in my rather limited repertoire. "Thank you for your feedback, sir. I'll be sure to tell the manager."

The man grunted, slapped a ten-dollar bill on the table, and stomped out of the room. Probably to head to some snobby wine bar. Fine with me.

Back behind the bar, I mixed up a Mai Tai for one of our local surfer bums who'd just arrived for his evening constitutional. The guy was probably sixty-five, had been married twice, divorced twice, and now just liked to hang out with the "cool kids," or so he said.

"Have you ever heard of Schrodinger's Cat?" Jeff the surfer

asked. Elbows on the counter, he leaned forward as if sharing a deep secret.

"Um . . ." Normally I loved Surfer Jeff's quirky facts of the day, but right now really wasn't the time. I scanned the rest of the bar, looking for evidence that the demon was well and truly gone.

"It was supposed to prove the absurdity of quantum physics, that until something is measured, it's both alive and dead."

"What?" Ezra and Tempest were laughing together in a corner. I'd never seen my brother quite so entranced with a woman, no matter how cute she was. And Tempest *was* cute, even from a very objective point of view. Tall and blonde, she could have been Heidi Klum's youngest sister, or eldest daughter.

Good for him, I decided. He might never be short of company but finding someone he connected with intellectually was a new thing.

"Exactly. It was a thought experiment. Put a cat in a box with a quantum bomb and seal it up."

I squinched my face.

"Not really of course, that would be felicide," Jeff hurried to add. "You know, cat murder. It's just a thought experiment, remember? But you don't know if the quantum bomb has gone off, so you don't know if the cat is alive or dead. Therefore, the cat is *both* alive and dead."

"That's . . . interesting," I murmured. My gaze returned to the room. Ty was working the bar closest to the front door, so I stayed nearer the dart board and the locals who preferred the dark corners. Gabi was . . .

Where was Gabi?

"Hold that thought, Jeff. I'll be right back." I slid down the bar a few steps to Ty. "Have you seen Gabi?"

"She went on break. Said she was stepping out to get some fresh air."

"Fresh air?" That didn't sound like her. She loved candy and books. Studying. I had never once heard her say a good word about anything in nature.

"That's what she said. She went out back."

To the beach. Shit.

"I'll be right back. You good?" I asked even as I threw my towel beneath the back bar.

Ty eyed the near-empty bar, noting Jeff who smiled mildly as he sipped his drink. "Sure."

"What's the matter?" Ezra asked. Tempest, hand on Ezra's shoulder, watched with a curious expression.

"Nothing. I'll be right back." I replied.

Whatever that demon had done to her, I hoped I wasn't too late.

CHAPTER 7

I burst through the back door, glancing to either side of the exit. "Gabi?"

She wasn't sitting at the tiny bistro table we kept in the alley for breaks and meals. To the left, the communal dumpsters were clear. Not even a homeless person loitered nearby. To the right, the faint sound of ocean waves pulled me toward the beach.

The woman had nearly been drowned by the biker dude.

The demon had manifested as ocean animals.

Gabi would have gone that way. I just knew it.

I ran down the alley toward the beach, coming out on the narrow sidewalk that bordered the highway. A few touristy pedestrians were heading south toward the busier town center and their next bar stop, but the streets were otherwise empty. It was, after all, eleven at night on a Tuesday. Most people had to get up and go to work in the morning.

I scanned heads, looking for Gabi's signature blue and purple streaked hair and curvy figure. I didn't see her, but I kept moving toward the sand, somehow knowing that's where I would find her. I didn't know how long she'd been gone from the bar, or how far she might have gotten, but I knew she would be heading to the water.

My hand drifted to my pocket and the napkin drawing within. If it had truly helped me disperse the demon from the biker dude, maybe it would help me get rid of the eel on Gabi's arm. I had to believe it would. And I had to believe that the eel was forcing Gabi to do what it wanted. She wasn't one to disappear from responsibilities.

I reached the crosswalk that connected the city with the beach. The highway wasn't busy by daytime standards, but it was still a highway. Cars passed at speed, and I was forced to wait for the walk signal. I slammed my hand against the button impatiently while scanning the empty volleyball courts and grassy area across the street. The lights from a passing car flashed on a figure near the lifeguard tower. A woman with blue and purple streaked hair.

"Gabi!" I shouted.

She didn't turn. She couldn't hear me.

I waited for a break in traffic and darted across the highway. A car blared its horn. I ignored it.

"Gabi!" I shouted again. She was still too far ahead of me. I doubled down, pressing my legs to dig harder into the shifting sand beneath my feet.

"Stop!" My lungs heaved. I mentally thanked my brother for all those training sessions.

Gabi strolled inexorably toward the waves. She paused at the edge of the low tide waters and gazed out onto the sea. I was almost there. She kicked off the clogs she always wore to work. Water lapped at her toes.

I grabbed her shoulder.

"Gabi!" I panted. "What are you doing?"

She turned to look at me. I gasped. My hands flinched up and away from her body. The demon eel had sprouted prehensile whiskers that now wrapped around her throat. A few waved in the air, grasping for purchase on her torso and stretching for her left arm. Her eyes looked glassy, dazed, as if she no longer saw the world around her.

"Gabi?" I asked.

"The waves are calling my name. Can't you hear them? A swim sounds lovely. You should join me."

"No, Gabi. It's the middle of the night. You'll freeze." I tried to draw her away from the water, but she took a step back, deeper into the sea.

"It's warm and wonderful. You'll see." She smiled, but the motion looked forced, as if hooks had been placed in the corners of her mouth to pull her lips upward.

I held out my hand. "Come back with me. We have work to do."

"I've worked so hard, for so long. I need a little break. Just a small breath of fresh air. That's all." She took another step backward.

My chest constricted. The demon hadn't possessed her, not like Mr. Button-Up, but it was doing a damn good job of controlling her and I couldn't seem to break through the connection. I needed to get closer, to touch her. I took off my poor, abused sneakers and stepped into the water. Despite being near the end of June, the water was frigid. I gritted my teeth against the cold.

Gabi smiled again, the same forced expression that had my insides twisting. "See? Lovely." She turned to face the open water. I grabbed her forearm. Her right forearm. The one with the eel attached. Tentacles oozed from its sides, stretching back to wrap around my wrist. I felt the draw of the waves, but they didn't have control. Not yet.

Still, I held on.

"No, Gabi. It's cold and wet. You hate the ocean." I pushed my hand into my pocket. The napkin was there, warm against my hand.

I unfolded the wrinkled paper with one hand, revealing the doodle the old woman had drawn. Except, instead of black ink, the design glowed with red heat, like the embers in the bottom of a fireplace.

The tentacles reached up to my elbow. The call of the ocean intensified. I still wasn't going to let go.

I blew out a breath. I hoped this worked. I had to believe it would. If not, I was fairly certain we were both doomed.

I slapped the paper face down on Gabi's arm, right through the head of the incorporeal eel. Gabi screamed and batted my hand away. This time, I let go. The paper clung to her skin, the image visible through the back. She scratched at the drawing, tried to pull it away, but it held fast.

The flaming red ink flowed into the eel's body to outline every horrifying curve. Its head opened in a silent scream. The body split in half, rolling back like a banana peel pulled away from the fruit inside. Its arms folded in on themselves. Everything seemed to turn inside out and shrink, until nothing was left but a bit of ash on the wind.

Gabi's scream had long since quieted when at last she blinked a few times and stared at me blearily.

"Gabi?" I asked for the umpteenth time.

"What happened?" she murmured. She glanced at the ocean over her shoulder and then down at her legs, submerged up to her knees. She was lucky she had been wearing shorts tonight. "Why am I in the water?"

I grinned and embraced her in what had to be the biggest hug I'd ever given anyone.

"It's okay, now. You're back." I held her at arm's length, staring into her eyes just to be sure they were entirely clear and free from whatever mind control the demon eel had put her under. "You're back." I repeated, feeling more certain with every passing moment.

"Where did I go?" She still seemed a bit dazed, but I supposed that was to be expected.

"It doesn't matter. You're okay. But we'd better get back to work before Ty has a hissy fit or Chaz comes in with his latest floozy."

"Okay," she murmured, following as I led her back up the beach toward our shoes.

"My socks are wet. And covered in sand. I hate sand."

I laughed, the relief welling up and out of me like bubbles in soda. "I know."

"Why is there a napkin stuck to my arm?" she asked after picking up her shoes. She started to pick at the edge of the paper, but it held fast like a sticker on fruit.

"Oh, here. Let me get that." I scraped my nail along the edge, found a gap, and pulled the napkin free. It ripped a little around the edge, and the fiery red glow was gone—a good thing, I thought—but otherwise the drawing remained whole, as if nothing had happened. Unfortunately, it also stayed on her skin.

"Did I get a tattoo?"

I licked my finger and wiped at the design. I blew out a relieved breath when it smeared a little.

"No, it's just pen ink. It'll wash off. Kind of a cool design though, don't you think?"

"The sign for Lilith? Queen of demons? I don't think so. Not my schtick," Gabi replied.

"You know what this is?" To me it just looked like a doodle. Other than the apparent power to disperse demons, I hadn't realized there was any significance to the design.

"My sister went goth for a little while, so yeah. But not with the crescent moons on either side like that. Just the symbol in the middle. But the moons make sense, I guess. But how'd it get on my arm?"

We paused at the playground to wipe off our feet and put

49

our shoes back on. "It was in my hand when I grabbed your arm to keep you from swimming. Must have stuck."

"Huh." Gabi shook her head and lifted her eyebrows. "I don't really remember that."

"You were kind of out of it. Are you stressed from school or something?" If I could distract her and lay the blame elsewhere, maybe she'd let it all go. Maybe, just maybe, I wouldn't be called a nutcase and chased out of yet another job.

"Must be a delayed reaction. Finals were last week."

Tension fled from my shoulders. "Let's finish tonight's shift, and then you can get some rest tomorrow."

She didn't seem to notice my relief or the way I carefully folded the napkin and put it back in my pocket.

CHAPTER 8

As we walked back to the Trident, Gabi paused to put a hand on my arm and pulled me to the side.

"Please don't tell anyone I had a panic attack. I don't want them to know I nearly walked fully clothed into the ocean."

"Not a problem. I can keep a secret." If she only knew.

"Thanks." She squeezed my arm. "Really. For everything."

"Of course."

"How did you find me, anyway?" she asked.

I paused, heart racing. What was I going to say? You were actually possessed by a demon that only I can see, and I followed you to the ocean because it reminded me of a sea creature? I mean, I guess that could've worked, if I didn't mind being sent back to the looney bin.

"Just a hunch, I guess." I shrugged, trying to keep my facial expression nonchalant. I wasn't good at it. Luckily, we had arrived at the back door by that point.

"Only one person on break at a time!" Ty practically shouted as soon as we entered the room.

I glanced around the near-empty space. Ezra was whirling

around the floor, dancing with Tempest to the mix playing on the overheads, and Surfer Jeff was still sitting by himself at the end of the bar. "Couldn't handle the rush?"

"I've had to take a leak for the last twenty minutes," Ty replied, dashing around the end of the bar and rushing past us, toward the restrooms at the back.

I grinned but headed toward the sound system to change the music. If Ezra wanted to dance, I'd give him a better song than the eighties nostalgia playlist that Chaz, our owner, had set up. The early aughts were more our style. A little "Poker Face" seemed appropriate.

Ezra spun his chair, popping it up on two wheels and grinned in my direction. "Not Lady Gaga!"

He'd never admit it to anyone but me, but he had that album on repeat for months.

I shot him two thumbs up and got back to work.

By midnight, Jeff had left, Gabi had gone home with a headache (I didn't blame her), and it was only me, Ty, Ezra, and Tempest left in the bar. Time to close up shop.

I cashed out the registers while Ty wiped down the tables and flipped the chairs on top.

"Twelve, twenty-seven, fourteen, a hundred and thirty-eight —" Ezra spouted off numbers, intentionally interrupting my count.

"Dammit Ezra, now I have to start over."

The little turd grinned. "Wanna spot me on a swim tomorrow?"

"I thought we were going on a run."

"Tempest has a boat, she lives on it, in fact. She's offered to give me some time in the real water to practice fighting the waves. The pool only takes me so far. If I want to place this time, I need more hours in the ocean. But I can take you on a run after, so long as we stick to pavement. I'll use the racing chair, not the handcycle."

"Like that makes a difference." The racing chair wasn't quite as fast as the handcycle, but it could still go faster than fifteen miles an hour.

"It'll be a recovery ride. I won't race you."

I rolled my eyes. "Thank the lord for small mercies."

"Come on, what do you say? A late morning on the water, and an afternoon run before work. It'll be relaxing."

"With you around? I don't think so."

Ezra pulled himself up a bit onto the counter, to lean toward me. "C'mon, sis. I need the practice, and things are going really well with Tempest. I don't want to miss this opportunity."

I glanced up at the blonde, who was waiting for him by the front door. She held a hairband between her teeth as she pulled her hair into a perfect bouncy ponytail. I couldn't mess this up for him.

"How about I take a recovery day myself. I'll sleep in and you can go out with your special ladyfriend without me."

Ezra tapped his knuckles on the wood, as he slid back in his chair. "I knew you'd understand."

"Just be careful, okay? Make sure she's got flotation for you, just in case."

"She used to be a lifeguard. It won't be a problem."

"Of course she was." The woman was truly his perfect match.

"I'll come by after, in case you change your mind about the run."

"I won't."

"I might be able to convince you."

53

I lifted a single eyebrow in disbelief. "You've *never* changed my mind. You've just bullied me until I gave in."

Ezra waffled his hand from side to side. "Tomato, tomahto. See you tomorrow."

He twisted his chair around and met up with Tempest. "Shall we?"

I rolled my eyes again and returned to counting the register.

T woke up just after noon the next day and threw on some running clothes. I knew my brother. He'd be here after his swim, as promised, and I wouldn't be able to wiggle my way out of the attempt to turn me into an athlete. As if.

Still, he wasn't entirely wrong. I'd only managed a semester and a half of college before dropping out, but even in that short span of time I'd managed to gain the dreaded freshman fifteen. It wasn't as if I knew how to cook anything other than mac and cheese at the time, and let's be real, my cooking skills hadn't improved much over the years. Compound that with a shot here and there at work, and a few beers after, and the only thing between me and becoming that big ol' round gal was a twenty-eight-year-old metabolism and Ezra's training regimen.

Unfortunately, the prospect of a run didn't look so good after all. After pulling open the blackout curtains that protected my sensitive night-owl eyes from the Southern California morning sun, I realized there wasn't much need for them today. Everything was gray and overcast. Dark clouds hung heavy in the sky. As I watched, a few big drops of rain fell on paving stones of the courtyard, and a roll of thunder boomed in the distance.

Ezra. He wouldn't be out on the water in this, would he? He would have checked the weather, known it was coming. He was responsible. Intelligent.

More drops fell. Another loud boom.

What the hell? We didn't get storms like this in June in Southern California. We rarely got storms like this at all. That's why everyone wanted to move here and tiny studio apartments cost a bazillion dollars a month.

Racing back to the phone charging on my nightstand, I called Ezra.

Please pick up. Please pick up. I prayed as the phone rang. Voicemail.

"Ezra, you better not be out on the water. When you get this, call me."

I hung up, my gaze returning to the storm now in full rage outside.

I didn't know where Tempest's boat was moored. It could have been Dana Point or Newport Beach. Hell, it could have been Long Beach or San Diego for all I knew. Ezra hadn't said where they were leaving from. He'd only asked me to spot him.

I wished I had. If I'd gone with them, maybe they wouldn't have left before the storm. I was always late, after all. They would have had to wait for me. It would have delayed them.

As it was, they had probably gone out before the clouds rolled in.

No, I couldn't think like that. They had stayed out late last night, too. Even Energizer Bunny Ezra would be tired, at least a little. They would have seen the forecasts.

I tried to bury my anxiety by making a coffee. I went all fancy and hand ground the beans before using the pour-over Chemex, if only because it was time intensive. Despite that, I couldn't keep my gaze from drifting back to the window between every addition of water to the filter.

The storm was getting worse. I couldn't believe my eyes. The rain was so heavy, the drains in the middle of the patio were backed up and overflowing. The plastic communal furniture the landlord had set up was knee-deep in water. The gutters on the building opposite my apartment were overflowing, the water falling from the edges as if they weren't there at all.

It was like Thor was emptying buckets from the clouds. No, that wasn't right . . . Thor was the god of thunder, not rain. Well, whoever controlled the rain was taking vengeance on our poor little beach town.

At least the drought would be over. Or something.

Ezra still hadn't called. I tried him again. No luck. I checked the weather app on my phone. Oddly, it listed us as scheduled for sun all day. No chance of rain. I refreshed the app just in case it wasn't capturing the current conditions. It still said sunny, seventy-four degrees, no precipitation.

What the hell?

Besides Ezra, I only had a few phone numbers in my cell. I wasn't about to call my father. He and his new wife lived in Newport, but that might as well have been the moon as far as I was concerned. Even if he knew that Ezra had gone out today, he wouldn't know any more than I did.

No, that's not true. He might have known which harbor they had left from. Or if they had left at all.

Dammit. I was going to have to call my father. I really didn't want to.

I blew out a breath and tapped my dad's name. The phone started ringing.

My father was a doctor in Newport Beach. Like most surgeons, he was always calm and serious, always practical. He believed only what could be proven or explained by science. A philosophy that was probably good in medicine, but not great when confronted with a wife and daughter who could see the spiritual influences on people. Why he'd married my eccentric, erratic mother in the first place, I'd never know. I just chalked it up to youthful rebellion, or escapism, or something. It didn't really matter.

After Mom died, my father receded even more from our lives. He already worked long hours at the hospital, but after that, he practically lived there. At first, we all did. Ezra had to suffer through multiple surgeries as my father brought in every specialist he knew to assess my brother's broken spine. But even then, Dad only visited when absolutely necessary. I was in the room with Ezra every day and only went home when Aunt Donna forced me to. She was the one who outed me.

I probably had it coming. I mean, I was a kid who could suddenly see the crazy demons wrapped up in people's lives. At first, I had no idea what I was seeing. I thought I was hallucinating. Aunt Donna agreed with me. She saw the same things in me that she had seen in my mother. She'd never liked my mother.

That summer was miserable. Between my own injury, Ezra's surgeries, Aunt Donna's sniping, and my father's absence, I couldn't wait to go back to school. The irony of what came next wasn't lost on me.

"Hello?" My dad's voice came on the line.

"Have you seen or heard from Ezra today?" I asked, not bothering with introductions or pleasantries. He had caller ID on his phone just like every other human being on the planet, and I wasn't calling to kiss and make up. He could kiss it, as far I was concerned.

"Lil?"

"Have you seen or heard from Ezra?" I spoke slowly, intentionally. "It's a simple question." Maybe that was a touch on the rude side, but this man had very nearly destroyed my life, just like he destroyed my mother's.

"No, why?"

"Never mind. Thanks for nothing," I replied. I took the phone from my ear, my thumb ready to tap the red button, when I heard his tinny voice.

"Lil, wait. Please talk to me. Just for a minute."

"I have nothing to say to you. Never have." I couldn't help but reply. It was a character flaw, I supposed. It would be so much easier if I could let things be, but I liked to have the last word.

"What's going on? Is Ezra okay?" At least he'd asked a sensible question.

"I don't know. He was planning an ocean swim today, but with the storm, I don't know if he went out or not. I can't get a hold of him."

"Storm?"

Was the man blind? "Yeah. The storm. The buckets of water falling from the sky, thunder raging across the coast. I haven't seen a storm this bad . . . ever."

"It's sunny and seventy-two. Hardly a breeze off the water."

"That's not possible." I lived only a few miles down the coast. The weather couldn't be that different between here and there.

"Lil, should I send someone over?"

I snorted. The man couldn't even be bothered to check on my mental state himself. Not that I needed it. I'd long since mastered my ability to hide my abilities. And this time, I knew I wasn't crazy.

I snapped a picture and sent it to him.

"Happy?" I paused for half a beat and listened to his sudden intake of breath. "I'm not seeing things. I'm not making it up. I'm not telling stories. And you know what? Even if I were, you couldn't do anything about it. I'm an adult and you can't force me into therapy anymore."

I hung up the phone, fuming. I knew I sounded like a petulant child, but I didn't care. How dare that man question what I was seeing right out my own window? This was why I refused to visit him. Why I hadn't been home since the day I'd left the institute. Why I hadn't taken a dime from his pocket.

I'd earn my own damn way, thank you very much.

I forced my hands to stop shaking long enough to take a sip out of my favorite coffee mug, the one that had *Crazy Like A* emblazoned across the side with a cartoon of a mischievous grinning fox to finish the sentence. Ezra had bought it for me while I was still in the institute. The guards—I mean, therapists —had thought it inappropriate, but I threw enough of a fuss that I got to keep it. I'd treasured it ever since.

Another boom echoed off the buildings. I tried Ezra again. Still nothing.

CHAPTER 9

"911. What's your emergency?" The Laguna Beach Police dispatcher answered the phone with polite authority.

"I need to report a missing person. Maybe. Or a boat wreck. I'm not sure." I replied. I honestly didn't know what to say. I'd never called 911 before. But it had been hours since I woke up and left the first message on Ezra's phone. He still hadn't called back or checked in. No word. Nothing.

"Did you witness a boat accident?" the woman asked. I could hear her fingers tapping away on the computer keyboard as she spoke.

"No. My brother went out for an ocean swim, but this freak storm blew in and I can't get a hold of him."

"Ma'am, this line is for emergencies only. Not being able to reach your brother does not qualify."

"Listen, he's a paraplegic, training for a paratriathlon. His girlfriend took him out on her boat and I can't get a hold of them."

"They're probably out of range, ma'am. I'm sure he'll return your call when he can."

"But this storm!"

"Ma'am, there's a small craft advisory in place and we've had no reports of any boats in danger. It's highly localized. I'm certain your brother is fine and will return your call shortly. I suggest you wait for his call. For now, this line needs to stay clear for actual emergencies." The woman's tone had shifted from polite to stern.

"Thanks for nothing." I hung up.

Why would no one believe me? I couldn't be the only one worried about this freak storm. She had admitted it was real.

I wasn't crazy. Ezra was in trouble. I could feel it.

No boats in danger. Maybe that was a good sign. Maybe they were outside the storm front, had gone down to San Diego or something. It was only a little over an hour drive, especially if they'd left early.

A thunderous boom shook my entire building, as if mocking my hope.

To say I was distracted that night would be the understatement of the year. It was a Wednesday, which meant Silas's band was back on stage, and the locals thronged. A lot of folks came for the vibe. We even had a few businessy-types who brought clients or out of towners for an after-work drink.

It was busy, but not busy enough to keep me distracted. Or maybe I was already too distracted to begin with.

"What the hell, Lil?" Ty demanded when I knocked over a shaker full of Blue Hawaiian. It spilled across the counter, soaking Ty's work area and dripping off the edge onto the floor.

"Sorry," I mumbled as I struggled to collect the ice and wipe up the mess.

"What's wrong with you tonight?"

I shook my head. "Nothing. Nevermind. It won't happen

again." I had to get my head on straight, but Ezra still hadn't called.

The storm had raged for about an hour before finally calming. It cleared out almost as quickly as it had rolled in, leaving puddles the size of small lakes glinting beneath sunny skies. And now it was all anyone could talk about.

"I got caught outside in that shit," one thirty-something hipster with a waxed mustache and suspenders announced. Given the amount of grease that had to be holding the shape of his facial hair, I figured the rain must have just rolled right off him.

"I heard the thunder, but I was stuck in my office. No windows. I missed the whole show," the woman he was with replied.

"You should have seen the waves. They had to have been at least ten-foot swells. Maybe fifteen."

A glass slipped from my hand, falling to the floor with a crash.

"You okay, hon?" Virginia asked, bending over to help me clean up the shattered glass. Two accidents in as many minutes. It might be a record.

I pressed my eyelids closed. "Ezra may have been out there." I could barely breathe the words out.

"Out where?"

"On the water. He was supposed to go for an ocean training swim with his new girlfriend. I can't get a hold of him."

"If he's with his new girlfriend, there could be a good explanation for that. A different kind of breaststroke, if you know what I mean." Virginia winked.

"Eww." She was clearly trying to cheer me up, but . . . "I do not need that visual."

"Never underestimate the male libido."

"That's my brother you're talking about."

"And you know perfectly well he's a scamp."

Scamp? Who even said stuff like that? "You use the strangest words."

Virginia shrugged. "*Lady and the Tramp* was one of my favorite movies as a kid."

"That explains a lot."

"Wanna guess what my second favorite movie was?"

"Not really?" I knew she'd tell me anyway.

"*Dirty Dancing.*" She wiggled her eyebrows suggestively and fanned her face. "Patrick Swayze, my oh my."

I couldn't help but laugh. "How old are you, anyway?"

Virginia grinned, unrepentant. "We didn't have cable as a kid. Just a busted old tube tv and DVD player. Remember those? All I had were my mom's favorites and what we could borrow from the library."

Long since done cleaning the floor, Virginia picked up her tray and swayed her hips as she headed back out to the tables.

"What was that all about?" Silas asked as he slid into a seat at the bar.

Heat lit my cheeks but I tried to stay nonchalant even as I was drawn to his presence. I wiped down the counter as I glanced up at him from beneath my lashes.

Silas wasn't totally alone tonight. A white essence perched on his shoulder. The demon, shaped like a bird with a long, curved beak, but with a prehensile tail that curled around Silas's back and twitched across his opposite shoulder, eyed me back.

"Virginia was just trying to cheer me up. Set break? What can I get'cha?" I asked without pausing, trying to change the subject before I had to tell the story all over again. No need to scare him away and ruin the night.

"Just an ice water tonight."

I lifted an eyebrow in disbelief. Usually Silas was all about the Blood and Sand. I'd had to learn to make them special, just for him. The demon puffed its chest and blinked at me. If I didn't know any better, I'd say it was trying to take the credit.

"I know, I know. I'm on a detox for a bit. Trying to get my head on straight. Stay present, know what I mean?"

"Not really." I should probably pay attention to all that health stuff that Ezra was always going on about. But I didn't. However, this demon seemed to be one of the more benevolent creatures if it had influenced Silas away from vice and toward a more balanced lifestyle.

Maybe. You never really knew with any of them.

"You look like you could use one, though."

I sighed. "More like three. But I'll refrain for now." I shot Silas a half-hearted smile as Virginia arrived with another order.

"She tell you about Ezra?" she asked.

Everyone knew my brother. He'd become a regular ever since I'd started working at the Trident.

"No! What happened?"

"He has a new girlfriend."

"That was not what I said, and you know it." I lifted the shaker over my shoulder and shook it back and forth as if the innocuous object had personally offended me.

"He'll call you back. He's in looooooove," Virginia teased before whisking the finished drinks away to her table.

Silas gazed at me with a question in his eyes, requesting information. Resigned, I told him the story.

"I'm worried," I finished. "He never fails to return my phone calls."

Silas frowned as the demon on his shoulder leaned in toward his ear. I had always thought it a little odd that the demons seemed to speak to their hosts, and yet no one but me could actually hear the words they said. This one encouraged Silas toward comfort and compassion. I sensed a push toward something Silas had learned earlier that day. Something that had given him an idea.

Maybe the idea that had allowed a benevolent demon to gain sway?

"Virginia's probably right," Silas said, drawing my attention to his soulful brown eyes. I'd always loved his eyes.

I quickly looked away.

"Maybe."

"He probably cuddled up with his lady during the storm. If I had a lady and the opportunity, it's what I would do."

I snorted. "Oh yeah?"

"Of course. It's not like we get this kind of weather all the time. Have to take advantage when we can." A crooked smile and a twinkle in those caramel eyes drew me in, but I couldn't hold his gaze.

"In fact," he continued, not seeming to notice my discomfort, "Grams told me today there hasn't been a storm like this in fifty years. Last time it happened, all sorts of strange stuff went down."

"Like what?"

"Like glowing waves, for one. They lasted three weeks, or so she said."

"Like red tide?" I scoffed. "That's not entirely uncommon."

"Yeah, except there was no algae in the water. Nothing red during the day. Just glowing at night. Scientists couldn't explain it."

Another customer slid up next to Silas and ordered a Pineapple Express. Silas shot the guy an annoyed glare, but I used the interruption to consider his words while I mixed the drink.

It couldn't be a coincidence, right? The ocean spirit possessing people, trying to draw Gabi into the water, trying to drown that poor woman. Then the storm. Ezra's disappearance.

"Did your grandma say anything about people disappearing around that time?" I asked, trying to keep my voice nonchalant. "An uptick in drownings, or anything?"

"No, not really. I mean, I only called to check on her, make sure the roof wasn't leaking or anything. With Gramps long gone and my dad out of town, I'm the only one around. We didn't talk very long."

"I wonder if it will happen tonight." I mused. A niggling thought at the back of my mind had me glancing over my shoulder to make sure there weren't any demons trying to latch on—I liked to maintain my independence, thank you very much—but there were no cloudy apparitions hanging around, except the one on Silas's shoulder.

Silas leaned his head to the side with a shy but hopeful smile. "I'll go with you after closing, if you want to check it out."

I wiped up the circle of water beneath Silas's now empty glass and put it in the bus bin that was overflowing with glassware. I was going to have to get after Ferghus to pay more attention to bussing my station. The barback idolized Ty, wanted to learn all the fancy shaker flips and tricks, but left me stranded in the meantime.

"Yeah," I said, returning my attention to Silas. "I'd like that."

My trombonist's eyes lit up. "Yeah?"

I nodded.

"Great! I have my car, so we can head to the overlook after you lock up. If they really glow like Grams said, it'll be a beautiful sight. She said after all these years, she still remembers the draw the ocean had for those three weeks. It never left her, which is why she never left Laguna Beach. Couldn't stand the thought of deserting her ocean. Her words. She thought she was being funny. You know, desert and ocean."

"Got it." I smiled.

Silas pushed his fedora back on his head. "I'd better get back on stage. The guys are already waiting."

"You know, that hat makes you look like a cheesy noir detective or something."

"Why do you think I wear it?" He grinned and tugged on the brim. "See you after."

Too flamboyant. I thought again. *But still cute.*

CHAPTER 10

Silas was as good as his word. He was waiting for me out front in his beat-up Ford hatchback. His smile was infectious. I felt like I'd given a kid a candy bar or something. All I'd done was agree to go to watch the waves with him. It wasn't even a date.

Right?

I shook my head. Of course not.

Ezra still hadn't called and I was still worried. I checked my phone every five minutes, obsessively making sure there was enough battery power, I had enough reception, and Ezra hadn't called or texted. Still no word.

Virginia continued to insist he was simply having fun times with the new girl, but a pit in my stomach told me that wasn't true.

There weren't any reports of damaged watercraft or any sign of boat debris—or so the police blotter claimed, and I was checking their updates almost as obsessively as I was checking my battery life—so I held out hope he was all right. I just couldn't shake the feeling that I'd missed something. Ezra didn't normally hold out on me.

I blew out a breath, trying to shake off the anxiety, and slid into the passenger seat next to Silas. He didn't have room for my bike, so I'd left it in the bar office. It would be safe enough there until tomorrow, and I opened anyway. Chaz, the owner, only popped in once every few days, and I didn't think he'd mind too much. It was pushed up against the wall and out of the way, unless he needed to get to the cases of liquor or something.

"So I thought we'd go up to Cliff Drive, and watch from the lookouts up there. I figured it would give us the best view, if there's anything to see at all." The excitement in Silas's voice leached into my distractions.

He had taken off the ridiculous fedora, thank goodness, but it left his dark brown hair a spiky mess that pointed in every direction, except where the hat band had pressed into his skull. There, it was so squashed it looked like no amount of combing or brushing would ever fluff it up. The combination was enough to make me want to laugh, but I refrained. At least my smile was actually sincere.

"Sounds good to me."

"Do you think they'll actually be glowing?" Silas pulled the car into non-existent 2:00 a.m. traffic. "I was checking social media, and no one has said anything that I could find, but Grams seems so certain it would happen again. I called her after our last set—she's a bit of a night owl—and she said this was just like back in those days. She said if she were still allowed to drive she'd be out here herself to see it one more time. As it is, I had to promise to take pictures and bring her back tomorrow night if it really is happening."

Silas's rambling was oddly soothing. His smooth, resonant voice cocooned us in the tight car, the flashing of the passing streetlights adding an extra syncopated rhythm to his words. He kept his eyes on the road, but a smile quirked up the side of his mouth as he spoke.

With a start, I realized he really loved his grandma, and honestly chose to spend time with her and check up on her. He was solid. Dependable. A family man at heart. A caregiver.

I'd never met a man who was a caregiver before. My father was a surgeon, and I still wouldn't qualify him as a caregiver. He was more interested in status and dominance than he was in taking care of the people under his charge. And Ezra, though I loved him, could be just as self-centered sometimes. Sure, he tried to get me to take better care of myself, but I secretly thought it was mostly so he would have a workout partner he could boss around. Or maybe it was his secret desire to quit his high-paying technology consulting gig and become an official gym rat for hire. The only reason he didn't was a secret fear that people wouldn't accept a trainer in a wheelchair and wouldn't take him seriously as an athlete. Hence the push to win a para-triathlon.

Of course, the money from his fancy job also may have been a factor.

But Silas wasn't like that. Despite being a musician, he was centered. Where I was a morose ball of anxious nerves close to spinning out of control, he was the calm in the eye of the storm, pulling everything around him into his orbit. Making them feel safe, even when everything outside was chaos.

My gaze traced the outline of his profile, sketched in the grays and blacks and whites of night in the city, yet highlighted by the occasional vibrant red of passing brake lights. His hair was admittedly a crazy mess, and his choice of hats amusing to say the least, but he had a straight nose with just enough of a bump at the bridge to keep it interesting, and full lips that continuously danced along the edge of a smile as he spoke. Smooth skin with a hint of late-night stubble—none of that hipster facial hair that required constant grooming.

The demon that had ridden his shoulder in the bar was gone, too, so this was just him. Just Silas. His true self, no influences drawing out his better nature for their own agenda. Nothing encouraging him toward base desires.

With a start, I realized he had parked the car and turned to catch me staring. The corner of his lips lifted in gentle amusement. My cheeks heated and I looked away, my gaze turning forward to stare through the windshield. I gasped.

"The waves are iridescent," I whispered.

Silas laughed. "I know. I've been admiring them for the last quarter mile, but you seemed a bit distracted."

I couldn't believe I'd been so lost in my own thoughts that I hadn't noticed the shimmering display on the ocean. Normally, you couldn't see a thing except maybe the lights of a passing boat in the distance, but whatever algae or chemical or plankton was making the luminescence, it lit up the ocean for miles in the distance. You could see the peak of every wave cresting from here to Catalina.

The colors ranged from a blue so pale it was almost white, to a bright royal lapis, to a violet so vibrant you could almost call it neon. Every so often, a flash of bright pink found its way into the mix.

"How is this not on social media?" I wondered aloud. I already had my phone out taking pictures. Surely, someone else had seen it.

"Maybe it started too late? Only us true denizens of the night can bear witness." Silas opened his door and the sound of the waves crashing against the cliffs below us battered its way into the car.

I cocked my head to the side. It wasn't just the sound of waves. There was something more. Something . . . odd. Like voices whispering in the wind, too quiet to make out. Almost imperceptible. Yet . . . singing. "Do you hear that?"

"Hear what?" Silas's brow furrowed in confusion as he studied my face.

I opened my own door and stepped out toward the grassy

area of the park that looked out over the ocean. Manicured lawn and carefully planned landscaping bordered the edge of the cliff and guided pedestrians toward the stairs that led down to the beach proper, but the view from above was breathtaking, and undisturbed. At three in the morning, there should have been a homeless person or two lying on the benches or beneath a palm tree, but either the police had already moved them along, or tonight was somehow special, because there wasn't a soul in sight.

Voices carried on the breeze that ruffled the loose hairs around my face. I pulled a wisp out of my mouth and tucked it back into the loose bun on the top of my head.

As I reached the top of the stairs that led down to the beach proper, I gasped. At last, I could see where the voices were coming from. The ocean was filled to bursting with demons. The glow of their aura was so strong, they lit up the night.

But how could Silas see them?

I grabbed his wrist, urgency coating my every word. I couldn't believe he could see them, too.

"You see them?"

"The waves are beautiful, aren't they? Grams was right. This is definitely something to see."

"How could you not have told me?"

Silas faced me, confusion lining the space between his brows. "I did tell you. Grams insisted tonight would be the same as what she saw. She told me to bring you here, that you would appreciate it."

I squeezed his arm tighter. "Do you know what they are?" I could hear the voices now, chanting the hunger of their desires. They sought souls to bring to the water. Worshippers of the ocean. They sought sacrifice and control.

My gaze turned back to the beach. An amalgamation of creatures crawled from the waves. Crab legs attached to deep-sea fish bodies—complete with hanging lantern bait—scuttled across the sand. Seals with tentacles and shark teeth. Eels with lobster claws. An octopus with the mouth of a barracuda. They crawled past the shore break and up the stairs, moving with purpose if not speed.

"It's just some kind of algae or something." Silas peeled my hand off his arm, opening and closing his fist a few times once he was free. "Are you okay?"

"You can't hear them?"

"All I hear is the ocean. It would be kind of cool to swim in all that light though, don't you think?"

"No!" I practically shouted the words. "Don't go near the water. Not even to the sand. Stay away from the beach!" That's what the demons wanted. They ached for self-sacrifice, for individuals to give themselves to the deep.

Horrified I looked again at all the empty benches. Had the homeless been drawn into the waves? Is that why we were alone?

Silas frowned. It might have been the first time I'd ever seen him not smiling, at least a little. I buried the sudden urge to touch his face, to erase the frown, but I couldn't afford to minimize the urgency. He should be frowning. He should be scared. He would be if he could see what I saw.

I had to protect him, to keep him from the call. Even if it meant looking crazy in his eyes, I couldn't let him succumb to the depths.

This is what had happened to Ezra. Somehow, I knew it. Ezra was out there, somehow pulled under by the spirits of the water.

I stepped toward the stairs. It was Silas's turn to grab *my* arm. "Where are you going? Didn't you *just* say to stay away from the beach?"

Worry etched the angles of his face.

I couldn't let him follow me. I yanked my hand out of his

grasp. "Leave me alone!" I screamed. "Go away! I don't want you here!"

Eyes wide, mouth gaping, he lifted both hands and took a step back.

"They're everywhere!" I kept shouting. "You have to go. If you don't, they'll claim you for their own. They've already taken Ezra. They can't take you, too."

"What are you talking about?"

"The demons! There are demons in the water. Demons on the sand. Demons everywhere!" I knew I sounded like a crazy person. I had worked so hard to hide what I was, but I couldn't—wouldn't —let them claim a good soul like Silas. I couldn't bear the guilt of doing nothing to stop them just to save my own reputation.

Silas shook his head, easing back another step, but not going away. "It's okay Lil."

"No it's not. Don't follow me."

I turned and sprinted down the stairs, refusing to look back. I wouldn't regret my choices, not when my brother needed me.

Before my toes hit the sand, the demons were pulling at me. Tugging at my very essence. They drew me toward the water, and for once, I let them. I didn't try to fight. I didn't push them away. I let them wrap their incorporeal forms around my limbs and take me where they would.

Ezra was in there. I knew it. I could feel it. To reach him, I had to accept the demon's influence. I had to let them take me, tell me what to do, guide me into their domain. I didn't know what I would do once I was there, but it didn't matter. I would find a way. And if I didn't, at least we would be together. He wouldn't be alone the way I had been for so many years.

I wouldn't let him down. He hadn't been able to stop our father, but I could stop this.

I would find a way.

I closed my eyes. I let the demons invade my psyche. They

sang of a great feast, of a never-ending party. I let them influence my body and mind, surrendering to their vision of a great hall, warm with drinks and laughter, fellowship, and pleasure. The waves would welcome me, they said. The waters would part for me. I would be one with the divine spirit of the ocean.

The sea beckoned and lapped at my toes, soothing and warm. The gentle shushing of the waves encouraged me forward. The voices shifted and changed, turning from natural waves to the promised laughter. The demons guided my progress as I stepped forward. A pop in my inner ear startled my consciousness, but the demons soothed my nerves once more.

CHAPTER 11

One would imagine that an underwater kingdom would be . . . well, wet, I suppose. Like King Trident's palace in *The Little Mermaid*, fish would calmly swim by, maybe singing a happy tune. You'd expect to see seaweed waving gently in the current, or maybe coral structures with mermaids gathering in the dappled light from the surface, their shell bras covering their private bits—or at least the human bits.

However, this was nothing like that. Despite the fact that I had entered from the water, I found myself in a dry hall bustling with activity. There wasn't a drop of water in sight. Not even my black work pants were wet.

How had I gotten here? I remembered walking into the ocean, surrendering to the demons, and then I was here. No doors, no windows, no entrance that I could see of any kind. It was as if I had simply popped into existence in the middle of some sort of elaborate Halloween party.

Men and women paraded the brilliant gold floor holding cups made of animal horn, or pint glasses, or beer steins. There were even a few martini glasses and cut crystal Marie

Antoinette coupes. A woman dressed in a Victorian bustled gown was bent over at the waist, laughing so hard tears were streaming down her face. Apparently, the man with the bright red beard and fur cloak had said something funny.

In another corner, a guy who looked like he could have been a floor performer at Caesar's Palace had his arm around the shoulders of a man dressed in Navy blues. There was even a woman wearing a cheongsam toasting a heavily tattooed man wearing nothing but a thin bit of fabric around his nether regions.

The space itself was all dark carved wood and hanging lanterns, with actual flames flickering behind golden lampshades. They clearly weren't worried about the fire marshal coming in for a visit. Pillars held up the ceiling at least five stories above my head. A balcony ran around the edges of the room and looked down on the happenings of the pub below, while a network of bridges connected the pillars and allowed people to move freely from one side of the room to the other.

The pillars and undersides of the bridges had been carved with images of sea serpents and sharks, octopuses and whales, schools of fish and turtles the size of minivans. The banisters and framing pieces had been shaped into intricate knots and fisherman's nets. It was like a bigger, classier, more polished version of the Trident, and I had to say, I approved.

"Welcome to Aegir's Hall!" a booming voice announced.

A push from behind had me turning in indignation. A sallow-faced man with sunken cheeks and puffy eyes wrapped a thin arm around my shoulders. He looked sick, worse than any of the drug-addled new admits I'd met at the institute. His pained smile revealed receded gums and yellowed teeth that I worried were going to fall right out of his head.

I shrugged away, putting some distance between myself and the revolting creature.

"Grab a drink and join the party," the demon encouraged in

the same booming voice. The sound didn't seem to originate from his mouth, which hardly moved, but from the center of his chest. Despite his sickly appearance, the power reverberated in each syllable.

He was a man, and yet not. Though he felt solid to the touch, he emanated an aura of spiritual energy that I'd only ever felt from the demons.

The demon-man swept an arm toward a bar in the middle of the room and curled into a partial bow, pointing me in the direction of the biggest bar I'd ever seen. A row of at least fifty taps wrapped around a giant golden brewer's vat the likes of which couldn't possibly exist in the real world. Casks of wine, their wood spigots inserted and ready, had been stacked three high on one side and shelves of every imaginable liquor lined the walkway behind.

This was not what I had been expecting. I wasn't sure what exactly I had expected, but this definitely wasn't it.

"Where are we?" I asked, finally finding my voice.

"Welcome to Aegir's Hall," the demon repeated. I glanced sideways at the creature and lifted an eyebrow. "Grab a drink and join the party!"

Apparently, that was all the thing could say. Maybe this one wasn't so much a demon as a golem. I'd read about them at some point . . . creatures created from clay or stone and imbued with the spark of life. More substantial than the spirits I was used to seeing, but also less intelligent, he didn't seem to notice or take offense to my inspection.

At a loss for what else to do, I let him guide me toward a seat at the bar. His cheeks spread into an unnerving grin before he turned away to greet the next new arrival.

"What's your preference?" Unlike the host who'd taken me to my seat, the bartender looked like a regular guy. Blond hair, blue eyes, broad shoulders . . . he was almost too good looking.

Too sculpted and perfect. It made me question his humanity as much as, if not more than, the sallow-faced host.

It made me miss Silas, with his unkempt hair and ratty fedora. My throat tightened and I clenched my hands together on the bar top. I'd abandoned him at the top of the stairs, screamed at him like a possessed banshee. He wouldn't want anything to do with me now that I'd exposed him to the truth of who I really was. Further proof that I couldn't even hope for any kind of relationship with him—or anyone. I was alone but for Ezra. Which was exactly why I needed to find him.

"Um . . ." I didn't want anything to drink. I needed to focus. But I couldn't let this guy know that. I had to play along, pretend I was one of the guests, at least for a little while. "What do you have?"

"Aegir makes the best mead in Aether; nothing in Gaia even comes close. But we're here to give you whatever you desire. Ale, wine . . . a Mai Tai . . ." The demon winked, as if he knew exactly who I was and where I came from. My heart lurched as he continued. "Name it and I'll make it and your cup will never fall empty."

I looked away, trying to hide my shock by pretending to examine the vat behind him. If he knew who I was, I had to pray that he'd keep my secret. And if he didn't, if it had just been a good guess, then I couldn't reveal anything. Play it cool, keep my head, find Ezra. That was it.

I took a cleansing breath and focused.

The bartender glanced over his shoulder, following my gaze. Wider than any brewing vat I'd ever seen, the structure had to be at least twenty yards across. The bottom actually extended down into the floor and several feet above his head. It looked like it was made entirely of gold, but if so, it would be the heaviest, most expensive brewing vat ever created. I couldn't even begin to imagine where all that precious metal would have come from.

Twisting knotted vines and stylistic animals of all types had been etched into rim and along the support braces that held up the sides. Between the supports, a Viking long boat sailed on a raging sea while a larger-than-life woman wielding a fisherman's net pulled the men overboard into the depths. Glancing toward the right, between the next set of supports, a woman with long flowing hair crouched on a rocky beach, her hand outstretched toward a dolphin with its head out of the water. Beneath the waves in the distance, a bearded merman carrying a trident watched them.

"The stories of the sea god and his wife, etched into the heart of Aegir's Hall."

"That one there," I pointed at the dolphin, "looks like Poseidon and Amphitrite."

"You know your myths!"

"My mother read them to us as bedtime stories." I decided not to mention that she'd ruined bedtime forever when she'd sliced my arm and abandoned us for the ocean. "I've never heard of Aegir."

"Most of the ocean myths are based on the adventures of Aegir. I can regale you with a few more of his tales—the true stories—while you enjoy your drink, if you'd like.

"Thanks," I turned away from the vat and searched through the laughing and dancing patrons out on the floor. "But I think I'll go look for my . . . friend."

I almost said brother. That would have been a disastrous mistake. If they suspected I was here with an ulterior motive, they would definitely try to stop me. Better to keep my information to myself as long as possible.

"Your friend, huh?" The corner of the demon's mouth pulled up in a teasing smile. "I could be your friend."

I lifted an eyebrow. I'd seen Ty make the same move on the women at the bar. Not very creative. "I bet you say that to all the ladies."

Laughter erupted from the demon's throat, surprisingly warm and somehow comforting. It made me want to laugh with him, and I couldn't stop the smile from turning up the corners of my own lips.

"While you're not wrong, that doesn't make it a lie," the demon replied after his chuckles quieted. He wiped a towel across the shiny varnished wood of the bar, keeping his hands busy, just as I would have done. "Let me get you something to drink, and then I'll help you find your friend. This place is endless, if you haven't noticed, but everyone passes through here first."

He was right. I'd been dropped into the center of the room. There were no doors, no windows, and yet it wasn't stifling. The room was crowded but extended so far into the distance I couldn't be sure I'd even seen the end. I had no idea where to start looking for Ezra. I was going to need some help, and the bartender was the first person to talk to me with any sense of rationality.

And yet, it wasn't so different from the Trident. The patrons were here to party. This was a haven. A release. Just like the surfers and the frat boys and the bachelorettes that came to the Trident, this was a place to let loose and forget.

My shoulders relaxed. I knew this space. I knew this atmosphere, and I knew his job. He was a bartender, just like me. It was the bartender's job to make their customers comfortable, to ease their burdens, to have some fun. I could work with this.

"I guess I'll have the mead. Always go with the specialty of the house, right?"

"Absolutely. Of course, now you have to decide which one. Aegir brews more than twenty varieties, plus seasonal offerings."

I snorted and sat back in my seat. I didn't know anything about mead. I had no idea how to choose, or where to start.

"What's your favorite on the lighter end? Not too strong?"

The demon tapped a finger against his nose. "I gotcha." He pulled a crystal snifter from beneath the countertop and turned to the row of taps attached to the vat behind him. He wiggled his fingers across the various handles, finally grabbing a purple flower with five heart-shaped petals. Golden liquid the color of an early winter California sunset splashed into the glass. He only filled the snifter halfway before pulling it away, giving it a swirl, and sliding it across the counter toward me.

"Give that a try. This is our Sand Dune show mead, made of honey from bees who have exclusively harvested their pollen from the beach sand verbena grown on Aegir's island estate."

I swirled the glass on the counter, fingers around the base of the stem, just like Gabi had shown me with wine. I didn't know much, but I figured I could pretend. After a few seconds, I lifted the glass to my nose, sniffed, then took a sip.

Flavor burst to life in my mouth. My eyes closed without conscious thought, better to appreciate the sensation. Not quite dry, but not really sweet either, the layers were complex and fruity, with floral notes that only enhanced the overall experience. I rolled the liquid around my tongue, letting it coat every tastebud before swallowing. A lingering sweetness on the finish.

"Wow." It was all I could say. It certainly was not what I would have expected in . . . the demon realm? Hell? Where was this, really?

"I know, right?" The demon grinned. "Aegir's the original master brewer."

"Aegir?"

"You really are new here, aren't you? Well, then, let me start with the basic orientation while you enjoy your first drink in our demesne."

"That would be great."

83

"You're currently sitting in Aegir's Hall, the biggest, best party in all of Aether and Gaia combined."

"Aether?"

"The Unseen spirit world, born of Heaven and Desire and home to the Aesir, the elemental gods. Gaia is the Seen world. Earth."

"Ah." I took another sip of the mead, hoping the drink would somehow help me understand. "So what you're saying is that we're not really here."

"No, you're here all right. At least, your spirit or soul or aura —whatever you want to call it—is sitting here at this bar in Aegir's Hall. I'm guessing your body is floating at the bottom of Gaia's sea, though."

"Excuse me?"

"You're dead, sweetheart. Welcome to your chosen afterlife."

CHAPTER 12

"I am not dead." And neither was Ezra. I was sure of it. Somehow this was all a big mistake, a big misunderstanding.

"Sorry to break it to you, but if you're here, you've left the Seen world. The only way to do that is to leave your body and everything else behind. But don't worry. You've come to the best of the possible afterlives. Valhalla and the Elysian Fields combined can't compare to Aegir's feast. And you've come at the perfect time. Aegir is getting ready to host another grand gathering of the gods. All nine daughters have been called home to prepare the mead and serve at the feast."

The bartender leaned forward, glancing from side to side and speaking out of the side of his mouth. "Rumor has it Tempest—the youngest—didn't want to come home. Rán had to cast her net and drag her down in a storm. Family, know what I mean? But now that she's back, the feast can start."

Tempest was here? Then so was Ezra. My heart raced. And yes, I was happy to say I could still feel it. The demon was wrong about being dead.

But . . . if Tempest was the youngest daughter of Aegir, did that mean she was a goddess?

"So Aegir is a god?"

The bartender nodded. "Primordial god of the ocean."

"Then who's Rán?"

"Aegir's current wife. Number ten, to be precise."

A gong reverberated through the room and all eyes turned to gaze at a beam of light that appeared out of nowhere. The revelers quieted.

"Perfect timing," the bartender whispered. "You get to see them in all their glory."

As I watched, three figures appeared as if formed of mist, then solidified. In the center, a giant of a man dominated the space. At least six and a half feet tall, he wore a long bushy beard with beads decorating the strands. Twinkling blue eyes shined from beneath heavy black brows. But like all proper hipsters, his mustache was curled and styled with wax, and his hair had been combed into a perfect wave on the top of his head. A few wrinkles around his eyes suggested he was a jovial fellow, used to having a good time. Sort of like a modern black-haired Santa, but without the giant bag of gifts. Or the jelly belly. So nothing like Santa at all, really.

When I was finally able to tear my gaze away from the man, I almost fell off my stool. Standing next to him was none other than my mother. Dark auburn hair hung loose in a tangled mane of frizzy tresses. Striking hazel eyes framed by long lashes sparkled with joy. I wanted to slap the sparkle right out of her.

My mother—though she could hardly claim the name—turned to the man who had materialized behind her. He was sitting in a chair, his face hidden from view behind her swirling skirts. Her free hand reached back to his shoulder, pulling him forward. In a wheelchair.

This time, I didn't even bother trying to stay on my stool. Ezra was here. With *her*.

I gripped the mead snifter so hard the stem broke off in my hand, spilling the mead across the counter.

"Easy there." The bartender kept his voice low, which was probably good since Aegir had started to speak. With quick movements, he cleaned the mess, then brought me a new cup with a fresh pour. I took a sip as I tried to figure out what to do.

"Ladies and gentlemen, I welcome you to my hall, and the Feast of Renewal! Today is a great blessing, for not only has my youngest daughter returned from her sojourn, she has also brought with her the lost son of our new mother, Rán!"

"Hold on a hot minute," I whispered. "That woman is Rán?" My mother's name was Raine, similar, but not the same. And she wasn't a goddess. Aegir might be a god, but not her. She was a bohemian wanderer at best, an attempted murderer in truth. Maybe an actual murderer, since Ezra was here.

"Mmm hmm." The bartender leaned in close, better to share the gossip. "I think this is the first time I've seen her smile since she bound herself to Aegir."

Aegir lifted a glass that appeared in his hand from nowhere. The bright colored liquid inside sloshed with his movement. "Let us drink and celebrate the renewal of our great demesne. With Rán by my side, our harvest will be bountiful and our feast eternal! Leave your regrets at the door. Join our party and feel the glory of your desires come to life. *Skål!*"

I grimaced, but the hand holding my drink lifted as if pulled by invisible strings and I drank to the coming feast.

"Welcome to Aegir's Hall!" the host demon's voice boomed right behind me. "Grab a drink and join the party."

A rather befuddled woman slid onto the stool next to me. The bartender tipped his head and shot me a grin. "Looks like I have a new customer."

I took another sip of the mead and nodded. "I think I'll take a look around."

"Enjoy! If you need anything, I'm Dion. Come find me when you're ready for something new."

"Thanks, Dion."

He was already leaning forward toward the new arrival. "What can I get'cha?"

As crowded as it had been when I arrived, it was ten times worse since Aegir's little speech. People appeared from nowhere. Literally. As far as I could tell, there were no doors in this place, no windows. It was a sealed building. So how were people getting in? How had I gotten in? I didn't imagine the gods needed a teleportation machine, but something had to beam them and everyone else into and out of the hall. Right?

I shook my head. I'd worry about that part later. I'd gotten here after all. I could find my way out.

In the meantime, I needed to find my brother. And avoid my mother. And somehow avoid being caught by Aegir, God of the Sea.

Right. Easy.

If only I knew where they'd gotten off to. As soon as the spotlight had turned off, the crowd had moved in and they'd disappeared from view. That didn't mean they weren't here though. They had to be.

I danced through the crowd of people, sliding my way between the gaps and into the empty spaces. I crossed through the boisterous masses and headed toward the wall. If I could find the stairs to the upper level, maybe I'd be able to spot them.

Unfortunately, this crowd was worse than a Thursday night

during spring break. A heavyset man in a rain slicker waggled his eyebrows at me and tried to pull me in for a dance. Not wanting anything to do with the sweaty guy who smelled like fish, I held up a hand and backed away. Luckily, he shrugged it off. Unluckily, I bumped into a red-haired woman wearing striped pantaloons and carrying a pistol on her hip.

"Watch where ye're going," she growled in a voice that sounded like a lifetime of drinking and smoking had caught up with her. Or would have, I supposed, if the sea hadn't caught her first.

I lifted both hands in a show of non-confrontation. "Sorry. Just trying to avoid the wandering hands."

The woman grinned, revealing a few gaps in her yellowed teeth. She lifted her stein in a toast. "Enjoy the attention, while you can."

Uh huh. I smiled, as if in agreement, but I knew it didn't reach my eyes. If I ever needed that kind of attention, something had seriously gone wrong in my life. Or death, for that matter.

Taking a more careful step away from the pirate, I slipped between a woman in a ball gown and a Navy sailor in denim dungarees and a white cap.

"Heya, doll!" the Navy man exclaimed, grabbing my arm. "What's the rush? Have a drink! It's a party!"

Dammit, I'd almost made it through. I tipped back my mead glass and smiled. "I need a refill!"

"Hold it up!" He pushed my hand up into the air, so the glass was above the heads of the crowd. The glass suddenly filled with the same golden mead as I'd been drinking before. "You only need to go to the bar to change your order." He grinned. "So now you can dance with me!"

He pulled me into a spin and moved me around the floor in what must have been a swing dance from the forties. I had no idea what I was doing, but the guy was a damn good dancer. He led me around the dance floor, hopping and twisting this way and that, never letting me go, and never losing the rhythm. I couldn't help but enjoy the ride.

We also never spilled a drop of our drinks. How that was possible, I couldn't say. Like everything else around here, I would chalk it up to magic.

I suddenly realized that truly, the best way to explore the room would be to stick with Mr. Navy and dance my way through the crowd. He seemed safe enough, not handsy at any rate, and no one else would bug me while I was with him. Of course, the downside was that he didn't seem to want to stop. The dancing was taking more out of me than a run with Ezra, and within minutes I was panting for breath.

Still, I kept up the pace while my eyes scanned the room. We traveled in small circles that progressively moved us in a larger circle around the central bar. I caught a glimpse of Dion watching from his position behind the bar. He grinned and lifted a glass as I passed, and then he was out of sight. We moved back into the crowd and through to the opposite side. Around and back. Still no sign of stairs, or of Ezra.

The space seemed endless, and with each passing breath, the gathering seemed larger, and more boisterous. Shouts picked up from one corner. A crash of glass from another. The music grew louder as if to drown out the noise of the crowd, but people only raised their voices in response. Individuals bounced into one another, barely making room for me and Mr. Navy as we passed. When they didn't, Navy man would bounce us off in a new direction.

At last, I spotted the staircase. I nodded my head in that direction, and Mr. Navy maneuvered us toward the wall. The crowd began to thin out some, and at last we slowed to a stop. My breath came in ragged gasps, but I grinned anyway.

"That was fun! Thank you!" I said sincerely.

"My pleasure, ma'am. You picked up the steps right quick."

I took a sip of my chilled mead while waving a hand at my face. "Well, I need a breather now."

"Would you like some company?" The man's brown eyes widened in innocent hopeful anticipation. He couldn't have been more than eighteen years old.

"Thanks, but you should probably find a new dance partner. I'm not sure I'll be up for another go-round anytime soon."

Mr. Navy's face fell, but like a true gentlemen of the Greatest Generation, he tipped his fingers to his little white cap and moved back toward the party.

I made my way up the spiral stairs, the polished wood of the banister smooth beneath my fingers. With the tight turns, I could only see a few steps ahead. Ten minutes in, I paused to lean against the railing. I still couldn't see the top. I felt like I was on one of those continuous stair climber machines at the gym. They just kept going and going.

At last, some hundreds of steps later, I reached the balcony level. Shockingly expansive decking stretched into the distance, way deeper than it appeared from below. But just like below, the balcony was crowded with people. They didn't dance, but mingled in tight groups, like high school cliques at prom. Except with sanctioned alcohol instead of clandestine sips from Daddy's flask hidden in their jacket pocket.

Seating had been arranged near the baluster to overlook the dancers, bar, and brewer's vat below. Looking out, I realized how big that vat—and the hall—actually was. Shaped like an oval, I'd been sitting on the narrow side talking to Dion. The length was at least double that, maybe fifty yards long. And the vat looked insignificant compared to the building in which I stood.

Finding Ezra was going to be harder than I thought.

CHAPTER 13

I leaned over the banister, frustrated. It had been hours since I'd started the search for my brother, and I hadn't seen any sign of him, Rán, or Aegir. They had all vanished just as they'd appeared. I had no clues, nothing to point me in the direction where I might be able to find them. I'd circled the floor, walked endlessly back and forth, but there were no doors leading out of this room, no windows to see out. Nothing but more people excitedly anticipating Aegir's feast.

I stared down at the brewer's vat, racking my brain for a new plan. I couldn't reveal myself. If they found out who I was, if my *mother* found out I was here, I was sure to be interrogated. They would capture me, imprison me. Murder me.

Or something.

Truth was, I didn't want to have to deal with her. I wanted to get in and get out and be done with this whole place, go back to my simple quiet life as a bartender making fruity rum-filled drinks and keeping people happy. I appeased their vices, kept their demons in check, fulfilled their desires whenever I could. It wasn't much, but I made decent money and it was a pleasant existence for the most part.

Sure, I had never liked my ability to see the spirits that influenced people. It had been the bane of my existence. It made me crazy. Literally, according to my father. And now, here I was, stuck in the center of demon activity and surrounded by the souls of the drowned. I knew what I saw was real. Ezra had believed me. He was the only one. Which was why I couldn't leave him here.

He was my brother. The only real family I had left.

I couldn't give up. I knew I wasn't dead. I knew Ezra was here. I would find a way to get us both back to the real world. Somehow.

Gaze trained on the golden vat of fermenting honey water, I watched the women tending the mead. It was a fascinating process, especially given the sheer size of the endeavor. After all, the vat was about half the size of a football field, and yet it only required nine women to process the fermentation.

The obvious boss-lady was a curvy woman with her hair braided into a crown on top of her head. Leaves and flowers were woven into the strands, making her look like an ancient Celtic queen or fertility goddess or something. Unfortunately, the surly snarl that twisted her lips ruined the tender impression. Queenie walked around the vat, pointing and waving her arms, clearly shouting at the others about one thing or another, though I couldn't hear the words from this distance.

A second woman must have been the sous chef. She climbed up and down the ladders, adding things from various jars and baskets stored under the bar counter. She was a skinny thing, all bones and right angles, and her billowy white dress practically swallowed her whole.

Four more women walked across wide planks that stretched across the vast width of the vat, pulling what looked like oars behind them. They sort of reminded me of those Venetian boat guys, but in rough spun tunics pinned at the shoulders instead of striped shirts and straw hats.

Then there was the pool cleaner. A big, broad-shouldered woman with a messy braided mohawk—like a shieldmaiden on one of those Viking shows—dragged a net through the top of the vat collecting all the floating debris. After each pass, she flipped the net into a wheelbarrow sized bucket. When the bucket was full, she lifted it up on one brawny shoulder and disappeared somewhere on the far side of the bar.

The last two looked to be on oven duty. They worked on opposite sides of the vat. The one on the far end was bedraggled at best, covered almost head to toe in soot and sweating profusely. She never stopped moving, except to wipe her face with her arm and smear the ash and charcoal everywhere.

The other—closer to me and wearing a simple ponytail—was equally diligent in her work, but far less destructive to her appearance. Every few minutes, she chucked a log into a furnace beneath the mead-cooking vat, then moved the logs into place using a metal poker longer than she was tall. She turned to wipe a few stray hairs out of her face.

Tempest.

I grinned. At last, I had a lead.

As quickly as I could maneuver through the crowd, I made my way back downstairs.

Dion's smile was wide and welcoming as I leaned across the counter and waved at him.

"Ready to try something new?" he asked.

"No, I'm really enjoying this one." I lifted my snifter into the air and it automatically refilled. I eyed the new level in the glass. "Clever that. I wish we had it at the Trident. Be a hell of a lot easier than having to pull a new order and add it to the tab each time."

"The magic of Aegir's Hall," Dion replied. "And we don't

have to keep tabs on people. Free drinks for everyone, so there's that. Did you work in a pub?"

"Tropical beach bar, actually. But that's kind of why I'm back. I have to know how this stuff is made." It was the best excuse I could come up with to meet with Tempest. I risked getting one of her sisters instead, but I figured they were all too busy with other tasks. She could probably step away from the fire for a minute without losing any steam.

I snorted at my own internal joke, then eyed the glass again. This stuff might be stronger than I realized.

"It's a family secret, I'm afraid. Aegir and his daughters are the only ones who know the recipes."

"Do you think they'd be willing to give me an overview? I was watching from the balcony, and it all seems so fascinating. I don't need a recipe—I wouldn't be able to do anything with it anyway—I'm just curious."

Dion lifted an eyebrow and pulled in a deep breath. "I supposed I could ask, but no guarantees. They're all pretty busy, and the work is precise." He frowned, twisting his lips to the side as he glanced over his shoulder. "Tempest is the nicest of the lot. I'll see if she's willing."

"That would be great!" I grinned, then patted my cheek. Truth be told, I was feeling a little numb. I had to get it together. `

I set my glass down on the counter, swearing I wouldn't take another sip. A minute later, the glass was back in my hand. The mead was just that tasty.

Dion was back a couple minutes later. "All right, she says she can't take a break or Eldoris will have her hide, but she can talk while she works."

"Eldoris?"

"The eldest. The one shouting and waving her hands around like a madwoman. She gives the orders and the rest obey . . . or else."

"Oh. Queenie. When I was up on the balcony, that's what I named her in my head, anyway."

Dion grimaced. "Don't let her hear you say that."

"Mmm-kay." I had no intention of getting anywhere near the woman with the snarl. I just needed to talk to Tempest, find out where they were holding Ezra, and get us both home. The fewer people I had to interact with the better.

Dion snapped his fingers, startling me. A flip top appeared in the counter.

"Nifty," I murmured as I stepped behind the bar. It made me wonder if something similar worked the entrance and exit to the hall. "Or else what?"

Dion furrowed one eyebrow quizzically. Right. We'd moved on, but not really.

"You said the rest obey . . . or else." I made the last two words all doom and gloom, deepening my voice and waggling my fingers like a bad movie villain. Then I straightened. "Or else what?"

They were gods, weren't they? I imagined it would be pretty difficult to hurt the gods.

"Or else they're grounded."

"Pfft," I spluttered. "Grounded? Like naughty teenagers? Ridiculous."

"Maybe, but you don't want to face Eldoris's wrath. Trust me."

We walked around the length of the bar, passing a few other bartenders and customers along the way. Since no one needed to ask for a refill, there weren't too many patrons at the bar itself. Those that were actually sitting down held the glazed expressions of new arrivals.

"A lot of new souls, eh?" I asked, trying to keep up some semblance of conversation.

Dion glanced over his shoulder. "Not really. This is barely a drip. Been this way for—I don't know—fifty, sixty years? We used to host hundreds, sometimes thousands of new arrivals every day. Those were the days. Ships sinking on the Atlantic crossing, Viking raids, conquistadors losing all their gold to the bottom of the ocean. Those feasts were epic. Truly. Aegir glowed with power, and we all were the stronger for it."

Sadness pulled at the corners of his mouth. "Now look at us." He waved a hand at the host who'd escorted me to the table. "Some have begun to regress, like Peithon over there. He used to be the master of ceremonies. He could turn a quiet little gathering into a rager with the snap of his fingers. Now all he can do is welcome you to the feast."

Regression? I'd have to think on that some more, but at the mention of food my stomach growled. Loudly.

"Speaking of feast, is there any food?"

The light returned to Dion's eyes. I was glad about that. He looked much nicer with a smile on his face.

"The feast is normally upstairs, but I'll bring you a snack."

"Upstairs? I didn't see any food upstairs." I looked up at the balcony, as if I could see the food from here.

"Don't worry about it. I'll be back in a minute. For now, I'd like to introduce you to Tempest, Aegir's youngest daughter."

We had come around to Tempest's workstation. It hadn't been noticeable from above, but she was actually standing a half level down from the main floor in a trench that ran about twenty yards in either direction along the base of the vat. I had been wrong before: the vat itself didn't sink into the ground, it rested on a cast iron cage that housed the fire. The bar had been built around the brewing vat. It just wasn't obvious until you saw Tempest's trench.

My thoughts were whirling in circles. I tried to put the snifter down again, but there was nowhere to set it in this section. Instead, I took another sip.

"Give me just a moment," she said before tossing another log into the fire.

"I'll leave you here, then," Dion said, "and be back with a snack in a jiff."

For the first time, I could see how the system worked. It was like a giant wood burning pizza oven. Tempest threw wood into the gap below the vat, moving it around until it caught fire and adjusting the distance to make sure the bottom of the vat was heated evenly across the entire bottom. When the wood was situated to her satisfaction, she finally turned to face me.

Her expression was priceless. Her mouth literally dropped open.

"What are you doing here?" she hissed as soon as she'd gathered herself together. She scanned me from head to toe. "You aren't supposed to be here. You heard Abdulbaith. You aren't supposed to interfere."

I pressed my eyes closed for a moment, trying to clear the fog from my brain. My stomach growled again, distracting me. I shook it off.

"Abdulbaith? Was he the spirit who possessed my customers? The one with tentacles and teeth and eels for friends?"

"He told you to leave it alone."

"You stole my brother!" I shouted.

Tempest's eyes widened. "Shh!" She grabbed my arm, frantically turning her head this way and that to see if anyone was watching or listening. When no one commented, she yanked me to the side.

"How much of that have you had to drink?" she asked.

"Dunno. Enough. Too much maybe. I can't seem to put it down."

She grabbed the glass from my hand and threw it on the floor. The crystal shattered.

"Hey!" I leaned forward to pick it up, but Tempest shoved me away. "Why'd you do that? That was good mead! What a waste."

"Leave it," she said. "Don't drink anymore. You have to go home. I assume you crossed without drowning, right?"

I shrugged. "I still have a heartbeat." I pressed my hand to my chest. I couldn't really feel anything, but I knew it was there. "I think."

"Good. Go back. However you got here, reverse it."

"Can't," I crossed my arms over my chest. "Not without Ezra."

"Ezra is with Rán." Tempest's shoulders sagged. "Even I couldn't keep him."

"No, he's with our *mother*. Raine. She is not a god."

"You're right. So am I. My father chooses a new wife every few centuries. They each become Rán until their usefulness is done. My mother was the last Rán. She faded half a century ago. When your mother arrived about fifteen years ago, she became the new Rán. Thus the cycle continues."

"Why should I believe you?"

"I don't know. I don't care. It's the truth. All I know is that if you are your mother's daughter, you do not want Aegir to find you."

"I'm not leaving without Ezra," I insisted.

Tempest shook her head, pressing her fingers into her left temple. "You don't understand. Rán refused to begin the harvest until her family was found and brought to her. I brought Ezra, even though I didn't want to, and she gave Aegir his new army. There's no separating them."

"I'll find a way. Just tell me how to find them."

CHAPTER 14

"Tempest! Where is your head? There's a cold spot on the Northeast corner. The boil is uneven." Queenie stomped her way around the stack of wood set aside for the fire.

Tempest ducked her head and hunched her shoulders as she spun toward the opening for the fire. "Apologies, Eldoris. I didn't see." This was not the woman I'd met in the bar, the svelte confident lady who had laughed and danced with Ezra. Where had she gone?

"Always excuses, never action. Get back to work. And you!" The woman's piercing blue eyes connected with mine. "Who are you and what are you doing here? Souls don't belong behind the bar. You must join the feast for our father."

I smiled, letting the alcohol float to the front of my brain. "I just wanted a peek at the action. I worked in the industry."

"I don't care if you were the greatest brewer to have walked Gaia's parasite infested dirt. Souls are not allowed behind the bar."

My smile turned into a grimace.

"Who let you back here, anyway? I'll regress them back to their base form and return them to the hunt."

"I let myself in. Jumped the counter." I replied. No need to get Dion in trouble. He had only been trying to help. "I'll leave the way I came."

"You do that."

I decided I was going to amend her nickname from Queenie to Bitch Queen Supreme.

"And Tempest," she spun back toward her younger sister, "fix the flame before I tell father that you've ruined his latest vat of Sweet Orange."

Tempest was already back at work, pushing the logs into place with her extra-long poker. She didn't say another word, but the hunch of her shoulders and bend of her neck said it all.

"Why you so mean?" I demanded, the slurred words slipping out of my mouth before my rational brain caught up with me.

"Excuse me?" Bitch Queen Supreme glared at me with narrowed eyes and both hands stacked on her rather broad hips. Childbearing, I think they used to call it. She had an hour-glass figure that any sex-pot celebrity would admire. I, however, found the shitty attitude overruled any beauty she may have had.

"You're sisters, aren't you? You should be nicer to her. You never know when something bad will happen."

"Leave it alone," Tempest hissed over her shoulder even as she continued to move the logs.

I returned Queenie's glare, staring her down like a dog defending its territory. Tempest may have kidnapped my brother, or aided in it anyway, but my first impressions were rarely wrong. She was still good people. Better people than Bitch Queen Supreme anyway.

"*I* am the eldest daughter of Aegir. My mother was the first Rán, the first goddess of the sea. *I* am the keeper of the secrets and mistress of the mead. Only my father outranks me."

"And my mother, apparently."

As soon as the words left my mouth, I knew I had made a mistake. I pressed my lips together, wishing I could take them back and hoping to prevent anything else damning from slipping out.

Queenie's eyes narrowed to slits. Her lips curled in a slow smile.

"You are Rán's second mortal child?"

"No," Tempest interrupted, eyes wide. "It's one of those jokes the humans like to tell. Like, 'your mama's so fat, when she sits around the house, she sits *around* the house.'"

"You knew who she was, didn't you? You found her before you brought the son home to us, and you said nothing." Venom laced Eldoris's voice, her words harsh and sibilant.

Tempest grabbed at Eldoris's sleeve. "She didn't want to come on the boat. I couldn't make her, not without drawing suspicion from the son as well. I did my job. I was only tasked with bringing him here. Not her."

I backed away a step, bumping into a cart holding random glassware. The goblets clinked together, sending those at the edges crashing to the floor where they shattered into a million sparkling pieces.

A cheer and laughter from the souls on the other side of the bar. "Party foul!" A man wearing nothing but board shorts shouted as he lifted his glass into the air for a refill. More curious eyes turned to see what was happening.

I did not want this attention. The last thing I needed was more people aware that I was here, aware that I wasn't quite like the rest of them.

I eased back another step but Eldoris tracked me with her eyes and her body. She slid forward, her movement sinuous. Something about her reminded me of the shadow eels that the demon in the bar had unleashed. Maybe it was the narrow chin that jutted out slightly from beneath a wide mouth. Or maybe it was the way that mouth gaped open. Or the wide set eyes that glared at me with emotionless focus.

Warning bells clanged in my brain. I turned, intending to sprint for the far side and jump the counter like I had said I would. Hide in the crowd.

I hadn't made it two steps before fingers clamped around my arm with a vise-like grip. Eldoris spun me around to face her, our noses just inches apart.

"There is someone anxious to see you. I am glad to be the one to bring you to her." The woman's grin was coldly gleeful, revealing pointed teeth. There was nothing human about her.

)●(

Trying to fight my way out of Eldoris's grip was an exercise in futility. She snapped her fingers, opened a passage in the counter, and dragged me across the dance floor. The revelers parted the way like waves at the prow of a boat. They never lost focus on their conversations or their drinks. They simply stepped aside without any recognition of their surroundings.

"Let me go!" I shouted as I dragged my feet across the floor. "You can't do this."

No one turned to look, not even Eldoris. She pulled me forward as if my wriggling and jerking was of no consequence. The rapid pace meant I could never set my feet, couldn't find the leverage against her. Every twist of my wrist only resulted in pinched skin and a friction burn.

We reached the edge of the oblivious gyrating crowd and I found myself in an area I hadn't seen on my self-guided tour. A set of grand steps led up to wide double doors carved with the image of a bare-chested, muscled man holding a trident. His bottom half was that of a curled sea serpent, and he wore a crown of what looked like coral, with a round gem at the top that shone with rays of light. There was some resemblance to Aegir, but the man who had given the speech didn't have a tail or crown, and the man in the carving didn't have the bedazzled facial hair.

The door cracked open with a resounding boom. The room beyond was decorated in plush fur rugs and more dark wood. Aegir the man sat in an overstuffed leather chair in the center of the room, backlit by the flickering light from a fireplace in the wall behind him. My mother was curled up on a couch to his right. Another dark-haired man sat in an old-fashioned wooden wheelchair with his back to us.

Their conversation stopped as Eldoris pulled me forward into the room.

Aegir lifted an eyebrow.

Rán's face lit up with undeserved joy.

Ezra's chair turned. Horror dripped from his expression.

Bitch Queen Supreme threw me forward onto the floor at Aegir's feet. A heavy fur rug cushioned my fall, but my hip still felt the reverberation from the stone beneath. I rubbed my arm. It was red and sore where she had gripped my skin.

"Ow." I glared at her but she didn't even deign to glance in my direction. She dipped her chin in deference to her father.

"Lil!" Rán exclaimed before Eldoris or Aegir could say a word. She jumped up and kneeled at my side, arms extended as if to give me a hug.

I flinched away. "Hello, Raine. Or should I call you Rán now? I hear you got a promotion after you drowned yourself."

I would not call her mother. The woman who had tried to murder me in my sleep, the woman who had triggered my visions and ultimately caused my incarceration in the institute, did not deserve any other title. Let her be the vengeful goddess of the sea. She had no other claim on me.

Rán's brows pinched together in a way that I remembered from childhood. It had always preceded a lecture. That is, when she was around for long enough to give one.

"Father," Eldoris interrupted, "I found Rán's mortal daughter at your feast. She was speaking with Tempest, distracting her from her sacred work."

"You were with Tempest? Did she steal you, too?" Ezra asked.

"No," Eldoris snapped. "Tempest is unreliable. Undisciplined. *I* found her at the feast. Tempest would have let her escape."

"So I guess I was just the lucky one," Ezra mumbled under his breath. I studied his face. He wasn't happy to be here, at least. He hadn't come willingly. My biggest question was whether he was somehow still alive, like me, or if Tempest had drowned him to bring him here. If he were truly dead, I wasn't sure I could bring him back at all. I was still going to try.

"How did you come to be here, in my hall?" Aegir's voice crashed through the room like waves against the cliffs.

"I came for my brother." I spit the words. "He doesn't belong here. You can't have him."

Aegir's laugh boomed from deep within his broad chest. Rán and Eldoris joined him, higher-pitched but equally cynical counterpoints to the mocking rhythm. "And how are going to stop me? We are all family, now. You both belong here, as much as my own daughters. My family doesn't leave unless I let them."

"You belong with me. I am still your mother." Rán patted her hand against my calf. I yanked my leg out of the way.

If I could have shot lasers from my eyes, I would have, right then and there.

"You have never been my mother. No mother in her right mind would wish her children dead."

"I never wished you dead!"

"Really?" I looked around, waving a hand at the room and gesturing back at the door that led to Aegir's feast. "Then why are we here? You stole us from our lives!"

"It's not like that. It's better here. Aegir has promised to fix Ezra just as soon as the harvesters bring in enough energy, and now that you're here, it will all be so much easier, so much faster. Then we can all live together as we were supposed to. As I always wanted."

I shook my head, disgusted at her selfishness. Mothers were supposed to want what was best for their children, not what was best for themselves. At least, that's what the tv made me want to believe.

"You're a monster."

Rán's eyes flashed and for a moment, I was back in my bed watching the blade strike down toward my head. I gritted my teeth and lifted my chin. I would not cower before her. Not again. Not ever again.

A boom of thunder rolled through the hall.

"Mom!" Ezra snapped, drawing the woman's attention. "I'm tired."

The storm quieted.

"Of course. You should rest. Take Lil with you. I'm sure she'll see things more clearly when she sees how happy you are here. How happy you both will be here. The feast will be all the more fun for the reunion that it celebrates."

Rán clapped her hands. A woman stepped forward out of a shadowed corner of the room. Lank hair draped across hunched shoulders. Watery eyes peered from the recesses of gaunt cheekbones. Thin lips pulled down toward a pointed chin.

I glanced at Eldoris, who had risen from her slight bow but remained in place in the center of the room. A smug smile twisted her lips. If I hadn't been watching so closely, I would have missed the subtle dip of her chin to acknowledge the woman.

Truth was the new woman could have been Eldoris's dying sister.

"Follow me." The words were a whispered hiss, barely audible over the still retreating sound of the storm.

Ezra turned his ancient chair with far more effort than the action deserved, and I fell in line behind him. There was no use protesting. It wasn't like I could run away right now. Besides, I needed to talk to Ezra, alone, and this might be the only chance I had.

As the doors closed behind us, Rán's voice slipped through. "Thank you, Eldoris. You have brought me my children and will be rewarded. What can I offer?"

The door sealed shut and I heard no more.

CHAPTER 15

I expected to see the great hall and the party still raging beyond the doors to Aegir's room. Imagine my surprise when we exited to an empty, carpeted corridor lit with a long line of skylights rather than the dim lamplight of the rest of the hall.

"What the . . ." I started to say, but I couldn't find the words to express my shock.

"Don't bother trying to figure it out," Ezra said. "As far as I can tell, the place changes based on the whims of Aegir. You see what he wants you to see, go where he wants you to go. It's like the stairs at Hogwarts, but you never see anything move."

"Then how do the demons know where to go? They must be able to determine their own path somehow."

"Demons?"

I nodded my chin toward our guide with the sallow skin and greasy hair. "Non-humans, like her."

"Oh, she's human. Dead now, but human. From what little I've been able to overhear, she's the soul of the first Rán and Aegir's most devoted priestess."

I couldn't help my snort. "Eldoris's mom? Makes sense.

Eldoris probably sucked all the life out of her while she was in the womb."

"Something like that." Ezra stopped his chair, turning it to face me and block my way. "Look, you need to get out of here as fast as you can. However you came, leave."

I shook my head. "Not without you. You're the only real family I have left, and I'm not going to leave you here. Besides, I don't really know how I got here."

"Follow me," Rán Numero Uno urged. Her voice was weak and hoarse, barely audible even in the silence of the hallway. She had stopped a few paces ahead of us, her gaze expressionless and face lax.

"That's what waits for you if you stay," Ezra whispered. "It's mom's future, and it'll be yours, too. Aegir wants power. He feeds off it. He'll find a way to twist you to his purpose like he has mom. You have to find a way out."

"I told you, I'm not leaving you here." I stuck my hands on my hips and glared. I knew I was being belligerent, but I didn't care. "We'll have to find a way together."

Ezra growled big brother frustration as he turned his chair back toward the woman. "I've already tried. There's no way out for me, not without Rán's gate. I can only go where Aegir allows, as he allows. Besides which, this chair is ancient. I can't go faster than a snail, and you can't carry me. But you got here somehow on your own without him knowing, and you can get back on your own."

"You've only been here what, a day? That hardly counts as trying."

Ezra's chair stopped so suddenly, I almost ran into him. He looked at me over his shoulder, his mouth agape. "That's not possible."

I frowned and shrugged. "How long do you think it's been?"

"Weeks at least. Months, maybe."

"There is no such thing as time in Aegir's Hall," the sickly woman suddenly chimed in. "As his power grows and wanes, so does his demesne. You are here at his call, by his whim, until he releases you."

She gestured one arm toward a door on the right side of the hallway. "For the mortal son." Her other arm moved toward the left. "For the mortal daughter. I will come for you when Aegir requires your presence. Until then, rest as Rán has decreed."

)⊕(

T he room smelled of fresh ocean breezes, plumeria flowers, and sunshine, reminding me of a summer day spent lying on a beach chair under an umbrella. Unlike the rest of the hall, the space was well-lit and cheerful, with pale blue and white decor and soft filtered light that came from everywhere and nowhere all at once. The fourposter bed was larger than my bed at home and draped with gauzy white curtains. It even had an en suite bathroom.

What it didn't have, was a way out. As soon as Rán Numero Uno closed the door, it disappeared. Literally. There wasn't even a doorframe to show where the exit should have been. I was locked in a comfortable box like Schrodinger's Cat.

I paced the length of the room. And back. I couldn't shake the feeling that I was missing something. Maybe my brain was still muddled by the mead. That was a fun phrase. Muddled by the mead . . . ha!

Shit.

I needed to sober up.

The bathroom was as done up as the bedroom and kept to the seashore cottage theme. Even the faucets were shaped like sea stars and the floor of the shower was tiled in actual seashells. Gag me. Too much. A watercolor painting of a boy and a girl playing in the waves could have been cute, if they hadn't looked eerily familiar.

Mother had painted this scene.

Rán.

I leaned my elbows on the counter and splashed cold water on my face. The blue and white striped hand towel was off to my right. I waved my hand around until I found it and patted myself dry. I still hadn't looked in the mirror. That was intentional. I didn't want or need the reminder of what—or rather who—I looked like.

I had my father's hair and my mother's eyes. That's what everyone who knew me as a child said. The eyes of a murderer who hadn't been able to stay in one place for more than a moment in time, and the hair of a narcissist more concerned with his own reputation than keeping his family together.

Awesome.

I set the towel aside. My narcissistic hair was a mess, my murderous eyes puffy from lack of sleep. How long had I been awake, anyway? At least twenty-four hours by this point. I reached in my pocket for my phone to check the time, but it wasn't there.

Double awesome.

I really didn't want to have to buy another one, but apparently walking straight into the ocean, only to be swarmed by demons, wasn't good for keeping track of things.

Quickly, to avoid staring at myself any longer than I had to, I rebraided my hair in a long tail down my back and pinched my cheeks to get a little blood back into the system. I wiped away the errant mascara crumbles and decided that was good enough.

Back in the bedroom, there was still no sign of the door. There was nowhere to go. I stretched out across the bed. A little on the fluffy side, but otherwise it was quite comfortable. A comfortable box to lull me into complacency and accept my imprisonment.

Was I dead, or alive?

I placed my fingers on my neck, feeling for my pulse point. My heart beat steady and strong. I was definitely alive.

And yet, here I sat in Aegir's Hall, surrounded by the souls of the dead and the demons who fed off them.

So which was it? Could it be both?

I closed my eyes. Listened to my breathing. Let my mind float free.

I'd had a stint of yoga classes once, gifted to me by one of my dad's girlfriends when I was on a brief home stay, who thought it might help with the "anxiety-induced hallucinations." Ha! But they had given me a tool to help me connect with my inner self. Or something. I liked the breathing.

I latched onto that now and sank deeper into the black.

Ten breaths later, I heard music. A horn. But not through my ears. It came from somewhere inside of myself. As if my deeper soul was resonating with the sound. It was sad. No, not sad. Mournful. Haunting. Kind of like the military's "Taps" song that they played at funerals, but not the same. More improvisational.

The sound called to me. Called me home.

CHAPTER 16

Freezing water filled my shoes. The soft shush of a wave breaching the sand filled my ears. I blinked.

"Lil!"

I turned my head and blinked another couple times. Silas was running toward me across the softer sand of dry beach. He held his trombone in one hand and waved at me with the other. A relieved grin lit his face from within. Or maybe it was the reflection of the sunrise.

An older woman walked behind him at a much more sedate pace. Her wild hair blew untamed around her head and a long bohemian-style skirt twisted around her ankles. She too smiled, though it was less jubilant and more knowing. She looked familiar.

I couldn't help but return Silas's smile as I made my way out of the cold surf. I honestly didn't know how people who lived in more northern climes ever dared dip a toe in the ocean. Even the Southern California summer didn't warm the water near enough for my comfort. I'd swim in Hawaii. Or Cancun. Maybe Tahiti, not that I'd ever been there. Anything north of the Tropic of Cancer and I'd stay on shore, thank you very much.

Silas wrapped me up in a giant hug, painfully thumping the trombone across my back without realizing. I gave an undignified grunt and he let go.

"Sorry. I'm just thrilled you're back. I couldn't believe you walked into the water and disappeared like that. Grams said you'd be fine, that you'd come back, but I have to admit I didn't entirely believe her. She's always been more of an optimist."

I rubbed my back where the bell of the horn had bruised my spine. "More of an optimist than you? How's that possible?"

Silas quirked his lip up in a half smile. With his free hand he reached out to brush a loose hair behind my ear. I shifted, uncomfortable, not from his touch, but how it made me feel. Connected. Appreciated. My heartbeat sped, reminding me that I was still physically in my body, grounding me to the present.

His hand lingered on my neck, thumb brushing across my jaw. "I was worried." His smile widened in a flash of straight white teeth. Nice, normal, human teeth. "She wasn't."

"You've done well for a first trip into the Aether." Grams announced as she finally drew closer. Smile lines creased her face and her skin had a little of that papery look that the elderly get with age, but she moved with confidence over the shifting sand.

I stepped away from Silas and cleared my throat. "Thanks, I guess."

"Silas was right to call me. The storm was stronger than even I anticipated, but you rose to the occasion. It would have been easier if your mother had taught you the way of things instead of trying to hide you away, but then, she always was unhappy with her lot. Luckily, you had Silas as an anchor. He was able to call you home."

I was lost. "What are you talking about? You knew my mother? And what things? Where was I?"

I had so many questions I didn't know where to start. They tumbled out of my mouth in a torrent.

Grams chuckled. "We'll get to that, my dear. Now, you really do need to rest up a bit. If you're willing, I'd like to invite you to my home."

I shook my head, then glanced over my shoulder at the ocean. "My brother. I need to go back and get him."

"You are a Daughter of Lilith. You can traverse between Earth and Aether any time you wish."

My face pinched. How did she know where I had been? I didn't even know where I had been. Aegir's Hall might have been a dream. Or a hallucination. Except, Ezra had been there with me. I was sure of it. "No. Really. I have to go. Time works differently there. Ezra said he's been trapped for weeks, maybe months, but it's been less than a day here, right?"

I glanced at Silas for confirmation, and he nodded, brow furrowed. "A few hours is all."

I couldn't tell if he was confused or worried for my sanity. Either would have made sense.

"I can't lose that much time again. They're probably already looking for me." My gaze drifted back over the waves, watching for the demons to emerge from the water once more. "They're probably already on their way."

"Perhaps, but that's of no importance. Time is of no importance. Time is, after all, a construct of the Seen realm. The Unseen has no constraints and therefore has no concept of urgency. We who walk—or walked, in my case—between have no need to rush."

The older woman turned and strode up the beach toward the steps that led to the parking lot. I had emerged from the water almost exactly where I remembered walking in. I glanced down at my clothes . . . still dry, except for my feet and the hem of my pants that must have caught the top edge of a wave. My shoes were well and truly ruined this time.

"I have no idea what you're talking about." But I followed, unsure what else to do. I didn't know how to get back to Ezra on my own. The old lady seemed to have all the answers, even if she were less than generous with her words.

Silas bumped me with his shoulder. "She's like that," he whispered. "She moves on her own schedule, does her own thing. I find it's easier just to follow along. She'll get to the point eventually. You'll get used to Grams."

"Used to her? I didn't even know she existed until just this moment," I whispered right back.

"Yes you did, dear," she called over her shoulder. "I've been watching you ever since Silas started playing at that lovely little night spot of yours."

Apparently her hearing was amazing for someone who looked at least eighty years old. A sprightly eighty, but still.

I eyed her frizzy hair and suddenly realized where I had seen her before. She had been the mysterious woman who drew the symbol on the napkin that had saved Gabi's life.

"She comes by almost every Saturday night," Silas added.

"How have I never noticed?" I thought I knew all the regulars, even the ones that didn't order a drink from me.

He shrugged. Then grinned. "Maybe you need to get your eyes checked?" He bumped me with his shoulder once more.

Twerp. My vision was perfect. Better than twenty-twenty, or so every doctor I'd ever seen said. But the mood lightened. A little bit of my anxiety slipped away, at least for the moment. When he stayed close, I didn't move away. It was nice to be home.

CHAPTER 17

S ilas's little hatchback turned off the highway just north
of the city of Laguna Beach onto a roughly paved access
road I'd never noticed before. It ran along the southern
edge of the wilderness area, and up into the hills overlooking
the state beach. The sky was just beginning to lighten into day,
casting odd gray shadows beneath the scrub brush of the native
chaparral that surrounded us. There wasn't a house or a car in
sight.

It was eerie.

"I didn't know you could even come up here," I murmured,
my gaze trained outside my window. Grams had been given the
front seat while I was crammed in the back with Silas's gear. I
didn't mind. At her age, the woman wouldn't have been able to
fold herself into the backseat even if she wanted to, and it gave
me time to think without anyone watching me.

"I'm not a fan of visitors, except for Silas here. He's been a
blessing, I'll admit. Everyone else can go right on to Hades as
far as I'm concerned."

I snorted, shocked by the vitriol that had been delivered in
the same kind, grandmotherly tone as everything else she said.

"Hades, huh?"

"Mmm," she replied noncommittally. "Heaven's too full these days. Of course, Valhalla's rising again with all of those new superhero movies. The Norse pantheon pivoted quite nicely from religious fervor to pop culture fandom. That actor who plays Thor draws quite the crowd." She leaned to the side and lifted a hand to her mouth, as if to whisper so Silas couldn't hear. "If given the opportunity, I'd take him for a tumble, that's for sure."

I slapped a hand over my mouth, but the laughter spilled out between my fingers.

"Graaammms," Silas whined between his own laughter. "I don't need to hear that."

The elderly woman shrugged unapologetically. "That's why I whispered."

The road twisted around another little hill and Grams's bungalow seemed to appear out of nowhere. The tiny house sat nestled in what looked like a natural depression and looked out on the ocean in the distance. There were no other houses between here and the water, just a mile or so of chaparral and the highway streaking by far enough away that you couldn't even hear the cars.

"Wow," I murmured, getting out of the cramped vehicle. The view was expansive, wrapping at least a hundred and eighty degrees.

"Thank you. I'm rather fond of it."

"I thought this was all government protected land."

"It is. I was 'grandfathered in' so to speak, though I hate that stupid patriarchal term. But if I said 'grandmothered in' you'd have no idea what I was talking about."

"I think I might have gotten the gist." I replied with a smirk.

Grams batted the words from the air with a wave of her hand. "Don't be a smartass. Come on."

She lifted her skirt with one hand and climbed the three

steps to the front door. The single-story rambling bungalow looked as if it might have been built by hand. It reminded me a lot of the Pasadena craftsman style houses, except more rustic. Two wooden rocking chairs with a small bistro table in between sat on the front porch looking out across the hills toward the ocean. Grams pulled open the screen door and entered the house.

I paused a moment, taking a deep breath and holding it in. The birds had already started their morning songs, warming up in watchful anticipation of the sun's rise over the hill.

"I love it out here," Silas said, leaning on the porch railing. "It's not that far from where I grew up, and yet it's in the middle of nowhere. You feel isolated, but not alone."

"It's peaceful," I replied. "Shockingly so. I mean, I run with Ezra just over that hill, and yet there are always people, and traffic, and just . . . noise. Up here it's like the rest of the world doesn't exist."

"It's a place out of time."

"Exactly."

"Coffee's ready!" Grams called from inside.

With one final wistful glance at the view, I went inside, Silas close on my heels.

"How long have you been here?" I asked, my gaze taking in the details of the house around me.

The inside was an odd combination of architectural eras. The front door opened to a cozy living room featuring an old-fashioned, wood-framed couch with lace doily covered side tables. A small potbelly stove sat in the corner of the room with a steel kettle on top. Yet the kitchen—visible over a half wall—was decked out in top-of-the-line stainless steel appliances. A breakfast nook with built-in nineteen fifties booth-style seating could just barely be seen nestled beneath a bay window that must look out on the spectacular northern view of the hills cascading down to the sea.

"My mother's mother's mother claimed this land before California was a state," Grams replied as she slowly pressed the handle of a French press coffee maker. "She built the first house, little more than a one room shack, but we've added on and modified over the years."

She handed one mug to me, and another to Silas. "Decaf for you, dears. You're going to crash soon, and rightly so. But I want to give you a couple more tidbits to mull over while you sleep."

Silas grunted his thanks and took a seat in the living room while the elderly woman went to the kitchen and rummaged around a few cabinets and drawers, still talking. "First, sit down before you fall down. I'd rather not have to clean coffee from my grandmother's best rug."

My jaw cracked with a yawn. She wasn't wrong. Exhaustion dragged on my limbs and my eyes felt swollen and gritty. I did as ordered and perched my butt on a small counter stool near the kitchen pass through.

"Now, we're going to start with the basics. You are a Daughter of Lilith."

"My mother's name was Raine," I interrupted. A headache was building at the back of my head, making it difficult to concentrate, but I still knew my own mother's name.

"Shush up and listen," Grams replied. She never raised her voice, never harshened her tone, but it was clear there was no arguing against her. Even while her hands were busy arranging biscotti and slicing fruit, she continued her lesson. "Before Eve, there was Lilith, the original woman and Adam's first wife. You are descended from her through your maternal line, as am I. We aren't as populous as the daughters of Eve, but we are spread around the world just the same."

I pressed my eyes closed and rubbed my thumb in circles on my temple.

"Lilith was created to tend the wilds, while Adam was granted dominion over the cultivated lands and domesticated animals. He thought that included Lilith. She disagreed. Unfortunately, when they separated, they made room for the beings of the Aether to invade and influence our world."

I lifted a hand. "I'm sorry, you've lost me. Adam and Eve were in the garden of Eden, right? Eve ate the apple from the serpent. That's the story I've heard."

Grams set her knife aside with more force than necessary. "I cannot believe your mother didn't educate you at least this much. You should have the real stories, the complete truths. They should have been told to you at bedtime, not buried away." She wiped her hands on a kitchen towel.

"My mother tried to kill me in my bed. I don't think she was too concerned with stories."

"Pfft," Grams replied.

My eyes flew open.

"Your mother was cutting your ties to the Aether, hobbling you in a twisted attempt to protect you. That her athame was used to cause harm was an abomination, but it was an accident." She passed the plate across the counter. "Eat something. You need to boost your blood sugar."

"That's not what happened."

"It's precisely what happened. It wasn't until after that night that you started to hear the spirits, right?"

I glanced at Silas, who had already fallen asleep on the uncomfortable looking couch. His coffee—cup still full and steaming—sat on the table by his head.

"Silas is out like a light. I may have put a touch of melatonin in his decaf, not that he needed it." She winked. "Poor boy really was worried about you."

"How do you know all this?" I asked as I took a bite of perfectly crunchy-soft biscotti. I nearly groaned with pleasure, but held it in. Most commercial biscotti were way too tooth shattering in my opinion. This one must have been homemade.

"As I said, I am also a Daughter of Lilith. I knew your

mother in passing, though we weren't friends. We have a loose organization—network might be a better term—to communicate with our sisters. Some participate more than others. Your mother never really did, but we were regionally close enough that I kept tabs on her activities. She hated what she was. Wanted to be 'normal' as if that's even a thing. She tried to conform, and it drove her mad. Allowed the spirits to control her."

"She's changed. She's Rán now."

Grams frowned. "I was afraid of that. I heard of her disappearance and figured she was in Aegir's demesne. I had hoped she would resist falling under his influence, but the man can be persuasive. She's not the first of Lilith's daughters to be tempted to his side."

My thoughts drifted to Eldoris's mother, and I wondered if she, too, had been a Daughter of Lilith. As if that was even a real thing. As far as I knew, Grams could be making the whole thing up.

"What should I call you?" I blurted. "I feel weird calling you Grams, like Silas does."

The woman's papery thin skin creased into a smile, her gaze once more traveling over Silas's sleeping form with affection. "That boy." She shook her head. "I'm not really his grandmother, you know."

"You're not?"

She shook her head. "No. But that's another story for another day. To answer your question, Grams is fine. My born name is unimportant. Or rather, it's too important to give away willy-nilly. True names have power, you know."

"So you are a Daughter of Lilith, like me, like my mother . . . does that mean you see the spirits, too?" I tried to keep the disbelief from my voice but wasn't sure I was successful.

"Yes. And no. Maybe? We all have a slightly different relationship with the Aether, which is why you had to make your first journey alone. It is sadly a sink or swim endeavor. Literally, in your case."

My lips twisted in a half smile at her joke.

"I have what I call an 'aural perception' of the spirits," she continued. "I don't see them with my eyes, but I can hear their influences like whispers all around. At least on this plane. When I travel the Between, I follow those voices and perceive my surroundings in the Aether through sound."

"Like echolocation?"

"Sort of. More like reading a good novel. I'm able to imagine my surroundings based on the voices and sounds that I hear. Then when it's time to return, I focus on the sounds of home. It's why I had Silas play his trombone for you. A solid anchor, that one. Now tell me, how did you experience it?"

I thought about how much I should share with her. How much I could even really explain in a way that made sense. I'd spent more than half my life trying to hide what I was, what I saw, from the rest of the world; it was difficult to bring myself to say anything now.

I chewed on a second bite of biscotti, sucking on a chocolate chip until it melted in my mouth. "I can hear their whispers, but only if I listen intentionally. Mostly, I see their forms wrapping around people, or sitting on their shoulders."

"So yours is a visual sense."

"Mostly," I replied with a nod. "But when I was there . . . in the Aether?" I made it a question, and Grams nodded encouragement. "In the Aether, I was there. It was no different than being here, now, in this room."

Grams pursed her lips and blew out a breath through her nose, considering. "That is a strong gift. A very strong gift. Well then, I think it's time for your rest. Let me show you to the guest bedroom."

"But Ezra—"

"Will be fine until your return. He still lives. He has not yet been tied to the Aether or Aegir's demesne. Aegir doesn't have the power. Not yet. You have time, and you won't do anyone any good if you're too tired to focus."

A yawn cracked my jaw. Grams smiled.

"Come with me, dear. Let's get you settled."

CHAPTER 18

"Sleep is as important as water. Did you know that?" Grams asked as she pulled closed the blackout curtains in the guest bedroom.

Like the rest of the house, the space was a place out of time. Scalloped navy blue and gold wallpaper covered the walls, accented by a large mirror over the dresser in a similar scalloped shape. Two nightstands on either side of the gilded bed featured lamps shaped like women with wings holding globes into the air. There was even a gold chandelier hanging from the ceiling—an earthquake hazard I thought, but then this house had probably been built before earthquake codes had been invented.

"I didn't," I replied with another ginormous yawn. Despite the ostentatious Gatsby-esque design, the bed looked damn comfortable.

I counted on my fingers the number of hours I thought I'd been awake. It hadn't quite been twenty-four hours since I'd woken during yesterday's storm, at least in Earth hours. It had felt like a lot more time had passed in Aegir's Hall, though.

Maybe even half a day. So that would have been what, thirty hours? Thirty-six? I couldn't be sure.

"After just thirty-six hours awake, you begin to take micro-naps, memory and concentration are impaired, and it's almost impossible to learn anything new. By forty-eight hours, you can begin to hallucinate. Sleep deprivation might not directly result in death, but the indirect effects certainly can. Imagine being so tired you accidentally port yourself into the middle of the ocean instead of the beach!"

Port? I wondered. What was she talking about?

Grams pulled back the blanket on the bed and ushered me in. "Time works differently in the Aether, as you've already noted, so whenever you travel the Between, don't forget to take a nap when you get home."

I didn't have a response. My jaw cracked in yet another yawn. My eyes felt like they had Acme two-ton weights tied to the lids. I could very easily imagine I looked like one of those cracked out, red-eyed cartoon characters. Almost as soon as my head hit the pillow, I was out.

"*Lil, come back! Come back, Lil. Come back.*"

A woman's voice called to me from the depths of a deep, impenetrable fog. I turned, spinning in a circle, looking for the source.

"*Lil, you should be here, with your family. Come back.*"

The hair on the back of my neck raised in alarm. I knew that voice. It had once been a comfort, but now was a terror. She had hurt me. She had hurt Ezra.

Ezra.

My brother appeared in the fog. He grinned. "She won't listen to you. She never forgave you, you know. She knew the truth that I refused to accept."

"Ezra!" I ran toward him, reaching out, but his image swirled and faded back into obscurity.

The female voice spoke from all around me, her voice echoing through my skull. "She has no family, no anchor in the Seen. She will return. She won't be able to help it."

"She is more powerful than you, Rán. And untrained. You should have told me," a deeper voice admonished.

)☽☾(

"Ezra!" I bolted upright. White sheets and blue blankets were twisted around my body, tangling my feet. The back of my shirt was damp with sweat, rapidly chilling me to my core despite the muggy warmth confined in my room.

I kicked my way free of my linen restraints and cracked open the bedroom door. Voices could be heard from the kitchen area, but I wasn't ready to see anyone yet. I needed to wash away the sticky fog that clung to the corners of my brain. Plus, I wasn't keen on Silas seeing me with sleep-matted hair and stinky armpits. That was a touch too personal—too *real*. If he wasn't already repulsed by my episode on the beach, morning breath would surely do the trick.

Even if he had been my anchor, whatever that meant.

Spying an open door that looked to lead into a tiled interior, I tiptoed down the hall. Unfortunately, in a house this old, there was no sneaking around. I hadn't made it three steps before the floor creaked and Grams called out.

"I left a spare toothbrush in the bathroom for you, dear. Toothpaste is in the drawer. And coffee's ready when you are."

I grimaced. "Thanks. I'll be right there."

"Take your time. There's no rush."

Time. Time. Time. I felt like I didn't have any, and yet Grams kept saying I had plenty. What time was it, anyway?

Hell, what day was it? I felt like I could have been asleep for weeks, rather than hours.

I scrubbed my face, bringing out the pink in my cheeks, and brushed the fuzz from my teeth. After loosely rebraiding my hair in an attempt to ignore the tangles and pressing my hands down the front of my work pants to try to release the wrinkles, I felt as ready as I was going to get to face Grams and Silas.

"There she is. Did you have a nice rest?" Grams asked as soon as I poked my head in the kitchen.

"I feel like a brand new person," I smiled.

Silas scanned me from head to toe, a gentle grin pulling at the corner of his mouth. "I like the look. Tousled goth-Hawaiian-chic. Very nice." He drawled the last in a bad impression of Borat and held up his fingers in an OK sign.

"Shut up," I pressed my lips in a self-conscious smile as I pulled on the rolled-up sleeve of my bright red and blue Hawaiian shirt self-consciously. It was tacky, but it was required for work and the only thing I had to wear. I'd briefly considered taking off the bold floral top, but all I had underneath was a black tank top, and that would have bared my scar for all to see. Even after all these years, I hated to show the damn thing. It raised too many questions that I simply didn't want to answer.

Even if Grams seemed to already know the story.

"At least I don't have hat hair," I teased.

Silas patted the fedora on top of his head. "Grams likes my hat, don't you Grams?"

"Yes, dear, but you know you shouldn't wear it in the house. It's not polite."

"I never understood that," he replied as he took it off anyway. "Why shouldn't you wear a hat inside?"

"Because it hides your adorable face." She reached up and pinched Silas's chin, wiggling it a little side to side.

Silas pulled his face out of her hand with a grin. "Makes me seem mysterious. And hip."

"What are you, a beatnik?" I asked as I put the coffee mug up to my lips. I blew the steam across the top and took a small sip. My eyes involuntarily closed in appreciation. Grams brewed a good cup o' joe.

When my eyes opened, the elderly woman was watching me with an enigmatic twist of her lips. "Good, right? Silas got me hooked on the expensive beans."

They tasted exactly like my favorite roast. I glanced at Silas and he shrugged, giving me a lightly embarrassed smile. "You brought in a bag of beans to the Trident once to make your own coffee. I tried a cup. It was good."

I lifted my eyebrows in shock. I hadn't realized he'd been paying such close attention.

"But here, have a scone." Grams pushed a small plate with a fist-sized triangular pastry across the counter. Dusted with powdered sugar, it looked like it could have been a feature in one of those cooking magazines.

I took a seat at the counter next to Silas, close enough that when I relaxed my leg, our knees touched. I didn't pull away. Neither did he.

I cleared my throat, forcing my attention back to the lady of the house. "This is all homemade, isn't it?"

"From scratch. I owned a small bakery in a past life and never could quite give it up. I don't often have people to bake for, though, so this is a nice treat."

The scone was at least as good, if not better than the impeccable biscotti from last night.

"Delicious," I said around a perfectly moist and crumbly bite. "Thank you."

"You're welcome." Grams smiled.

I glanced at Silas and hesitated. I had so many questions. So many things I needed to know. I still needed to find a way back to Aegir's Hall to bring Ezra home, which meant I needed to talk to Grams and find out what she knew, but I didn't want to have this conversation in front of observers. Even nerdy-hot musicians who didn't seem bothered by my late-night disappearance on the beach. Especially *this* nerdy-hot musician.

I didn't know how much Grams had told him, or how much he inferred from her behavior or mine, but the risk of talking about what I could do had been ingrained in me over the last fifteen years. I wasn't about to break my silence now.

"I should probably get back to my apartment soon so I can get ready for work..."

Silas hopped up from his seat. "Not a problem. I'm happy to take you home."

"Not yet, dear. Lil and I need to have a chat. Why don't you go out to the canyon and practice for a bit and give us some privacy for girl-talk."

"You sure?" He looked to me for confirmation, his brow lightly furrowed in concern.

I nodded and took another delicious bite of the scone.

"Okay then. Just stand on the porch and give a shout when you're ready to go."

One warm hand gently squeezed my shoulder as he passed on his way to the front door, his fingers trailing a tingling path across the back of my neck and leaving me oddly wishing I'd asked him to stay.

I shook off the feeling and blew out a breath. As soon as the door closed behind him, I faced down Grams.

"How do I get back to Aegir's Hall?"

"Blunt and to the point. I like it." She took a delicate sip from her coffee mug, which was shaped like an owl. It was actually pretty cute. But she hadn't answered my question.

"So?"

"Truth? I don't know."

CHAPTER 19

G rams was lying. She had to be. I just didn't
understand why.

"You seem to know everything about everything.
How can you not know how to get back to the Aether? You
claim you've been there before yourself!"

"That is true. Yes. I was once able to walk the Between."
Grams wouldn't look at me.

"Then teach me how to do it. My brother has been stuck in
some underwater afterlife for two days, which seems like weeks
or months to him already. I'm not about to just leave him
there."

"I would teach you if I could, dear, but that was your mother's responsibility."

"She's a murderous bitch!" I was shouting, and I couldn't
stop. My coffee sloshed on the counter, and I had to put the
mug down or risk throwing it across the room. "She can't be
trusted."

"No. She can't." Grams took another sip. Her tone remained
calm and patient, if a bit condescending. It made me want to
scream and yet I also felt guilty for acting like a toddler

throwing a tantrum. I was twenty-eight goddamn years old. I shouldn't be having a hissy fit at my age, and I knew it, and yet I couldn't seem to stop myself.

I took a deep breath, holding the air in the bottom of my lungs for a solid five seconds before releasing it in a gush. I measured my words carefully. "I don't understand."

"I'm too old." The words came out a whisper, sad and ashamed. "My powers have faded along with my hearing, and my time as a Daughter of Lilith has nearly come to an end."

"Your hearing seems just fine to me. Better than most people I know half, even a third of your age."

"Perhaps, but I used to have the hearing of a forest-dwelling bat. I used to be able to pinpoint the sound of a mouse rustling through the canyon floor from inside my kitchen with the dishwasher running. The old one, before the renovations. Just as you have the sight of a bird of prey. Now I am but a fraction of what I once was. I cannot show you the way to the Aether. Your mother should have been your guide."

"You must have something you can tell me. Something that will help me find Ezra and bring him home."

Grams shook her head, gaze still trained on the countertop. "I spent most of last night trying to figure out what I could do, how I could help. But the path through the Between is precarious at best. The gods—" she paused and rolled her eyes. "I hate that term, but it's a shorthand most people understand, even if it's entirely inaccurate. But I digress—"

She sipped her coffee and cleared her throat. "As I was saying, the spiritual beings that rule the Aether either protect their borders against us or attempt to use us to their advantage by binding our will to their purpose, using our Lilith-given power to their own advantage. Like your mother. She is lost to the Aether, bound to Aegir's side. She cannot leave. It was her choice, and now she must face the consequences of that choice."

"What consequences? She seemed pretty content to be there."

Grams shrugged. "Maybe. For now. Aegir promised her a normal life. He promised to bring you and your brother to her side, that you would all be one big happy family. All she has to do is fuel his power, and she will have everything she ever wanted. Except, to do that, she has to sacrifice her life and yours, as well as the poor souls she draws to the sea. She doesn't yet see the paradox—she's been promised a normal life that is fundamentally abnormal. Worse, it's amoral and contrary to her base nature."

"Base nature?"

"We daughters of Lilith are not meant to be tamed. In binding her, Aegir will consume her from the inside out. The longer she is with him, the less of herself she will retain. He will use you and your brother as leverage against her, and by the time she realizes what has happened, it will be too late."

I pressed my lips together, unsure of what to feel. I didn't want to care what happened to her. She made her bed; she could sleep in it. Her actions had destroyed my life. But pity thrummed in my heart.

"That doesn't change our current situation. In fact, knowing that, it's even more important I get Ezra out of there. I can't leave him to be a pawn in their games."

"Nor should you. As a son of Lilith, he does not carry the ability to walk between—only the daughters gain that strength —but he carries more inherent Aethereal energy than a son of Eve. If Aegir claims his soul or binds him, he would grow immensely stronger. The good news is that even though I cannot help you, your mother can. If you focus on her, call to her for help, she can be the beacon to light your way through the Aether. Without her, I'm afraid you will be lost."

"I can't ask my mother for help. I dreamed of her last night. She's gone mad."

Grams's gaze snapped to my face, and she lifted an eyebrow. "What did you see?"

"My mother called to me. She wants me to return to her. She said I don't have an anchor in the Seen world, that I won't be able to help but go back because she's there, and Ezra's there. But Ezra said she underestimated how much I hated her, and he's right. *I* was right not to trust her."

"You were. But that leaves you in a quandary. If you want to save your brother, you must forgive your mother."

"I'm not sure I can do that."

Grams shrugged. "Then you're shit out of luck, and so is your brother. The storm is coming, and you either find a way to stay afloat, or you lose yourself to the depths."

"I'd rather not be out in the rain," I replied.

"Alas, we can't control the weather. We can only choose whether to bring an umbrella. Or a life vest. I think we're mixing metaphors." She waved a hand through the air, batting away the words.

I pulled the doodle napkin from my back pocket—it was still there, thankfully—and slid it across the table toward her. "Then what is this?"

"That is Lilith's sigil."

"And what does it do?"

"Do, dear? It does nothing. You do everything."

"It glowed. And got hot. It chased away a demon that was trying to eat my friend."

"See? Your mother is wrong. You have friends. Maybe even more than friends. Anchors to bind you to this world."

I shook my head. "That's not the point. You're confusing things. I need to know how to stop this. How to get back to my brother. How to go back to normal!"

Grams patted my arm. "Haven't you realized yet? You're not normal. There is no normal."

136

"Then help me go back to my life. As not normal as it may have been, it was still my life."

"Life is choices. Choices have consequences. Choosing not to choose is still a choice. Your mother learned this the hard way. Are you sure you want to follow in her path?"

"I am not my mother," I ground out. "I will never be like her."

"Then your choices must be different than hers. She chose to hide herself from those she loved, tried to conform. She tried to do the same for you, and never gave you the freedom of your own choice. It is what allowed her to be influenced and bound by Aegir. But now you are grown and are recognizing your power. What will you choose to do with it?"

My mind whirled, lost in this conversation that made no sense, and yet also made too much sense.

"You still haven't explained the napkin."

Grams sighed, leaning on the counter with one elbow and rubbing her eye with her thumb. "In the right hands, in the right moment, the symbol of Lilith channels power. It calls to the part of you that protects the wilds and the creatures of the night. But it is *your* power, not the napkin. It is your choice whether or how to use your abilities."

"And the heat? The glow?"

"A manifestation of your personal power. Lilith had many facets. Her daughters each inherited some, but not all of her powers. How you meet her and interpret her gifts is individual to you."

"What do you do, then? You must have a strategy, or a ritual, or something!"

"Your path is your own, as was mine."

"Cagey much?"

"When you get to my age, dear, you learn that not every question must be answered. However, it is now three in the

137

afternoon, and I think you'd best hurry if you want to make it to work on time. I'll call Silas."

The batty old lady leaned her head out the window and put her fingers between her lips. A shrieking whistle louder than a train pierced the air, and my hands shot up to protect my ears. She pulled her head back inside as if it was all no big deal.

"Silas will be in in a minute, I'm sure. He's a good boy, that one."

"You keep saying that."

Grams shrugged. "I only speak the truth."

"And vague random facts."

"Perhaps." She pressed her lips together in a tightly mocking smile. "I've never been much of one for small talk and social graces. The wilds are where I belong and where I'll stay. Well, there, and the kitchen. But we each must learn to accept who we are and improve where we can. Thus is the purpose in life."

"Not love? Not family?"

"Born family can be overrated. Love can be abused. Not always, mind, but at times. Best to find strength and comfort in oneself, first. Once you love yourself, you can see the truth and love in others."

CHAPTER 20

"So . . ." Silas glanced at me from the corner of his eye as his thumbs drummed a random rhythm on the steering wheel. He was back in the driver's seat, taking me home to change before heading to the Trident together. He had a show, I had a job, and I couldn't do anything for Ezra until I could find a way back to Aegir's Hall. One that didn't involve asking Rán for help or binding myself to whatever scheme she'd hatched. I was not about to take Grams's advice on that one.

"What's the deal with your Grams, anyway?" I demanded, frustration leaking into my voice. "She seems to know everything, yet refuses to explain anything, and you don't even blink at the weirdness."

Silas chuckled and the side of his mouth lifted in a half smile. "Grams is a character, isn't she?"

"Is she for real? Or is she just another eccentric artist type?"

"Both?" He made it a question. "Grams is hard to explain."

"Why don't you start with how you know her. She said you're not related by blood."

"No, but it sure feels like it. She's been in my life for practically my whole life."

I waited for him to say more.

"I'm not getting out of this one, am I?"

"Nope."

Silas tipped his head to the side, thinking, even as he kept his eyes on the road. Two hands on the wheel. He was a safe driver. He didn't speed. Didn't run the yellow lights. He was . . . safe. Good.

"My biological grandma died kinda young. I mean, not really young, she was maybe seventy? But young enough that I don't remember her real well. I was only two or three. When I was about six, Gramps introduced the family to his 'wild woman of the woods', as he called her. He moved out to her house against my family's wishes—my dad and aunt thought he should move into a retirement community with caretakers and stuff, not some backwoods house without even a street sign to give people directions—and lived there until he died. He was ninety-one, and apparently had a heart attack in bed . . . if you catch my drift." He waggled his eyebrows suggestively.

"Anyway, Gramps was a musician, too. Strictly amateur, for his own pleasure and I guess for Grams, but he was a phenomenal fiddler. He's who I got my musical talent from, or so says Grams. She was the one to give me my first trombone after I grew out of the student rentals. She's been to almost every local gig I've ever had, even my high school performances. She says she can listen to me play all day and can tune in to my sound from miles away." He laughed. "I know that's an exaggeration, but I've always appreciated the support. After Gramps died, there was no one to take care of her, so I stepped in. I mean, she'll probably tell you she doesn't need any help, but that old house requires work, if nothing else."

"Not the kitchen. That place looks top of the line brand new."

"Yeah. I finally convinced her to remodel a couple years ago and get rid of the old 1950s setup she had in there. Really, she just needed a new stove. The old one barely functioned, but she was sentimental about it because it had been her mother's. She knew all the tricks to make it work, but ultimately, she was a baker and needed professional tools. Once she started shopping she kind of went overboard and what was supposed to be a simple appliance swap ended up being a full tear down. She insisted on keeping the booth table, but had the cushions reupholstered and all the wood refinished as part of the process. Everything else went down to studs and was rewired and updated. I was actually relieved when I realized just how dangerous that old house had gotten. She didn't even have proper grounding on the electrical! It was a mess."

I swallowed. It was time to ask the really hard question—at least, hard for me. I'd never revealed my own abilities to anyone but Ezra, not since the institute at any rate, but I had to know what he knew. I had to understand. How could he be so calm? So accepting? I'd disappeared into the water, he'd played music to call me home, and I'd reappeared on the beach, dry, just a few feet down the shore.

"But what about this descendent of Lilith stuff?"

Silas shrugged. "Weird stuff happens around Grams. I've never really worried about it; it's all I've ever really known of her."

"Is she like, a witch, or something?"

Silas lifted an eyebrow and smiled. "No more than you are, I suppose. It's funny though, I always feel calm and centered around her. Same as I feel around you. Except, different, too. Of course. I mean . . ."

If I hadn't been staring at him, I would have missed the red spots that lit his cheeks.

He cleared his throat. "She has some odd ideas I'll grant you that, but it's all harmless."

"But why did you call her when I disappeared and not the police or paramedics or something?"

"Because . . . I don't know, you disappeared! You didn't dive into the water, you were just there, and then you weren't. It seemed like something Grams would know about. I just had this urge to call her. I knew it was the right choice. And then she told me to play the trombone, hopped in an Uber, and found me on the beach."

"Hopped in an Uber? At four in the morning? From her house in the middle of the woods?"

"Yeah. She's actually pretty tech savvy when she wants to be."

I shook my head. That didn't make sense. No one would be able to find that house in the dark, not without already knowing where it was to begin with.

Silas stopped the car in front of my building and I got out. Silas rolled down the window and leaned over the passenger seat. "I'll be back in about . . . maybe twenty minutes? To pick you up. I just need to take a quick shower and change clothes is all."

"That's okay, I can walk." I didn't have my bike, but it wasn't the first time I'd chosen the slow route.

"You'll be late. It's no problem. I'll be right back."

I reached for my phone to check the time and remembered that I'd lost it on the beach. "Crap," I murmured, patting my pocket forlornly.

"Oh! Right! I can't believe I forgot!" Silas leaned over the center console and into the back seat, rummaging around in a bag on the floor. "You dropped this last night. I grabbed it and threw it in here when I came up to get my horn."

"Thanks." Relief washed over me. I really didn't want to have to buy a new phone. Bartending made a decent living, but it wasn't like I had a ton of money to just throw around.

"No problem. You were pretty out of it."

"Why are you still here?" I blurted. Anytime anyone found out anything unusual about me, they backed away with their hands up, as if I was toxic waste that they wouldn't touch with a ten-foot pole.

Silas frowned, the furrow between his brows deep and dark with shadows. He leaned back in his seat, his expression showing his hurt.

"Sorry, I was just trying to help."

"No, I know, it's just . . ."

"Never mind. I'll leave you alone. See you at the Trident." He shifted the car to drive and rolled up the window as he drove away.

"Dammit."

CHAPTER 21

Silas had been right. I was late. My freshly-washed long-sleeved Hawaiian shirt was no longer as fresh as it had been. Sweat dripped down my back beneath my black tank top. I'd rolled up the cuffs of my standard black work pants, and since my sneakers were still covered in sand, I was wearing heavy soled black boots. They were comfortable for standing and walking, not so comfortable for jogging.

"Dammit," I reprimanded myself for the umpteenth time.

Silas had been trying to help. He'd been so understanding —too understanding—and I'd ruined it. For the first time, someone other than Ezra hadn't run away when they discovered that I wasn't exactly normal. What did I do? I verbally abused him and made him feel like he wasn't wanted.

What I should have said, if I wasn't such an asshole, was *'Thank you, for being so thoughtful. I'd really appreciate a ride.'*

Or even, *'I'm so glad you were with me last night. Thank you for being so wonderful.'*

Instead, I made him feel like a jerk. What kind of irredeemable bitch did that?

Me, that's who. I'd never been good with people, never learned how to have friends. The institute made sure of that.

"Bastards."

No, it wasn't their fault. Not entirely. I was damaged goods. My family was broken, my life a mess. I'd spent my teenage years locked in counseling with people who believed I was a nutcase. I'd learned to hide who and what I was from the world.

Maybe, just maybe, I didn't need to hide from Silas? I rolled the thought around my head as I half walked, half jogged to the Trident.

I would apologize. It wouldn't solve anything, not really, but maybe it would be a start in the right direction. Maybe we could still be friends if I just explained . . . a little. He didn't need to know everything. No one did. But a little wouldn't hurt. Not with someone who had grown up with a woman like Grams. Someone who didn't blink when she talked about alternate realities and ancient gods and multiple afterlives.

I let myself into the bar and got to work with the opening prep. First things first, music. I recognized the irony when I put on the ska playlist that Silas had built for the bar after some of the locals asked for it. I'd learned to love the sound of the horns and the upbeat rhythm. It was better live, of course. You couldn't get the same power of sound through the speakers, no matter how good they were, plus the energy of the band always fed the room. But it was definitely better than the pop crap the college kids were listening to.

I bobbed my head to the beat as I chopped fruit and made sure all the glasses were stocked in the right places.

Virginia showed up right on time, logging into the computer at four thirty on the dot.

"Hey girlie!" She smiled as she wrapped her half apron over black short-shorts. Unlike me, she liked to show a bit of skin and had the long legs and cleavage to pull it off, even going so far as to knot the required Hawaiian shirt at her waist. She wasn't quite Hooters scandalous, but close.

"Hi," I replied, still setting up the bar just the way I liked it.

Virginia started pulling down the chairs from the tables. We opened at five, but all she had to do to prep was pull down the chairs and give the tables a quick once over, maybe double check the darts were set up properly.

"How was your date with Silas yesterday?" She smirked at me as she wound her way around the room.

"How do you even know about that?"

"Small bar. Word travels fast. Besides, I've been having a bit of fun with Ben."

"The drummer?"

Virginia's smile got even wider. "Rock hard abs and energy for days. It's been wild. You're not getting out of answering though. How was it? Did you have fun?" She lifted an eyebrow and wiggled her shoulders side to side.

"We just went to watch the red tide. It was pretty." I wasn't about to tell her the truth of everything that happened.

"Come on, I need the deets. Did he stay over? Did you?"

I shook my head. "I met his Grams."

Virginia frowned. "The little old lady that comes to listen to him play? That's kinda big. I mean, meeting family? Shouldn't you wait until you've been dating awhile for that? Like, months?"

"It wasn't intentional. She wanted to see the waves, too." I couldn't tell her that Silas had seen me disappear into the water and his Grams had told him how to bring me back. There was *no way* someone like Virginia would understand something like that. We weren't close, but I still considered her a friend. I didn't have many of those.

"Hmmph. He could have taken her some other night," she groused. "First dates are supposed to be special. And private. Especially with someone you've been flirting with for months."

"Yeah, I suppose. But it wasn't a date. Not really."

"Well, with the way you two have been eyeing each other every night, it won't be long. Trombonists might not have the energy of drummers, but those lips! I hear good things. You'll have to confirm."

Our first customers came in, saving me from having to respond.

A couple on their honeymoon, judging by the pink and gold spirits that swirled in a dizzying motion between them. Deep lust but also pure joy, mixed with a steady commitment. The demons on their shoulders fed off their love, encouraging and growing the connection. It was actually kinda sweet. But also headache-inducing.

Now that I knew about Aegir's demesne and the function of the demons that had come in off the waves, I wondered who these demons served. Was there a marriage god that drew power from weddings? That would be interesting.

"What can I get'cha?" I asked.

"Our hotel said this bar serves the best Mai Tais in all of Southern California. That true?" The groom asked with a bit of a sneer.

Goddamn Mai Tais. Most cliché of all the cocktails on the menu. I plastered a smile across my lips. "It's not wrong." I leaned forward over the bar, glancing to the side as if to tell them a secret. "Tell you what, though. You two look like you could use something a little more . . . decadent." I winked. "Like a drink with two straws kind of decadent." I glanced at Virginia. "Or a single spaghetti noodle for two."

Virginia rolled her eyes, catching the *Lady and the Tramp* reference.

"Lil makes the best concoctions this side of New York City," she contributed.

"I don't know, I've been craving a Mai Tai since the day we

arrived," the bride replied. "He promised me a beach honeymoon."

I tapped my nose. "Gotcha. Mai Tai base, but I'm going to make it better. I promise you won't be disappointed. And if you are, the drink'll be on me."

The bride smiled, "Okay. We'll give it a shot."

I snapped my fingers. Time to get to work.

I made the Honeymooner Special, then returned to chopping fruit. They asked a few questions about the area, but by six, we were hopping. I was actually glad when Gabi and Ty arrived to start their shifts. Bruce would be last—the big guy being our extra bouncer got him the best shifts, but I didn't mind. He earned it. As did Ty, with his bottle acrobatics. My skill was more subtle than theirs. Thanks to my special ability, I could diagnose a customer's deeper desires faster than anyone else in the room.

However, tonight, I was distracted. I was counting down the minutes until Silas and the band arrived. They usually got in at eight to set up for the show at nine. I ran through different conversations in my head as I watched the clock and tended to the pre-dinner crowd. The energy hadn't ramped up yet. It was busy, but not crazy. I kept the flow and danced the back-bar shuffle, dodging Ty and our barback, Ferghus, as I mixed up the fruity drinks our customers craved, but my head wasn't in the game.

At quarter to eight, I spotted the drummer—Ben—cozying up to Virginia. Still no sign of Silas. It was early, yet.

The crowd had gotten thick with people. Someone—probably Gabi—swapped the music from Silas's playlist to heart pounding dance tunes. I shook a tumbler over my shoulder prepping a drink for a woman wearing so much perfume I could hardly breathe, even three feet away and surrounded by alcohol and juice.

I scanned the crowd of shouting, gyrating bodies. The

trumpet player was on stage, adjusting the mics to where he liked them. The bass player was in the corner with a girl in a bikini top and jean shorts. Summer in Laguna.

Still no Silas. They couldn't go on without their trombonist and lead singer. Could they? No. Never. He had to be here somewhere or be on his way. He wouldn't shirk his responsibilities. Right? He was a musician, but he was a good guy.

Finally, I couldn't take it anymore. "Have you seen Silas yet?" I shouted when Virginia came in to drop off some dirties and place another table order.

"What did you say to him?"

"What?"

"He's out back, warming up, I guess. Ben says that he doesn't want to come in until the last minute. What happened?"

"I'm taking my dinner break," I replied, not answering.

"Now?"

"Yes, now." I waved at Bruce and shoveled a pretend fork toward my mouth. He gave me a thumbs up. We weren't slammed—not yet anyway—and I had been the first one in, so I got the first, and longest break. "Bruce'll handle your drink order."

I patted the big guy on the shoulder as I passed him on my way out the flip-top end of the bar and headed out toward the bathroom hallway and back exit.

Stepping outside was like stepping into a different world. I could still hear the music and crowd from inside, but it was muted, sort of like putting on cheap noise canceling headphones. The sound was still there, it was just softer, less invasive, letting me focus on the melancholy trombone at the end of the alley.

I approached Silas carefully, not wanting to startle or disturb the music. The sound he could create out of that horn was something to behold. Pure notes, drawn out with expression and emotion. No spirits had attached themselves to his shoulder. It was just him. Purely him. Strong, and yet sad, controlled, and yet tormented. I had done this to him. I was the source of his turmoil. I knew it, and I didn't want to be that. Not to him.

When the last note faded into the night air, I cleared my throat. "Hi, Silas."

I'd been practicing my speech for hours in my head, and yet somehow the words stuck in my throat, and I didn't know how to start.

"What are you doing here?" He asked, throwing my words back in my face. I flinched, knowing I deserved it.

"I need to apologize. I'm not . . ." I trailed off, trying to find the right way to explain myself.

"Not what?" He demanded. "Not nice? Not interested? Not who I thought you were? So I gathered."

"No . . . that's not it . . . I just . . . I'm not good with people," I finally stuttered. I stepped forward, hand raised, palm up. "If you knew where I came from, what happened . . ."

"So tell me. Who are you, Lil? It's all I've ever wanted to know."

"I'm not normal." I swallowed and let the words sit in the air like hummingbirds, ready to dash away at the first sign of rejection.

"That's a bullshit excuse. There's no such thing as normal. Try again." Silas held his trombone in front of him like a shield and dipped his chin in challenge.

"Fine. You want to know the truth? I can see demons. All around us. All the time. Sitting on people's shoulders and hovering over their heads, wrapped around their bodies, and telling them to do things. They whisper of sex and death, betrayal and sacrifice, vanity and pride. When I was twelve, my mom tried to kill me. She was being controlled by one of them and ever since that night, I've been able to see them. My dad thought I was crazy. Everyone thinks I'm crazy, but I see what I see and I'm not making shit up."

My voice had risen over the course of my little speech, and by the end I was practically shouting. I threw my hands up in the air and turned away from him, breathing hard. I didn't want to see the rejection in his eyes, the change from angry challenge to pity, or worse, fear. It wouldn't be the first time someone had emotionally distanced themselves from me when they found out the truth. I was sure it wouldn't be the last.

"I believe you," Silas said. His voice held no pity, no fear, no uncertainty.

I still couldn't look at him. I wrapped my arms around myself as if I was cold. I wasn't. Not physically, at least. The freeze came from deep within. "I don't know how to be around normal people. I don't know how to have friends. Other than Ezra, I've never had any kind of real relationship, of any kind, since I was twelve years old."

"I believe that, too." His voice was closer.

"I'm broken."

His breath picked up the tiny hairs around my nape that had come loose from my braid. "That, I don't believe."

"You should." I glanced at him over my shoulder. His face was just inches away. Our gazes connected. Electricity zinged between us.

"No. You're strong. Stronger than anyone I've ever met, save Grams. Maybe. You put up walls, keep people out, and yet they gravitate toward you with every breath you take. They're drawn to you, as if they're dying of thirst and you're the only oasis in the desert. You heal them. Give them something they need, even if it's just a smile or a point in the right direction."

"That's the demons. Not me. I just satisfy their desire."

"You *see* people. Do you know how rare that is? And imagine how much more you could do if you let people help you. Let them in."

Silas's free hand came up to my cheek. He brushed a hair behind my ear, his thumb trailing across the skin of my neck, sending jolts of heat through my system.

"I can't. They'll run away."

"I won't."

I searched his face for any sign of hesitation or subterfuge. There was nothing. No demon on his shoulder. Nothing. Just him. Just me.

CHAPTER 22

A scream shattered the night air. I jumped away from Silas as if we were teenagers caught making out on the couch. We both turned toward the alley door to the Trident.

"Was that . . .?" I trailed off.

A second scream. Shouting. We ran toward the bar. Silas still had his trombone in his hand.

We entered into chaos.

A man stood in the center of the bar, tentacles outstretched.

Okay, so maybe he wasn't so much of a man after all.

Dozens of wriggling tentacles lashed out from his back, reaching for customers and employees alike. Twenty feet long —or more—and thick as my thigh, they looked like elephant trunks on steroids, but with spiked suction cups running up the entire length.

Octopus-man grabbed Bruce around the waist and throat— the biggest guy in the entire room—and lifted him into the air. Bruce kicked and clawed at the thick tentacle, but the suckers just squeezed harder. The appendage throbbed as it sucked the life out of my friend and carried him over the bar toward the creature.

Ty fought off a second arm, swinging his ice pick like a hammer. Gabi and Virginia huddled in a back corner with another group of customers, while drummer-boy Ben attempted to protect them with an overturned chair.

"Holy shit!" Silas shouted. "What the hell is that thing?"

"Carlos!" I screamed, hoping the bouncer hadn't already taken off. He and James might be able to do something. Right? They were experienced bouncers, used to throwing rowdy miscreants out of the bar. Surely . . .

Carlos popped his head inside the door. His eyes widened. "Oh, hell no."

He was gone.

The creature turned to face us. He looked familiar, and yet not, but when his gaze met mine, he smiled. Sharpened shark teeth glistened from beneath too wide lips.

"There she is," he murmured. His voice was grating, and yet sweet. It called me to step closer, to give in and follow him to the depths of the sea.

I remembered him now. The demon that had possessed the wine snob, that had already tried to claim Gabi once, with his eel minion. But how was he here physically like this? Demons shouldn't be able to cross the Between, right? They were spirits, formless influences, not solid, flesh-and-blood monsters.

"I warned you not to interfere," Sharktopus-man taunted. "But you didn't listen, did you? You came to Aegir's Hall, and you insulted his hospitality. Now we will do the same to yours. But this time, you won't get away."

Even as the monster taunted me, his tentacles attacked customers and employees alike. I watched, stunned and help-less, as he batted away the wooden seat and grabbed Ben's arm. He wasn't even looking at what he was doing. Suction cups slapped up onto Ben's face and connected to any and all exposed skin. The tentacle began pulsing.

Bruce had stopped moving. Ben would soon, too.

Sharktopus-man had grown stronger than human, stronger than anything I'd ever witnessed—at least here on Earth. The result of the harvest that Rán had supposedly started? Maybe. All those demons that had come up on the shore—they had to have had a purpose. They had been sent to draw power and influence for Aegir, to fuel his feast. Apparently, that power had a trickle-down effect.

Ty slashed through the meat of the arm closest to him and ducked under another flailing limb, then leaped over the counter to race out the front door. The monster ignored him. I hoped Ty went for help.

Except, he wouldn't know the real help we needed. He would go to the cops, and they would have even less hope of stopping this thing than I did. They would be caught in its grip and pulled down to the bottom of the sea, just like everyone else. Aegir was taking revenge, and it was all my fault.

"You will watch as I absorb their will and send their souls to the feast. You will suffer for your defiance, as will they, and then you will submit to Aegir's will as do all of his guests. And when your spirit is drained, your soul consumed, only then may you find the bliss of oblivion."

I had no response. What could I say? I had only just become aware of the existence of the other realm, of Aegir's demesne. I had suppressed my abilities my entire life, hidden them away, attempted to pretend they didn't exist. I was unprepared for this battle. I couldn't do it.

At least, I couldn't do it alone.

We needed someone with more power. Someone with knowledge of the Aether, who could see the demons as I did. Or rather, hear them.

"Run, Silas," I said as I placed myself in front of him. It was time to step up, to do more than just appease the demons that influenced the people around me. It was time to fight back.

"Get Grams. She'll know what to do."

"I'm not leaving you here."

I turned halfway to face him, while keeping the demon in my peripheral vision. "Please, Silas. You have to, or we're all lost." I gripped his free hand. A surge of energy connected us for a fraction of a moment. I didn't want to let go. I'd found an ally, a friend, maybe more, but right now I needed him to leave. He was too important.

"Get Grams and be ready to play me home."

Silas squeezed my hand, eyes imploring. I swallowed and released him. He would get Grams. He could be relied on. I knew that. And yet, the loss of his presence felt as if I had taken off my jacket in a snowstorm.

I took a breath and tried to focus on the task at hand. There had to be a way to solve this, to stop the monster and rescue my friends. I had traveled into the Aether to rescue Ezra, and I could do no less for the people who had gotten caught up in my madness.

"Let them go," I ordered with as much confidence as I could muster. I was no fighter. I couldn't save them with physical strength. Hell, if Bruce hadn't been able to fight him off, I had no chance.

"They are the sacrifice you have chosen to make." The creature sneered.

"I chose nothing," I replied. "I don't sacrifice those I love. Not for anything."

"You chose to disrupt Aegir's sacred feast, to deny his wife Rán her greatest desire. When she is unhappy, so is our god, and the ocean will take its due."

"You talk in myth and riddle." I stepped forward, feeling in my pocket for my little slip of paper. The napkin had freed Gabi from the demon's touch. Perhaps I could free Bruce and Ben if I could just get close enough to touch them with it, as I had done with her.

From the corner, Gabi squealed.

"Gabi!" Virginia shouted. She beat on the tentacle that had grabbed our friend with her bare fists, but all that served to do was attract another arm to grab her. The women struggled, but the muscled arms were too strong for them. Between one heartbeat and the next, they were both wrapped up tight, like a boa constrictor about to swallow its prey.

I bounced on my toes. Bruce was closest. Three. Two. One. I sprinted toward the center of Sharktopus-man. Ducked beneath the first tentacle that swept my way. Hurdled over the second. Reached forward. Slammed the napkin onto the tentacle where it wrapped Bruce's waist.

Nothing happened.

Sharktopus-man laughed. He actually laughed.

"Is that it? That was your plan?" he asked. Another tentacle lashed out toward me.

I spun out of the way, but just barely, and retreated into the short hallway that led to the bathrooms and the back door.

"Lil, you can't defeat me. I have gained too much strength from the bodies of your friends. Your only hope is to join us beneath the waves and serve Aegir as your mother Rán does."

"I am not my mother."

"Are you so certain? You hide your powers, suppress your abilities, and attempt to live life as a daughter of Eve."

"Not anymore. I am not my mother. I will not suppress who I am to please another."

The bar was nearly empty now. Everyone who could had fled. I was glad for it, though I hoped Grams would get here quickly.

Sharktopus-man used his tentacles to lift himself from the ground like a spider in the center of dozens of sinuous, suction-cupped legs. He hovered a few feet off the ground and glided forward. He sneered down his nose while two empty arms wriggled toward me.

"You have no athame. You have no power. You will fall and you will succumb. You will spend your life to please Aegir. And I will be rewarded for bringing you home."

No. That way madness lay. Grams had warned me—said that dear old mom had rejected her heritage, had tried to conform. It was what had driven her mad, not the demons.

Grams also said true names had power. Tempest had given me his name.

"Abdulbaith, was it?"

Sharktopus-man flinched. The tentacle that had been reaching for me paused in midair. The tip curled and twisted, as if unsure where it was supposed to go. His eyes narrowed to slits and his lips pulled back into a grimace. "Where did you hear that name?"

"Doesn't matter, Abdulbaith. You will let them go."

The creature hissed. His tentacles twitched. "It is too late. They are with Aegir. If you want them, you will have to beg him on hands and knees."

"Abdulbaith." I emphasized the name, strengthening my voice with my will, infusing it with as much command as I could manage. "You will let them go. You will release their souls and you will do it now. And then, and only then, will you take me to Aegir and Rán."

"Done."

Abdulbaith grinned. He dropped my friends to the ground and snatched me up. None of them woke. None of them twitched. Before I could check on them and make sure Abdulbaith had upheld his side of the bargain, he took us out the door and to the water as fast as his tentacles would carry him.

CHAPTER 23

Abdulbaith didn't drop me in the center of Aegir's Hall, as the incorporeal demons had done. He took me straight to his master's suite and threw me at the feet of his god.

"Abdulbaith! Well done!" Aegir's booming voice filled the room. "And I see you are well fed. That is good. Good! The Feast of Renewal will be spectacular."

I stood from the floor and dusted off my black work pants. Rán lounged on her couch in the same position as when I'd seen her last, but now she wouldn't meet my gaze. She stared at her hands as they picked at the floral-patterned fabric, so feminine compared to Aegir's leather chair.

I faced Aegir and lifted my chin. Whatever had happened, I was not responsible. It was not my job to fix her situation or make her feel better. I was here for one thing, and one thing only. To get Ezra and my friends back to our lives.

"Where is Ezra?" I demanded.

"Rest assured, he is safe and comfortable."

"Where?"

"You may see him in time. If you give your allegiance to me."

"Never."

Aegir's beard twitched in amusement.

"Oh, I like your spunk, girl. But all who are lost to the ocean's depths come to serve me. Until their usefulness is complete, anyway."

"Lil—"

I cut my mother—Rán—off with a brusque wave of my hand. I didn't want to hear what she had to say. I wouldn't allow her to sway me. The tiny bit of pity that had taken root in my heart would not be allowed to flower. Grams said I needed a teacher, that I needed to forgive her, but I couldn't. I wouldn't. She had destroyed our lives once and was trying to do it again.

"Ezra and I are not lost to the ocean. You have no dominion over us."

The humor in Aegir's eyes drained away. He pressed his hands into the armrests of his chair and rose from his seat. Standing at full height, he was a monster of a man. At least two heads taller than Bruce and twice as wide, he looked as if he could eat me whole without choking. The expression in his eyes said he was considering it.

"I am Aegir, jotun of the ocean, host of the gods of the Aether." The room literally shook with his words. Dust rained down from the ceiling and the glasses on the tables clinked together. "Anyone who so much as dips a toe in my waters is under my dominion. You have insulted me once with your rejection of my great hospitality. Do so again and you will learn why the ancients feared my wrath."

I understood already. My hands trembled. Still, I couldn't leave without Ezra. When Silas played for me, I had to be ready. I had to be with my brother.

"Let me see my brother. Please." I could be polite. There

was no reason to further antagonize the giant. All I needed was to get to Ezra and I could get us both out of here. I hoped.

Aegir's eyes narrowed as he sneered down at me. "The Feast of Renewal begins soon. You may see your brother at the right hand of your mother Rán. Until then, you will join the feast in the hall with the others."

"I'm not exactly in the mood to party. I just want to see my brother, to make sure that he's alright. You can't keep me here."

Aegir's smile was as cold as the darkest depths of the Mariana Trench. "You're right. I cannot, Daughter of Lilith. But if you leave, your brother's soul is forfeit. He is of no use to me except as another soul to build my empire in the Aether."

I swallowed. I didn't know the rules of this place. I didn't understand the Aether or his empire. I only knew two things. I was here, and I wasn't dead. And if that was true, it had to also be true for Ezra.

"He's not dead. His soul is not yours to claim."

"That is not a difficult obstacle to overcome."

"No!" Rán exclaimed. "That was not our deal."

"Our deal was that your children would join you, here in my demesne. They are here. How they are here was never discussed."

Rán's eyes widened, and her mouth gaped. "They are my children, Aegir. They are part of *our* family now. You promised they would be honored as your own children."

"Yes. They are honored to serve me, as my own children serve. My daughters are the mistresses of the mead. My sons are the harvesters of my power. Did you think your children wouldn't also have to serve?" Condescension dripped from every word.

"But I gave you what you wanted. I sent your spirits to the Seen realm, brought new souls to the feast. I have increased your power." Her voice trembled and her hands shook.

Still, I was unmoved. She had made her choices, as I would make mine. I would not become my mother.

"Our deal is done, Rán. You have sworn it. And soon, so will your daughter." He turned to face me. "One way or another, child, you will add to my power." He quirked a finger. A tentacle grasped me around my wrist, the suction cups sinking their barbs into the delicate skin before I had a chance to pull away. "You may join the feast and drink with the souls of the lost, or Abdulbaith can drink from you. Either way, if you wish to see your brother, you will not leave this place again."

Abdulbaith dragged me to the bar. The feast was much the same as I remembered, except now I saw it for what it truly was: a trap to allow the souls of the drowned to drown themselves over and over again. Over-flowing cups of endless drink, an ageless party that would last for eternity, all designed to keep the souls from ever wanting to leave. To keep them from remembering those they left behind in the pleasures of the moment. To hide from their sadness.

It was enough to break my heart. I'd been a bartender for years, my purpose was to help people have a good time and ease their troubles, or at least appease their desires. We had regulars, like Jeff, who came almost every night to chase away the loneliness and feel part of something, and I'd never questioned it. Here, it was as if the entire point was to forget who they once were, forever, not take a moment to relax and release.

Abdulbaith shoved a glass in my hand. "Here. Drink this," he ordered.

"Now, now, Abdulbaith. You're scaring my customers." Dion smiled as he approached from behind the bar with a glass already in his hands. "There's a reason you're not a server. You draw them in, Peithon greets them, and I serve them. And I happen to know this beautiful woman likes the Sand Dune show mead, not the standard sack mead."

"Fine. But keep her drinking. Aegir's orders."

Dion saluted Abdulbaith with two fingers on his forehead. "Aye, captain. 'Tis my job after all."

Abdulbaith grumbled something under his breath about showy two-faced entertainers, but his tentacle released my arm. "Don't attempt to leave again. We'll be watching."

He moved away, the crowd parting before him without seeing him for what he was. An interesting trait that Eldoris had shared.

"He's a right toad, that one," Dion pulled my attention back to his blond hair and baby blue eyes.

Unlike Abdulbaith, he looked entirely human. All the other demons were stitched together from various sea creatures, as if Frankenstein had a fish fetish when he created his monsters. Even so, I knew he was a demon and not human. It was hard to pinpoint *why* I knew that, but I did.

I cocked my head to the side and examined him closer. Maybe the better term would be not *fully* human.

"Why are you not like him?" I tossed a thumb over my shoulder, as I took a sip of the mead. It really was good. However, knowing that I was giving Aegir more power with every drop that touched my tongue, I paced myself and set the glass on the counter, just touching the base with a finger.

"Are you the same as every other Earth-born woman? No? Then why would I be the same as any other servant of Aegir?"

I scanned him up and down. "You don't have fish parts, at least not that I can see. You're made differently. You behave differently. Why?"

Dion shrugged. "I am what I was made to be." He leaned over the counter and dropped his voice to a whisper. "Some of us are better able to empathize with the human condition than others. Even amongst Aegir's children, some have more capacity for higher emotion."

"Higher emotion?" I took another careful sip of the sweet nectar.

"Sure. Love, family, friendship, loyalty . . . the good stuff. Everyone feels lust—whether for physical satisfaction or power, it doesn't matter—and everyone feels hate—the desire to dominate, the need to set themselves apart from and better than others. But love . . . love is harder. It puts the bearer in a position of vulnerability."

"Someone once told me love can be abused, so it's better to find strength in yourself."

"Love yourself so that you don't mistake lust—or desire—for love. That's good advice."

I frowned. That wasn't exactly how I had heard it. "No, love yourself so you don't have to rely on others."

Dion shrugged one shoulder as he mindlessly wiped another glass. Like me, he was always doing something with his hands. "That's a lonely road bound for nowhere." He nodded his chin toward the dance floor. "Even the souls of the dead find succor in each other."

"They forget who they were, who they left behind."

"Maybe. Or maybe they choose to exist in the now. Who they were no longer matters. They can't go back. This is who they are now."

"This is who I am now." Something resonated within those words.

"The past has passed. Hence the name, right?" Dion's gaze traveled out across the hall and up into the rafters. "Mistakes are made, accidents happen, but if you dwell on them they become your reality. Move on, I say. Accept what was and move on. Who are you now?"

"Welcome to Aegir's Hall! Grab a drink and join the party!"

Peithon boomed his words to a new arrival, ushering the man to the bar.

Without another word, Dion moved down the wood to serve his new customer.

I turned in my seat to watch the gathered masses and took a sip of the mead.

Who am I? Who do I want to be? And what do I want for my existence?

Because unlike the souls of the dead stuck in Aegir's Hall, I could go back.

CHAPTER 24

Someone sat down at the stool to my left. I didn't turn to look. The scent of lavender and vanilla, her favorites, wafted toward me on the air.

"Rán." I stated in lieu of greeting.

"I'm your mother," she replied tersely. I didn't care. I still wouldn't look at her.

Who was I now? Who did I want to be? The questions kept tumbling through my brain.

"I am a Daughter of Lilith, not a daughter of Rán."

"You are *my* child."

I took a sip of my mead and kept my calm. In the past, I would have risen to the challenge and let the anger and the hate rise to the surface. I would have attempted to scare her away with harsh words and acrimony.

That was no longer who I wanted to be.

"I am who I am, and I will not reject who I am to please another. Not even you. Not anymore. Never again."

I unbuttoned my long sleeve Hawaiian shirt and took it off, leaving my arms bare in a simple black tank top. The skin of my scar, bleached white compared to the rest of my olive skin tone, shone in the flickering light of the lamps. I leaned back, with my elbows against the counter.

Rán hissed. Her fingers fluttered around my elbow and upper forearm, tracing the curve of the long-healed wound. Still, I did not look at her.

"It was an accident, you know. All of it. I was trying to protect you."

"So I've been told." My eyes traced the crowd. I found Mr. Navy swinging with a dark-haired beauty in pin curls and a red polka dot dress. She knew how to move, too. The two of them twisted and turned. She slid between his legs and back. Another few steps, then her legs were up in the air.

"Told by whom?" Rán asked.

"Grams." I took another tiny sip of mead, barely letting the liquid touch my lips. I was being careful. I knew that if I stopped drinking entirely, Abdulbaith would be back, and the last thing I wanted was his tentacles attached to my arm. But at the same time, I couldn't let my judgment get cloudy, like last time. I couldn't make another mistake. Not with Ezra's life hanging in the balance.

"That old biddy? How'd she find you?"

I thought about Silas and his trombone. Thought about how Grams had brought me back the last time and taken care of me when I'd needed help. Whatever Rán thought of her, she at least had taught me a little of what I truly was. Had given me a few tools to navigate this nightmare.

"What do you want, Rán?" I didn't owe her an explanation. I didn't owe her anything at all.

Her fingers stilled on my arm. "Would you just look at me?"

I shook my head. I wouldn't give her the satisfaction.

"You are so much like your father."

"Nope." I shook my head again. "You don't get to do that. I am nothing like him, as I am nothing like you."

"So stubborn."

"What do you want, Rán?" I asked again. "I don't want or need you here."

"You are my daughter. I looked forward to being able to sit with you, talk with you, adult to adult. And now you're here."

"By your order, against my will, at the expense of my life. You are not my mother. You are Rán now, sending your net up to shore to drag the souls of the living to the bottom of the sea."

"You think I wanted this? You think I chose it?"

"This is who you are now." Funny how the words I'd just heard minutes ago were so applicable in so many scenarios.

"That means nothing."

It meant everything. The woman who had brushed my hair and given me baths was gone. The woman who had jumped in puddles and fed us ice cream before dinner was no more. All that was left was a selfish megalomaniac on a power trip who thought to manipulate me into subservience.

At last, I looked at her. I met her gaze and let the disdain drip from my expression. "You are your choices. You are the demon that haunted my childhood nightmares. You are Rán. But I am no longer a child, and I will not fear you."

She sucked in a pained breath. "You hate me. Truly."

"No. I don't hate you. I've been told hate is a base emotion. Easy. Instead, I choose to love myself, which means you no longer influence me. I choose to love my brother, which means I will not leave him here to your whims."

"I've saved him. I will fix him. Fix my mistake."

"Yeah, see, that's the problem. He never asked to be fixed. There's nothing wrong with him. He rebuilt himself years ago and never needed your help. Unlike me, he never blamed you for his injury. He forgave you. If you hadn't succumbed to Aegir, you might have been around to see that."

"How could I face you, either of you, after what I had done?" Rán whispered. "All I ever wanted was to protect you, to give you the life I couldn't have, but I knew after that night you would never love me again. Now, with Aegir's help, I can fix my mistakes. I can make it right. I can make us a family again. Aegir's power grows with each new arrival and soon he will be strong enough to fulfill his promise so that I can fulfill mine."

"You can't change the past, but you can shape the future. Accept who you are *now*, not who you wish you were."

Rán's expression closed down, and she stood from her seat. "And if Ezra chooses to stay?"

"He's a grown man. He can make his own choice. But I will give him one."

"Good luck, my dear. Aegir will not let you go so easily."

I grinned. "I am a Daughter of Lilith. I am not so easily tamed. Now, where is Ezra?"

"Aegir is ready. He will mend Ezra's spine, allow him to walk again, here in the Aether at least." Rán's voice was distant, as if her mind was already elsewhere, her body just hadn't yet followed.

"In the Aether, but not on Earth, I take it."

Empty eyes turned toward me, looked through me. Rán was here but not here. "The altar is arranged, the primordial waters prepared. I must go."

My mother—Rán—took a single step and disappeared.

CHAPTER 25

"Daughter of Lilith, huh?" Dion's voice surprised me. I hadn't seen him approach.

My shoulders tensed. "Yes."

"No wonder Abdulbaith wanted to keep you drinking."

"Why's that?"

"Aegir's mead has been brewed special. Beyond the normal alcoholic euphoria, it ties the souls who drink it to him, ties them to this place. Not the worst way to go, mind, and many—maybe most—consider themselves lucky to be here. They willingly sink into the mental oblivion." Dion paused. His lips twisted to the side. "I don't see that being true for you, though."

"I had assumed something along those lines. But no, I think it's about time I faced my demons. Living and . . . less than living."

"Like your mother?"

"She's not my mother. She's Rán, now. Goddess of the sea, bound to Aegir's side."

"True. True. But she still gave birth to you."

"And taught me nothing." I shook my head. "No, I just need to get Ezra and get out of here. Get home."

"No one leaves, once they're here."

"I already have, once. I can do it again."

Dion frowned. "You really are a Daughter, then? With the power to walk between Earth and Aether?"

"So they tell me."

Dion leaned forward and scanning the people around us with narrowed eyes, as if to share a secret.

"Welcome to Aegir's Hall," Peithon boomed before Dion could utter a word.

The bartender straightened, swallowing down whatever he was about to say. A stiff smile spread across his features, the mask of the host welcoming his guests for a good time.

"Grab a drink and join the party!" Peithon finished his mantra and Dion prepared to serve his drinks. The moment of sharing truths had passed.

"Holy shit!"

I recognized the woman's voice. I spun on my stool.

"Virginia? Gabi?" My two friends stood gaping, not ten feet behind me, their eyes wider than their serving trays at the Trident.

As I stared at them, Bruce and Ben materialized another ten feet to their right.

Were they dead? Were they alive? I'd demanded Abdulbaith release them, but I hadn't been able to check to make sure they were still living before he snatched me up and drew me down to the depths. I'd hoped they would wake after we were gone. Their presence here didn't bode well for them.

But I'd already been here for hours it seemed, and they should have arrived first. Right? But time worked differently here, or so Grams said. There was no time and all time and everything in between.

"Lil?" Virginia gasped. She darted forward, catching me up in a massive hug. I thought for sure you were a goner, the way you stood up to that . . . thing. What the hell was that? Where are we?"

I patted her back. I wasn't used to signs of affection and didn't really know how to respond, but I could at least answer her questions. Sort of.

"Like the man said, welcome to Aegir's Hall."

"Is this like some kind of kinky speakeasy or something?" Gabi asked, snapping the gum she somehow still carried in her mouth. For a woman focused on the sciences, she seemed rather nonplussed.

"No," Bruce replied. His gaze lifted to the ceiling, taking it all in. "This is the home of Tangaroa. My grandmother told us stories of the sea god and his palace beneath the waves."

"The Norse named him Aegir, the Greeks, Poseidon," Dion chimed in. "All different aspects of the same elemental born of the Aether, the union of Heaven and Desire."

"So what? Are we dead or something?" Virginia demanded. "'Cause I don't feel dead."

"Welcome to your afterlife," Dion smiled and spread his arms to draw attention to the taps and brewing vat behind him. "What can I get'cha?"

"Nothing," I said. "They're not drinking."

"Can I get a Sunset Ale?" Ben asked, ignoring me. His fingers drummed on the counter in a syncopated rhythm I recognized from one of the band's songs.

"No," I put my hand on top of Ben's drumming fingers to silence them and make sure he was listening. "Seriously. Don't drink anything. Don't eat anything."

"Aww, why not?" Ben whined. "You heard the man. It's a party. We're supposed to have fun."

"Because if you do, you might be stuck here. I don't want you to be stuck here." I didn't know how, or even if I'd be able to get everyone home, but I had to believe there would be a way I could.

The Trident was home, odd as it sounded, and Gabi, Virginia, and Bruce were my family, almost as much as Ezra, and more than my own father. I didn't know Ben that well, but he was part of Silas's band, so I wouldn't leave him behind. I wouldn't leave anyone behind. Not if I could help it. And the one thing I knew with certainty was that the mead drained the souls of the dead, tied them to the Aether, and wouldn't let them go. If there was such a thing as a near-death experience, I was going to make sure that was what my friends had now. Not the real deal.

"I have to find Ezra, and then we'll go." I didn't care what Grams said. Time was of the essence. If I wanted to save my friends' lives, I needed to get them back to their bodies ASAP. "Dion, where's my brother? How do I find Ezra?"

Dion's face was unreadable as he responded. "To get anywhere, you have to know where you're going."

"Obvious much?" Gabi snapped her gum.

Dion twisted his lips and narrowed his eyes. Hesitated. Then glanced around and leaned forward. "Are you really going to steal souls from Aegir's Hall?"

"These ones, yes. But I'm not stealing them. Or at least, I'm only stealing them back. Abdulbaith stole them first."

"I want out. I don't want to end up like Abdulbaith, for all his upgraded power. Take me with you, and I'll personally lead you to Ezra and do everything I can to help you take them home."

"It that even possible? I mean, you're one of Aegir's minions."

"Not by choice. I was born into this just like you. If you're truly a Daughter of Lilith, then it's possible to get me out. Rán sent Tempest and Abdulbaith, after all."

"Isn't Tempest a Daughter of Lilith, too?" I asked, suddenly realizing a truth I hadn't considered. If the former Rán, the one with the greasy hair and wasted figure, was a Daughter of Lilith like my mother, then Eldoris would be a Daughter of Lilith, too. And if that was true for Bitch Queen Supreme, then it must also be true for Tempest.

"Yes, but so am I. I mean, I'm not a daughter, I'm a son, but my mother was the ninth Rán. I'm Tempest's brother."

"That's why you look more human than the others!"

Dion nodded. "But even though we're half human descendants of Rán, we're stuck here. Aegir's blood is too strong. We didn't inherit the ability to walk the Between. It's Aegir's greatest disappointment, and why he keeps binding himself to any living Daughter of Lilith he can coerce to his side. He's hoping someday to breed the perfect minion, one who can walk between and gather the souls he needs to conquer the Aether."

"Conquer?"

"What else is there? When you live forever, your only entertainment is trying to outmaneuver and dominate your competition."

Dion shrugged, but I didn't understand how he could be so nonchalant about it. I had to imagine it would be a pretty dismal existence to always be fighting and scrabbling for position.

"So far, only a full human Daughter of Lilith can cut the path between Earth and Aether," Dion continued. "We have enough humanity to exist in the Seen realm so long as we maintain enough Aethereal energy to support our independence from Aegir, but even then, it is Rán who creates the passage between. We don't have the skill to make the journey without her guidance."

"Then won't she just bring you back if you leave?"

"Not if you kill her. Which you'll have to do to escape her yourself." Hope filled Dion's eyes implored me to accept, to help him escape.

I flinched back. "I'm not a killer. I don't even kill spiders. I scoop them up and release them outside. I can't kill anyone." No way, no how. No matter how much I hated my mother, I couldn't do that.

"She'll find a way to bind you here, just like she's binding Ezra now."

"What are you talking about?"

Dion sighed, exasperated, as if it were all so obvious. "She took him to the primordial waters. She's going to bind him to the Aether so that he cannot return home."

"No. I have to stop her."

"Promise you'll take me with you. Swear it, and I will lead you to them."

My gaze connected with Bruce. Then Virginia. Both seemed to agree. Ben was still gazing longingly at the various taps and Gabi just popped another bubble.

"Fine. Okay." I would do anything to save my brother, and honestly, I could almost tell myself she was already dead. She'd died fifteen years ago when she wrote that note and disappeared from our lives. Even if her body still lived, she'd surrendered her life to Aegir. I didn't know that I could kill her, I didn't even have a weapon, but I would find a way to stop her. "Lead the way."

"They'll have to stay here. It'll be hard enough trying to keep you from being noticed. They'll draw too much attention for sure. And anyway, the souls of the dead can't pass beyond the feasting rooms. At least, not until they're spent."

"Spent?"

"Wasted. Drunk. Intoxicated to the point of falling down. Shit-faced."

"Are you serious?"

"That's how this works. The souls drink. Aegir gains their power. They pass out. If they can recover, they come back to party some more. If not, they move on."

"Move on where?"

Dion shrugged. "There are options, I guess. I've heard Hel takes some of them. Samael others. Woden likes the noble warrior types. All the majors have agreements with one another. It's how they stay in power, while the lesser spirits and demigods struggle for handouts."

"Then why can I go behind the curtain?"

"You're a Daughter of Lilith. No one can stop you. Unless you're not truly what you say you are?"

I swallowed. "I am who I am."

"Then let's go."

"Doesn't someone need to take your place at the bar?"

Dion passed out empty glassware to my friends. "If I'm not here, Peithon won't bring anyone to my station. All you guys have to do is pretend to have a good time."

"Why can't we *actually* have a good time?" Virginia asked.

"Right?" Ben chimed in as he wrapped an arm around her waist. "This is a great party. We should take advantage."

"Weren't you guys listening?" Gabi asked. "I don't want to be someone's food. Or dead. Do you?"

"Dunno. Could be worse." Ben replied.

Gabi rolled her eyes

"I'll watch them." Bruce crossed his arms over his chest, flexing his giant muscles and shooting Virginia and Ben a stern glare. "Go get Ezra. We'll be ready when you are."

"Wonderful." Dion slapped a hand on the counter and a pass through magically opened in the wood. He motioned for me to join him.

"Aren't we leaving?" I'm sure I sounded stupid, but there was no obvious entry or exit behind the bar. It was just the ginormous brewing vat and taps as far as I could see.

"You can't get to where we're going from there. Trust me."

I lifted my eyebrows but followed his lead. He shut the pass through behind me and it disappeared.

I glanced nervously at Bruce, but he dipped his chin in

encouragement. "I'll be back for you. I promise," I said. "I'll find a way to get all of us home."

"I know you will. Find your brother."

Dion led the way around the side of the brewing vat. We passed another bartender, who glanced at us curiously, but his station was crowded with what looked like an entire swim team wearing those funny-looking overall shorts and swim caps. As we passed, one of them took off the rubber helmet thing and shook out his brown hair.

Must be new arrivals.

Dion hardly spared them a glance.

"Are all the bartenders like you?" I asked once I thought we were out of earshot.

"No one's quite like me," he replied with a wink and a teasing smile.

I rolled my eyes and snorted a laugh at the innuendo. The odd thing was, even though I was more comfortable around Dion's obvious flirting than Silas's more sincere admiration, I didn't feel anything for the blond half-demon. He was good for a laugh, but he didn't make my heart race.

"I thought we were past that."

"Never."

I noticed he hadn't actually answered the question, but I let it slide as we approached a hatch set at an angle beneath the counter, the entrance pointing down and away from the vat. Like nearly every surface in this room, the wood was carved with images of the sea, but this time it was the hybrid demons that I'd seen on the beach that night. Malformed creatures made of multiple different sea animals. Dion pulled on a ring set into the hand of a mermaid with wide set fish eyes and a long eel tail.

The door opened without a sound; the hinges oiled into silence. Dion motioned me forward.

I glanced back once more toward where my friends waited.

They'd disappeared around the gentle curve of the vat, but I knew they were there. I felt like I was entering the belly of the beast, that once I passed through this door, I would no longer be able to claim I was normal. Maybe not even really human. After all, they apparently couldn't cross this threshold. But I could. And so had my brother. I was going to get him. There was no other choice.

I descended into the dark. Torches flickered to life as I walked down a narrow set of stairs, their flames lighting the way forward. There was only enough room for one person to descend at a time. The darkness pressed in around the edges of the flames, and I thought of ancient castle dungeons and torture chambers, or basements dripping with chains and saws.

In other words, it didn't seem like a friendly place.

The temperature dropped. The walls dripped with condensation. We must have descended three or four stories beneath Aegir's Hall when at last the floor leveled out. Yet still, we walked down a narrow hall, single file.

"Where are we going?" I asked in a hushed voice.

"This is the heart of Aegir's demesne," Dion replied, equally subdued. "The ocean from which he and all his servants are born. Or turned."

I glanced over my shoulder, but his face was unreadable in the faltering light. I pressed my lips tight, foreboding tightening a vise around my shoulders. Had I been right to trust him? Was he trying to entrap me into this life? Into this world?

"Your brother will be here," he said, as if answering my unasked question. "Aegir promised him the use of his legs. He'll perform the conversion here."

"Conversion?"

Dion frowned. "Aegir can't give him legs from nothing."

My heart raced in my chest, speeding along with my breath. "What are you saying?"

"Aegir is a god of the ocean. He will grant Ezra some of his spirit to build a new body for your brother. A new form. And when he's done, your brother will be tied to the Aether permanently."

My lip curled in horror. "Like Abdulbaith?"

"Abdulbaith is the first of Aegir's sons." Dion replied, as if that was an answer.

A male scream reverberated down the hall.

I broke into a sprint.

CHAPTER 26

Ezra lay writhing on a stone slab in the center of an underground lake, two flickering torches illuminating his figure. He was naked, except for a white cloth that thankfully wrapped his waist and upper legs. There were some things a sister shouldn't see.

Aegir swam in a lazy circle around Ezra's little island like a sea monster in a castle moat. The god of the ocean had transformed into a less human version of himself, the one from the carving with the fish tail. He even carried the trident and wore the coral crown.

Under any other circumstance, I would have told you that a merman was a wussy sort of mythological creature. Sure, the Disney versions had killer abs, and they could probably kick my ass on land if they had legs, but that wasn't exactly saying much. Especially since they didn't have legs.

Of course, neither did Ezra—at least not functional ones—and he was pretty badass without them.

But now Aegir was truly in his element. His tail was long and writhing, less a fish tail and more a sea serpent. Like those grainy old pictures of the Loch Ness monster, he curled up and out of the water in a sinuous ribbon of muscle. In addition to at least twenty feet of boa constrictor strength that I would barely be able to wrap my arms around, two spiny fins extended from the back of his hips and another down the length of his back. Dorsal, I guess. Blue-green scales covered his torso from about his rib cage down, and his hands had transformed into webbed monstrosities with talons at the end of each digit. Lightning flashes of bioluminescence pulsed down his entire length, revealing muscled legs with webbed feet about halfway down his tail, just underneath the water.

The carving on the door hadn't done him justice. Or maybe it was some sort of idealized version of himself as the kind benefactor of the ocean. What I saw here was worse than a sea monster out of medieval legend.

Meanwhile, Rán paced barefoot along the shore, moving in the opposite direction of Aegir. She paused every so often to light a torch that had clearly been prepared for her flame. When all five were lit, she finished her circle, ending at the beginning. She stepped into the water and lifted her hands, palms up, fingers pointed toward Ezra and the altar that held his insensate form.

Aegir's humanoid half rose up out of the water. He spread his arms wide and pressed his chest out. A burst of white energy pulsed from his core and a misty spirit coalesced in front of him, slowly forming into one of the hazy hybrid sea animals I'd seen rise up out of the waves that night with Silas.

How long ago was that? It seemed like weeks but must have only been a couple of days.

The creature began to take form. First, a lobster's legs and tail. Then the body of a lizard—one of those Galápagos iguanas —grew from the shell, rising up in a mockery of the human torso. The demon hissed and flicked its tongue. Aegir relaxed back down into the water and the pair began to circle Ezra's island, slowly at first, and then faster and faster.

As Aegir and his minion picked up speed, Rán began to chant in a language I didn't understand. She threw her head back and closed her eyes, giving herself over to the powerful rhythm.

Ezra's back arched. His hands clenched and unclenched against the stone. He twisted his head from side to side, and his forehead glistened with sweat visible even from my hiding spot in the shadows at the edge of the cavern. Dion clenched a hand on my shoulder, but I couldn't tear my gaze away to look at him or find out what he wanted. Right now, it didn't matter.

I stared, transfixed as Aegir swam faster, the demon at his side. Water splashed onto the stone from his wake. They swam impossibly faster. The demon broke away, toward Ezra's island. The waves grew higher. With a final dash, the water poured over Ezra's immobile legs. The demon surfed the crest, landing on Ezra's prone form and grasping at my brother's body as it pulled itself onto the rock.

Ezra twisted and turned, as if trying to escape a nightmare. His eyes were closed, he couldn't see what was coming, but his hands spasmed and he moaned in distress. The demon relentlessly crawled over my brother, lining its translucent crab-like legs alongside Ezra's atrophied human ones. I watched in horror as the spirit sank into my brother's skin.

Ezra screamed.

I lurched forward.

Dion yanked me back. His eyes were wide, scared. This was his worst nightmare. I could see it in every shallow breath and rigid muscle. He wouldn't challenge his father. Couldn't even fathom it. He wouldn't challenge Rán. He had spent his life following orders, living at the will of others, afraid of stepping out of line or doing anything that would draw attention to himself.

I had, too, but I wasn't going to do that anymore. I was tired of it, tired of pretending to be something I wasn't for someone else's benefit.

I turned toward the lake again, trying to pull my arm from Dion's grip, but he only gripped tighter.

I turned to growl at him, but his eyes were all on Rán.

The woman grinned. She grinned! She was hurting her son, the only child that still cared a thing about her, and she was excited about it.

My lip curled. I was going to stop her. I started forward, but once more, Dion pulled me away.

"What is your problem?" I hissed, tearing my arm out of his grasp.

"What are you going to do? How are you going to stop this? Aegir will wipe you away with a flick of his tail. Rán will swarm you with siphons to suck your soul before you take two steps toward the lake."

"I'm going to save my brother. Take him home."

"Look." Dion pointed back toward the island. "It's too late."

Ezra's scream quieted. The hazy outline of lobster legs surrounded the natural ones. The remainder of the tail stretched out behind him. Despite the horror of the Franken-stein-ish form, I couldn't tear my gaze away.

My brother's leg twitched. His real leg. He moaned, eyes still closed, but his hands slowed their spasms.

"Again!" Aegir shouted. "He is not yet strong enough!"

The sea god dove into the water, his tail undulating behind him. Rán lifted her arms.

What should I do? Should I stop them? If I stop them, am I destroying Ezra's chance of walking again? Would he want that? Would he prefer to go home?

"Stop this!" Tempest sprinted into the room from another passage on the opposite side of the lake from us. My gaze zeroed in on the blonde woman. Her face was flushed, her ponytail askew. "He doesn't need new legs. He was perfect the way he was, and he didn't ask to be transformed."

Rán's empty smile never left her face as she turned toward the out-of-breath intruder. It was the same smile I'd seen on her face when I was twelve years old. "He will be whole. He will be well. And he will love me again."

Aegir lifted himself up out of the water, like a cobra about to strike. The fins at his hips flared to the sides and shook in warning. "Do not desecrate the temple, daughter. You have done your part. You brought him home. Now it is Rán's turn."

"If I had known—"

"You were given a task. You accomplished it. You earned your reward. Unless you wish to have your brother's existence returned to what it was, you should return to your station."

I glanced at Dion, but he was gone. Whatever had happened, it didn't matter now. I couldn't worry about Aegir's son. I could only worry about my own brother.

"Please," Tempest begged. "Do not do this. Do not turn him into Abdulbaith."

I slipped into the room. I moved slowly to avoid drawing attention, but my nerves screamed at me to hurry. I didn't know how long Aegir's patience would last. He and Rán were focused on Tempest as she continued to beg and plead. I had to make the most of it.

Aegir's tail lashed an angry ripple through the water. I was going to have to enter the water. I was going to have to swim to the island and pull my brother from the stone. I didn't know if I could do it. I didn't know if I was strong enough. But I had to try.

Aegir and Rán were still focused on Tempest. I couldn't tell if she saw me, but I prayed she would keep them distracted.

I crept forward toward the edge of the water. Aegir's body had coiled beneath him, the legs just visible pushing against the bottom, holding his human torso up high. Still, the tail extended another ten feet behind him and lashed back and forth in agitation.

I took a breath. Too late to go back now, not that I would anyway. Not with my brother's life—and sanity—on the line.

I took off my boots. They would weigh me down. Black pants, black tank top, black hair tied back in a braid, I hoped I would be able to hide in the shadows.

Staying in a low crouch, I shuffled into the water. I sucked in a breath as the cold crept over my toes and ankles, then my calves and butt. I couldn't make a sound. I avoided any kind of splash. I moved slowly, keeping my ripples to a minimum.

When the water reached my shoulders, I took a deep, silent breath and sank beneath the surface. I pushed off the bottom. My best chance was to make it to the rock underwater on a single breath. I wasn't a great swimmer. I hadn't trained for this, but the rock wasn't that far away.

The water was deep though, and dark. The farther I got from the shore, the deeper it became, until I could no longer see the bottom.

Instead, I turned my focus forward. My eyes strained to see the island ahead of me. There was nothing. Only more water. Only more darkness. It had to appear soon. It hadn't been far.

My arms pushed through the water. My legs kicked. My lungs burned. I wasn't going to make it.

I kicked for the surface. How had it gotten so far away? White spots appeared in my vision. I was in the deepest depths of the ocean. Alone. A bubble escaped my lips. I followed it upward. About to scream and suck in the water, my head breached the surface at last.

I gasped in the precious oxygen as the booming sound of laughter echoed around me.

CHAPTER 27

"Did you honestly think you could sneak past me?" Aegir's voice dripped with cruel disdain. "Did you believe you could keep me from my purpose? In my own demesne?"

A thick coil of Aegir's tail brushed against my legs as I tread water, gasping for air. Ezra's island was no closer than it had been from the shore. Only now, the shore was equally distant. It was as if the island had moved at the same pace that I had been swimming, always unreachable. I was at the mercy of the ocean god.

"Leave my brother alone!" It wasn't great, as far as defiant comebacks went, but it was all I could think of while trying to stay afloat when my clothes were weighing me down and my arms were quickly tiring. A lifeguard, I was not.

Aegir shot forward, lightning fast, his face stopping just inches from my own. His eyes bored into mine. His mouth hissed open, wide rows of pointed teeth making him even less human than before. "He is mine now. Just as your mother is mine. He has absorbed my spirit and I have given him the ability to walk again. I have granted Rán her greatest desire, and she is bound to me. As will you be."

"Never," I spat.

"We shall see." Aegir's tail wrapped around my waist, tightening until I could barely breathe. The shore was suddenly under me. With a heave of his muscled length, he tossed me up on the rocks at Rán's feet. Tempest was already there, on her knees, sobbing. I had missed whatever had happened to her while I was underwater. Apparently, she had been stopped in her attempt to rescue Ezra, just like me.

"Take her to the brig and keep her contained," Aegir ordered Rán. "If she leaves, your son's life is forfeit. None of you will ever see him again."

The brig was dark and damp, a cave dripping with calcified water and smelling of sharp rock and salt water. Or maybe that was me. My teeth chattered. My clothes were still soaked, and without a fire or any other source of heat, I wasn't sure they'd ever dry.

"You brought this on yourself, you know." Rán jeered at me from the simple wood-framed doorway.

"Said every evil stepmother ever." I was in no mood for her games.

"If you'd just stop, *look,* and *listen* for once. Aegir is powerful. He's not evil. He's doing what he can to help us, to help me."

"You're the evil one," I replied. "I thought that was obvious."

"Your brother can walk again. That's not evil."

"You gave him a lobster tail!" I shouted, unable to control my temper and still horrified by what I'd seen. "Those aren't his legs. You can't fix what you did. I know my brother. All you've succeeded in doing is turning him against you. He loved you once, even after the so-called accident. He would visit your empty grave with Dad every year. But I've always known the truth, and now, so does he."

Rán shook her head, pity washing across her expression. "You'll see. He will be happy here, and one day so will you. One day, you'll forgive me."

"Never," I spat and stepped away from the bars. "What little I had, the small life I'd built for myself, you've stolen from me. You've hidden away here for the last fifteen years, unwilling to face your mistakes. You should have been there."

I turned my back on the bitch and slumped into the corner.

"Lil—"

"Go away, Rán. Just go away. I don't need you, or your empty excuses."

I wrapped my arms around my knees and pressed my forehead into them, refusing to look up even when the door clicked shut. My thoughts whirled. I knew I wasn't trapped here, not really. Just as I had escaped the more comfortable prison of the room Rán had prepared for me, I could escape this actual prison. Hell, who knew? Maybe this was even the same room. The laws of physics didn't apply here, and I had no idea how things worked. The whim of Aegir was all anyone would say.

But I couldn't leave. They still had Ezra, and despite what Rán had convinced herself, he wasn't going to like being turned into some weird sea monster just so he could walk. He'd come to terms with his injury years ago, had moved beyond it and excelled. If anything, he would be pissed he couldn't compete in the paratriathlons anymore. He had been working for years to move up the ranks and nearly placed in the last one. There was very little that he couldn't do.

He was stronger than me.

Still, the image of Ezra, laying on that rock, twitching compulsively as the demon spirit of Aegir's making fused with his spine . . . I would never forget it. How had they done it? It had taken both Aegir and Rán to remake Ezra's body. They'd both put their magic into the ritual, or ceremony, or spell . . . whatever you wanted to call it, it had been a perverted distortion of the natural order. It wasn't right. It didn't *feel* right.

I thought back on Grams's little history lesson. If Lilith had been created to tend to the wilds, to protect the chaos of nature, then it was no wonder the ceremony had felt like an abomination. It twisted nature to the whims of man. Or god. Whatever.

If only Grams were here, I was sure she'd know what to do. I could just see her, standing in her kitchen making some kind of dough in one of those big countertop mixers. As always, the countertops gleamed, absolutely pristine despite whatever recipe she was making. She formed the dough into a log shape on a pan and slid it into the oven, simultaneously pulling out a similar log that had already been baked.

She sliced the log into pieces. I recognized the chocolate chip biscotti.

"Well, come through, dear, if you'd like one. No need to mope about in the Aether if you don't have to."

I sat upright, startled. I opened my eyes. I was still in the dank cell they'd shoved me in, but when I closed my eyes again, I could easily see Grams. "You can see me?"

"Of course not. That's not how my ability works, remember? But you're muttering loud enough for even my old ears to pick it up."

"I don't mutter," I muttered.

"Step through, dear, and let's have a chat. I made the biscotti for you."

"If I leave, they'll kill Ezra."

"Pfft, as if the waning god of the ocean has any clue what you do. Come, dear. Sit."

"How did I do this? How am I seeing you?" I asked, still not accepting Grams's offer. As much as the biscotti looked delicious, I wouldn't risk Ezra's life. I needed to find him, needed to free him. Not sit and eat a cookie.

Grams began slicing the baked log on an angle, carefully arranging the pieces on the pan. "Now, that's a good question. What did you do?"

"I'm stuck in a prison cell."

"Bah. You are a Daughter of Lilith. You can't be stuck anywhere. So what did you do?"

"I sat down. I closed my eyes, and I pictured you in the kitchen. I could see you there, working."

Grams placed the cut biscotti back in the oven with the first log. "You stopped. You centered yourself. And then you envisioned the help you thought you needed. Interesting."

"*Stop, look, and listen.*" I repeated my mother's words. Had she left me clues intentionally?

My brain hiccoughed. "Wait a second. What are you doing here at home? Why aren't you at the Trident? Didn't Silas call you? You were supposed to help our friends. Bruce and Virginia and the others. That's why their souls are here! You were supposed to save them!"

Grams lifted a hand, interrupting my tirade.

"Time works differently in the Aether, remember?" She pointed a finger over her shoulder and her phone rang. "There's Silas now."

"But their souls are here! That means they're already dead!"

"My dear, have you never heard of a near-death experience? If they have a heartbeat, even a faint one, I can bring them back. You just need to mark their souls so I can find them in the Aether and pull them through the Between."

"What? How?"

Grams shook her head. "The mark of Lilith, dear. Draw it on their hand or arm or something so I can connect. I'll take care of the rest."

"So they're going to be okay? What about Ezra? I'm stuck here in this cave and he's half-lobster."

"That is a problem, isn't it?"

Her calm, unflustered attitude was worse than nails on a chalkboard. I wanted to scream and flail, and she was baking biscotti.

"What do I do?"

"Look for him. Listen for him. And you'll find what you need."

"Can't you pull him through like the others?"

Grams frowned as she sliced through another biscotti log. "Sadly, no. Like you, his physical body—not just his soul—is there in the Aether, and I'm too old to make the crossing anymore. You'll have to bring him home with you."

"But he's half-lobster. He can't come home like that."

"Then you'll have to find a way to break him out of his shell. Without killing him, of course. Your mother would be best suited to teach you the unbinding."

I rubbed a hand over my face. "She's the one who bound him." I growled.

"Precisely. Which is why she can unbind him." The phone rang again, and she paused. "I'd better answer that. Silas is already such a worrywart. I'll tell him I'm on my way."

With a wave of her hand, Grams dismissed our conversation. "Don't forget to mark your friends when they're ready to return." Her last words whispered into my mind as the image of her kitchen faded from my view.

I opened my eyes. Water oozed down the stone walls of my cell. I shivered, then stood, wrapping my arms around me as I paced a circle around the small space.

I touched a hand to the wall. The stone was real. The water dripped in the corner was wet and salty. It was real.

And yet, it couldn't contain me.

The mind is stronger than the body. Where the mind goes,

the body follows. Ezra had said it a million times during our runs.

I leaned against one wall and closed my eyes. I stopped moving, let my mind calm. I focused my thoughts on my brother. His dark hair, the same color as mine, but just long enough to curl over the top of his ears. Normally brushed back in a loose wave, now tangled and sweaty, lying flat on a white pillow.

I peered at him as if through an open doorway. Rán sat in a chair at his side, and I dared not enter. If she could sense me watching she didn't show it, but she didn't know I could reach out with my mind like this. She thought I was untrained. That I didn't have an anchor. I had been isolated my entire life, unable to connect with anyone . . . except Ezra. He had always been there for me, as much as he was able, and I would always be there for him.

Rán had her back to the doorway, and Ezra kept his back to her, choosing instead to stare at the blank wall on the other side of the bed. Like my room, there were no windows in the space and yet it was lit as well as if it were a sunny day in a greenhouse. His room was decorated in greens and blues, emphasizing the natural feel of the unnatural space.

"It's okay, Ezra. Accept the change. Accept the support. Aegir has promised that soon it will be like an extension of your body. You won't even notice the extras."

My brother had been grossly transformed. His legs—his natural human legs—bent and twitched, as if he couldn't keep them still, but it was the translucent outline of the lobster legs and tail that drove the movement. The spirit had begun to fuse with his body, growing more opaque even as I watched. Little by little, it was taking over control of his limbs, but hopefully not his mind.

"I have eight legs and a tail, Mother. I'm never *not* going to notice that."

"But you're able to walk! We've fixed you. My mistake has been corrected. I've given back what was taken away."

"I didn't need to be fixed, and I never asked to be this monster." His hand clenched the bedspread as another spasm wrenched down the length of his new body. Rán placed a hand on his shoulder, but he jerked himself out of her grasp.

I had warned her. Whatever misguided thought made her believe Ezra would welcome her intrusion in his life, she was wrong.

"You'll see. You'll thank me soon enough."

"You've ruined me. Twice." Ezra snapped.

Rán's shoulders jerked as if she'd been hit. "Well then. I'll leave you alone for now. But you're expected to attend the feast. The priestesses are preparing something suitable for you to wear."

"You mean your boy-toy's previous conquests?" Ezra growled.

"That's not fair."

"It's the truth. They are what you will become, and you don't even care. You will be twisted to his purpose. You already are."

"He is a powerful man."

"Monster."

"He controls the oceans. He has given me everything I've asked for, and more. He is good and kind. You'll see."

"No, Rán. What he has given you he has taken from me. So go. Go run back to your fish-man. I want nothing to do with either of you."

"You *will* attend the feast." A rumble of thunder echoed in the distance.

"Or what? What can you possibly do to me to make me go?"

"We have your sister." The words came out of Rán's mouth with cruel intent, like a villain ready to monologue their plans. There was no emotion buried in its depths, no sense of pain or love or regret. Not even a general fondness. It served to confirm my feeling that this woman was not my mother, no matter who she looked like. Fifteen years in Aegir's Hall had fundamentally changed her.

"You mean your daughter?" Ezra asked. "The child that you gave birth to? The little girl who had nightmares for months—years—after you stood with a knife over her bed? The one you *left behind* when you abandoned us to a father who buried himself in work rather than face the memory of you in her eyes?"

"Enough," Rán snapped. The boom of a crashing wave pounded against the side of Ezra's room, as if we were sitting in the bowels of a ship sailing through a storm. "If you fail to appear at the feast, she will take the punishment. Do not force our hand."

As she moved to turn toward the doors, I opened my physical eyes. Once more, I paced the confines of the cell.

So. She would use me against Ezra just like she would use my brother against me. She thought I was helpless. Trapped. But she had accidentally taught me all that I needed to know to escape this place.

Stop. Look. Listen. Like crossing the street, I could—and would—cross the Between.

And no one, not even the god of the ocean, was going to stop me.

CHAPTER 28

I paced a circle around my cell. I needed to think, dammit. I was confident I could walk the Between, like Grams had suggested. The problem was, I didn't know what to do next. I could go to Ezra now that Rán had left, but I couldn't get us home. Not both of us. Not while he had a lobster tail fused with his spine. I had no idea how to fix that, but I knew someone who would.

Rán.

But Rán wasn't going to help. Not on her own. Not without extra motivation.

I needed leverage. But what? I couldn't think of anything, and that was a problem.

The door to my cell cracked opened. I stopped pacing and faced the newcomer. Fingers wrapped around the edge of the door. A blond ponytail swept into the room. Tempest eased the rest of her body through the gap as if she was afraid she would be seen.

She pressed the door shut behind her, with a near-silent snick of sound.

"Hello." I couldn't think of anything better to say. I crossed my arms over my chest. I was still wet, but I must have gone a little numb because I no longer chattered from the cold. Maybe it was hypothermia. Maybe that was why I couldn't think properly.

Tempest tiptoed into the room, glancing nervously over her shoulder every few seconds.

"You're still here?" She asked.

"Where else would I go?"

"You could go anywhere."

"Not at the cost of Ezra's life."

"I'm so sorry, Lil," Tempest blubbered, hunching as she crossed her arms over her chest. "I really am. I never meant to bring you into this."

"No. Just my brother."

"At first, yes. But then I got to know him. I like him Lil. I really like him. I didn't want to hurt him, or you. They forced my hand."

My throat tightened as I tried to contain my emotions. I wouldn't let her see me cry. Ezra wasn't gone, not yet. I could still make this work. I didn't know what the hell I was doing, but I knew I could do *something*. I had to.

"It doesn't matter what you intended. You shouldn't be playing with people's lives. I don't know much about this after-life stuff, but to kidnap the living, to shorten their lives for your own gain? That's murder. Rán is a murderer, and now, so are you."

Tears poured down Tempest's cheeks. "No. I am partly to blame, it's true. I found him. But I wasn't the one who dragged him down. I needed to protect someone. Like you, they used him against me. It was Rán who crafted the storm and opened the gates. It was Rán who sent the harvesters. I only found him for her."

"Who were you protecting? Dion?" I asked, lifting one eyebrow.

Tempest gasped. "How did you know?"

"He told me. He led me to Ezra. He begged me to get the two of you out when I leave. But I won't leave without Ezra."

"Your brother's gone, Lil. He's been transformed. Mutated. Like Abdulbaith. He won't be the same. Not anymore."

"Explain."

Tempest somehow managed to hunch down even further at the command in my tone. "There was once a time when Abdulbaith wasn't so different from Dion. He served the mead at the feast and worked to bind the souls to Aegir's Hall, to encourage their worship. But as the new arrivals slowed and Aegir's power waned, Aegir needed a more direct approach. He twisted Abdulbaith into his current form, and Rán sent him into the Seen realm to attract souls into the deep. I think he enjoyed the drownings a little too much."

"I'll say. He told me he likes to make the bodies he possesses uncomfortable. Make them do things they don't want to do. Like drown their girlfriend."

Tempest frowned. "Unfortunately, that sounds about right."

"Wait a second. You were there. When Abdulbaith tried to take my friend Gabi."

Tempest winced. "I was. I couldn't say anything. Abdulbaith had his job and I had mine."

"What I don't understand is why you both didn't try to take me like you took Ezra."

"Haven't you figured it out yet?" Tempest released her arms and paced closer. "No one can make you do anything. The spirits can't attach to you unless you allow them to. They can't influence you unless you listen. Ezra was always intended to appease your mother, but also to be leverage against you. If Abdulbaith had succeeded with Gabi, she would have been leverage as well. The fewer ties you retain to the Seen world, the more isolated you are, the easier it is to convince a Daughter of Lilith to join with the Aether."

"So they were targets because of me? My friends are in danger, because of me?"

"Yes. But also, they are protected by you. You affect their influences."

"That's why my mother cut the spirits away from me."

"I can't speak to her motivations, but most likely. She thought she was protecting you."

"She really was just trying to help. Misguided, but doing her best." I lifted my gaze to the rough stone ceiling, trying to internalize the changed perspective.

Tempest shook her head. "It doesn't really change anything though, now. She allowed Aegir to influence her into the sea, and then bound herself to him."

"But she loves her children, all the same." She just didn't know how to show it. She couldn't let go of her own desires—likely exacerbated by the spirits that Aegir twisted around her—and see how she made us suffer. She didn't want to hurt Ezra. She wanted to protect him. To protect us.

And if there was one thing I had learned since coming to this damp hell, it was that leverage could work both ways.

I nodded, the beginnings of a plan forming in my mind. "Okay then. Tell me everything you can about the feast and the elementals who will attend."

Tempest took a deep breath and pulled her shoulders back. Her lips twisted in contemplation, and she absentmindedly pulled her ponytail tighter.

"Right. Okay. The Feast of Renewal is essentially the beginning of a new season. It's Aegir's declaration that a new cycle has begun."

"Cycle?"

Tempest shrugged. "Like a new year?" She made it a question. "We don't deal with time the way you do. All of the gods maintain their own demesne however they like, so it's not like they have seasons the way Gaia does. Unless they want to, I suppose. This is Aegir's reset. He has a new Rán, new powers. He's refueling and refreshing, reconsidering his role in the Aether and on Earth. Finding a new way."

"But the others aren't?"

"Probably not. They're just here for the diversion. It's actually an honor to be invited. Aegir's parties are legendary."

"Then who's coming?"

"The old gods. The elementals who've been around since the beginning of all things, or pretty close to it. His closest friends and rivals. He doesn't particularly care for the 'upstarts' who've risen in power over the last few millennia."

"What's your role?"

"The daughters are the escorts and secondary hosts. We make sure that the gods have everything they need—including the proper adoration of souls. The sons keep the mead and the party flowing. They each have different roles to play, everything from master of ceremonies to barback to bouncer. Not that they would bounce any of the gods, but sometimes the souls can get a little too unruly—or too familiar, if you know what I mean."

"I know precisely what you mean." Images of barhopping drunk girls celebrating a twenty-first birthday came to mind. Carlos had been called in to tear a group off the stage that had decided Silas and the band would look better without their shirts. Carlos had been a lot gentler than I would have liked.

"How do I get in?"

"Why would you want to? They'll tear you apart. As unforgiving as Aegir can be, he at least attempts to make life pleasant for his denizens. Some of the others . . . well, let's just say the human version of hell isn't too far off in some demesnes. Aegir's daughters have some protection from them—no one wants to offend Aegir and be disinvited from the feast or face Rán's temper. But souls? They're pretty much fair game."

"It's a good thing I'm not a soul, then. And I've witnessed Rán's temper. It's not as scary as all that."

"She hasn't come into her power yet, hasn't fully been twisted by Aegir's desires. Trust me. Even my own mother couldn't stand up to him for long. She became his weapon and he used her ruthlessly, as he will yours. The only reason I'm not as twisted and insane as Eldoris is because of Dion. Unlike the others, we were born close enough in age to rely on each other."

"Like me and Ezra."

"We're lucky."

"Yes, we are," I agreed. If it hadn't been for Ezra fifteen years ago, I was pretty sure I would already have ended my misery. But I helped him through his and he helped me through mine and together we survived. "So how do I get in? I'm assuming I can't just walk in uninvited."

"Couldn't you just, you know, walk through? Port yourself in?"

I shook my head. "I don't know. I don't think so. Not until I've seen it? I've never actually done this before, you know."

"Never?"

I shook my head.

"But you left! You disappeared and Abdulbaith retrieved you."

"It was an accident. I fell asleep and was . . . I don't know, called home, I guess? I think I know how to do it. Theoretically, anyway. But I—"

Tempest groaned, interrupting my excuses. She dropped her head into her hands and slumped to the floor against the far wall. "This is never going to work. Ezra is gone. You can't get out. I'm stuck here and Dion will be mutated like Abdulbaith."

"Why? Why has Dion been singled out?"

"Because he's a son. With the exception of Abdulbaith, he's the most powerful of Aegir's children, and gained more from our father. He contains more of the Aether, can siphon and shape it better than any of the rest of us. Because of that, Aegir holds him on a tight leash. So long as our father controls him, keeps him weak, he can use him like a battery. But Dion has the potential to become more than a demigod. With every transformation, Aegir binds Dion to his will, until what remains of his humanity is gone."

"Well, that's not acceptable." I liked Dion. He seemed like a decent guy. I couldn't let Aegir warp him into some kind of monster. Not if I could help. "I already gave Dion my word on this, but I'll make the same to you. Help me return Ezra to his fully human body and I'll do everything I can to get all of us back to Gaia."

All of us. Me, Ezra, Tempest, Dion, Bruce, Gabi, Virginia, and Ben. Easy peasy lemon squeezey, as my mother used to say. You know. Before she became the megalomaniac wife of the ocean god.

I took a deep breath, held it, blew it out fast.

"Thank you," Tempest murmured. She reached out and gripped my hand. Tears glittered in her eyes. "You don't know what this means to me. To us. I swear, I won't do anything to hurt you or Ezra. Not on purpose, anyway."

My throat tightened. No one had ever depended on me before. No one—except Ezra—had accepted my gifts. Tempest not only accepted them, she actively appreciated them. It was a new experience. "You're welcome."

Without losing eye contact, Tempest dipped her chin in a quick nod. She squeezed my hand and let go. She glanced over her shoulder at the door, as if someone was calling for her. "I have to go, or Eldoris will notice I'm missing. Dion may have a better idea than I do about how to get into the feast without being seen or noticed. Talk to him. Once you're in, I'll do what I can to help."

With that, she pushed herself off the ground and away from the wall. I rose with her.

"Be careful. The gods are ancient beings, long used to their own power. They have plans within plans, and agendas that play out over millennia. They do not fear humans. Quite the opposite. Whatever you're going to do, you'll have to do it quickly and get back to Earth. The Aether is too dangerous for mortals."

Wrapping me in one more quick hug, Tempest crept out of the room and was gone.

CHAPTER 29

Before I could put any kind of plan in place—even an obscure, barely formed idea—I needed to know if Ezra truly wanted to return to his life on Earth, especially if it meant once more losing his ability to walk. If he didn't, I would understand. It would break my heart, but I would leave him behind if he wanted to stay. I had made a promise to Tempest and the others, and I intended to keep it. Which is why, after Tempest left, I turned inward once more. Time to prove I could walk the Between like Grams said.

Stop. I stood in the center of the cave and closed my eyes. I focused on the water dripping slow drop by slow drop, pinging against the stone. I cleared my mind of distractions and paced my breathing.

Look. I pictured Ezra in my mind: dark hair, quick smile. I forced myself to consider the new spirit-formed additions—the legs and tail of a lobster. He was still in his room, in his bed. Still wallowing.

Listen. His shoulders lifted with each breath, shuddering as he exhaled. A soft sob. I couldn't see his face, but I knew he was crying. My tough, thirty-two-year-old brother was *crying*.

207

I took a step forward.

And tripped over the chair Rán had been sitting in. I guess I'd forgotten to imagine that piece of the room. The chair squeaked as it scraped across the tile floor.

Ezra flipped over, using the lobster tail to launch himself upright on the bed. When he saw it was me, he groaned and lay back down, tucking the tail under the covers beneath him. He scrubbed away the tears with the back of his hand.

"Go away," he groaned. "I don't want you to remember me like this."

"Remember you? You sound like you're dying."

"Death no longer scares me. This is way worse."

"Bah humbug." I pulled the chair forward to sit next to him and made sure my face didn't show any of the sickening horror that I felt. "You're like a centaur, but instead of a horse's butt, you've got rear-end armor. Have you tried the legs out yet?"

"I'm a monster, Lil. They warped me. Sewed me together like Frankenstein."

"Frankenstein was the doctor, not the monster."

"Shut up."

"But have you tried the legs out yet? I bet with eight of them, you could move pretty fast if you wanted to."

"Have you ever seen a lobster move? They're not fast. And besides, it hurts. Like fiery pins and needles that have been dipped in acid and implanted into my nerves."

"So, acupuncture?"

Ezra rolled his eyes. "Seriously, Lil. You have to go. You have to get out of here. Before they do something like this to you."

"Tell me you're happy here, that you want to stay, and I'll go."

"Of course I don't want to stay. This is not my idea of a good time."

"Even if it means giving up the ability to walk?"

"You call this—" he waved down at his covered up crustacean anatomy "—walking?"

"Well, scuttling might be a better term, but it's still moving without the use of a wheelchair."

"I like my chairs. I can do anything you can do better."

"True. Except reach the top shelf." I grinned.

"Pfft. Overrated."

I let my gaze travel across him, noting where the demon had attached itself inside his skin. It was way more complicated than anything I'd seen back home. Which, I guess made sense. Here, Aegir was in his element. He was the master of his demesne, and his will was law.

The shell emerged from Ezra's torso just below his ribs. Mottled brown, it almost matched his skin tone at the top, then darkened the lower it went, until it disappeared beneath the sheets. It looked hazy around the edges, like it wasn't totally formed yet. Definitely of the Aether and not of the Earth.

"May I touch it?" I asked, hesitantly.

"Do you think you can get rid of it?"

"I don't know yet. It's a lot different than the pitiful demon you had attached to you after the accident. I don't think salt is going to work."

"It's a lobster tail. It probably prefers salt water."

"Right. So . . . may I?"

"Go ahead."

I poked a finger into the shell. As I expected, it hadn't totally hardened. It was like the shell of a crab right after it had molted. Softshell crab. I'd eaten that at a Thai restaurant once. It had been delicious. I decided I'd keep that to myself.

"Can you feel that?" I asked, poking him again.

"Kind of. Not really."

"I don't think it's totally fused, so that's maybe good news?" I thought back to Abdulbaith. He had full control over his tentacles when he attacked the bar. "How much control do you have? And where are your natural legs?"

"Control is—" he spasmed on the bed, hands clasping against the sheets, but a leg lifted the covers about a foot, "—painful," he finished. "As to where my legs are, I think they're inside the damn shell."

"So really like armor? If I cracked you open—"

"It would kill me, I think. They're part of me now." He paused, looked me full in the eyes. "There's nothing you can do, Lil. You really do need to get out of here, the sooner the better." He glanced at the doorway. "How'd you get in, anyway?"

"I've got witchy ways, now," I wiggled my right eyebrow. Ezra didn't laugh. "Let's just say, I've learned a thing or two about my abilities while being here."

"Good. Then go."

"Nope. I'm going to figure this out. I might not be able to cut you out of that shell, but the woman who put you in could."

"She'll never do it."

"We'll see. I'm working on that."

"Whatever you do, you'd better do it fast. I'm supposed to go to that feast thing."

"Yeah, I know."

"If the shell hardens all the way—"

"I got you. We're going to make this work. I'm not going to abandon you."

"Thanks, Lil."

I started to stand, but then thought better of it. "Um . . . one more question . . ."

"Yeah?"

"What are your thoughts on Tempest?"

Ezra frowned, his face puckering like he was sucking on sour candy. "She brought me here. She tricked me. She never cared about me."

"What if that wasn't true? What if they trapped her, like

they're trying to trap me? What if she didn't exactly have a choice."

"What are you saying?"

"Tempest has a brother. Aegir was going to drain him of his spiritual mojo, but she made a deal with him that if she brought you here, he would leave her brother alone."

"I don't believe it."

"I've met them both. And the guy that was drained instead. Not pleasant. He looks like he's being eaten from the inside out." Peithon's repetitive mantra ran through my brain. "And he has the mental capacity of a parrot." I shuddered, scattering the thought, then looked Ezra directly in the eyes.

He returned my gaze, hope warring with obvious—and arguably justified—cynicism.

"She tried to stop them from hurting you, too."

"How do you know that? You can't believe anything she tells you."

"We were both there when they did this to you. I tried to swim across, to the little island altar thing you were on, but failed. Aegir caught me. But she was there, too. She begged for your life. Begged them not to change you. They didn't listen."

"Really?" Hope was winning. He cared for her. He really did. I didn't know if it was love, but it was close. And I liked Tempest for him.

I nodded. "If you had the option, would you want to see her again?"

Ezra thought about it for a few minutes, his gaze dropping to the floor at my feet. A slow nod turned into full agreement. "Yes. It'll take a while to trust her, but I'd like to hear her side of things."

"Fair enough. She'll be at the feast, too. She'll be serving the gods, apparently."

"Will you be there?"

"I've gotta break you out of your shell, don't I?" I grinned.

"Aegir will be distracted with all his frenemies nearby. It'll be my best chance to change things, so be ready."

"Okay, sis. Whatever you say."

I closed my eyes. Time to go visit Dion and figure out how to get into the feast without being spotted.

"I can still see you, you know." Ezra chimed in, unhelpfully.

I cracked an eyelid. "Shut up. I'll see you later."

"Promise?"

"Promise."

I closed my eye again and blew out a breath. I'd done it once, and I could do it again.

I envisioned the space I'd entered in Aegir's Hall: the bar, with its polished wood counter, the raw edge of the bark pointing out toward the customers, the brewing vat with its golden etchings, the taps with their diversely shaped pull handles. I thought about Dion, standing in his spot behind the bar, dirty blond hair falling into his eyes, drying off a pint glass, as always. Now that I knew they were siblings, I could easily see the resemblance between them.

My friends were gathered more or less where I left them at Dion's station. Gabi had her hands crossed over her chest and blew a giant pink bubble, while Bruce scowled at Ben. I hadn't realized they didn't like each other all that much. Ben was trying to pull Virginia out onto the dance floor. She seemed willing to go but was trying to placate the big Samoan who clearly didn't want them out of his sight. Good man.

I turned my mental gaze up to the balconies where the souls of the drowned feasted and laughed, looking down on the dancers and merrymakers below. The sound of the room drifted into my consciousness: the pounding of a bass drum beneath a fiddle playing an Irish jig. No wonder Virginia and Ben wanted to dance.

"We'll be right back!" Virginia's words traveled into my inner ear. "Don't worry so much!"

"She said to stay here."

"She said don't drink anything. She didn't say anything about dancing!"

The scene opened up before me. I took another deep breath. Blew it out. Stepped forward.

CHAPTER 30

I tripped over the bar stool, stumbled into the counter, and bruised my lower ribs against the wood.

"Ouch."

"That was graceful." Dion's lip curled in a teasing half-smile.

"Practice makes perfect." Dammit. I was going to have to work on that. Clearly, I needed to get better at the *look* part of the equation and try to remember everything in the space. Details mattered.

"Finally," Gabi grumbled. She nudged Bruce with her elbow, dragging his attention back from where Virginia and Ben had disappeared into the dancing, partying mob. "This one," she jerked her head toward Dion, "told us you got caught."

Dion lifted his hands in the air, a rag hanging from his fingers. "I also said you'd be back. Aegir can't keep a Daughter of Lilith against her will. It's impossible."

"Not for want of trying," I replied.

"Is Tempest okay?" Dion asked, face suddenly pinched in worry. "Did he hurt her? Drain her?"

"Why didn't you try to stop him?"

Dion grimaced. "I couldn't stay. I couldn't be there, or . . ." he glanced over at Peithon. "Is she hurt?" he asked again.

"No. At least, I don't think so."

"Thank the gods of mercy."

"Did you find Ezra?" Gabi asked, popping another bubble.

"Yes. I couldn't get him out for . . . reasons . . . but I have a plan. Sort of."

"That sounds less than promising," Bruce grumbled.

"I need to find a way into the feast, but without being noticed by Aegir. I'm going to make Rán understand her mistake and undo what she's done."

"Riiiiight." Gabi drawled. "Then I guess I can start drinking now."

I ignored Gabi as Virginia and Ben bounced their way back toward us. "You're back! Did you see my *Dirty Dancing* moves?" She patted Ben on the chest. "No surprise, this one's got a great sense of rhythm. Not as much pizzazz as Mr. Swayze, but enough enthusiasm to make up for it."

"I even managed to lift her over my head!"

Virginia shoved him away. "Are you saying I'm fat?"

"No! That's not what I meant."

"Guys. Focus. It's time for you to go home." I interrupted before the spat could turn into a full-on drama queen throwdown.

I reached back to my hair, but my pen wasn't there. I must have lost it somewhere along the way—perhaps while swimming through endless water.

"I need a pen. Dion?"

The demon bartender shrugged. "No receipts. No pens."

"Right."

Gabi rolled her eyes, pulling a blue ballpoint from her short apron pocket as Virginia dragged one out of her bun.

"Don't lose your pen!" They said in unison, then looked at each other and laughed.

I chuckled. "Right. Sorry." I took the offered writing implement along with Gabi's hand. Quickly, before she could protest, I drew Lilith's sigil on the back of her hand. It was hard to see on her dark skin, but I hoped it would be enough for Grams to connect with. She couldn't see the Aether, anyway, right?

I shook my head. It would have to work.

"The symbol for Lilith?" Gabi asked.

I grabbed Virginia next. "Silas is calling in reinforcements, and she'll be able to put you back in your bodies. This isn't your end."

"Lucky day for you lot, to have a friend like Lil," Dion quipped.

A chill of apprehension swept down my spine. My friends hadn't known about my abilities prior to this little jaunt through the afterlife. None had seemed too concerned, but then they were probably in shock from being mostly dead already. What would they say when they returned to the Seen? If history was any guide, they'd run screaming into the night, and I'd be out of a job by morning.

The thought hurt a lot more than I expected. I'd been in and out of jobs all my adult life, but somehow the Trident was the only one that had ever felt like home. Even if I barely socialized outside of the bar, they'd never stopped inviting me. Maybe that was Silas, but Bruce had watched out for me, insisting on making sure I got home safe at the end of the night. I would miss Virginia's innuendo and old movie references, and Gabi's candy-eating tough-girl attitude.

I chewed on the side of my lip as I finished drawing the sigil on Virginia's hand and moved on to Ben, who stuck his hand in range without making me ask.

Whatever happened after, it didn't matter. I owed it to them to get them back to their bodies. I owed it to Ezra to get him home safely, and Tempest and Dion for helping. If I was run out of town after that . . . well, I could find another bar. Maybe I'd move out of state. Start over completely. Get away from the ocean and the sand.

I reached for Bruce, but he shook his head and stayed out of reach. "I'm not leaving you here. You're going to need help."

"Bruce, you're married. Give me your hand so you can go home to your wife."

"I'll go home when you go home. I trust you. And like I said, you're going to need help. If my grandmother's stories are true, Tangaroa is not to be trifled with. He will not let Ezra go easily."

"I can't let you stay. Your soul is separate from your body. The longer they are apart, the harder it will be for you to return."

Bruce gave a stubborn shake of his head. "I want to help."

"I have Dion to help."

"Is he trustworthy? He left you to be captured."

"Hey! That's not fair. I was afraid for my own essence."

"My point exactly. You feared for yourself and abandoned someone who would help you." Bruce lowered his head to stare into my eyes. "I'm staying. I'll watch your back."

I sighed. There was no getting out of this. "Fine. But only until I can get close to Ezra. Once I'm at the feast, you're going home."

"Deal."

I closed my eyes and thought of Grams. I pictured her in the Trident, standing next to Silas with her hands on her hips. Chairs and tables had been knocked over, my friends left to lie on the sticky floor, but everyone and everything else had been cleared out.

The police and paramedics have been called and are on their way, Silas told her.

Grams crouched next to Virginia, cupping her hand over my friend's forehead, as if feeling for her temperature. *Then we must bring them back now, before the nulls arrive.* She moved her fingers to the pulse point in Virginia's neck. *Before their bodies are closed to their souls.*

Silas visibly tensed. *What are you saying?*

Their souls have left their bodies, but Lil will send them home.

And Lil? She's coming back, right? Silas gripped Grams's shoulder, pulling her around to face him. Worry etched deep lines between his eyebrows. *She came back from the water. She'll come home again, right?*

Grams shrugged. *She has her own path to walk. A choice to make. Her brother needs her.*

The muscle in Silas's jaw twitched. *So do we.*

Grams placed her hand over Silas's where it still rested on her shoulder. *I know, dear. All will work out as it's supposed to, in the end. Trust and acceptance.* Her hand squeezed his, bones pushing against her thin skin.

I swallowed the lump that had suddenly appeared in my throat. Silas worried for me. He wanted me back. He'd seen the monster, knew my truth, and still, he accepted me for who and what I was.

Grams was right, I would make sure my friends were safe. I would find a way to break Ezra free. And together, we would return home.

Home . . . I hadn't had a real home since the accident. Except, that wasn't entirely true. I was coming to realize the Trident was more than a bar. It was community. Family. And it was time to send them home.

"They're ready for you," I murmured, knowing Grams would hear me. "Bruce will be last."

Understood. Grams cracked her knuckles and returned to Virginia's side. Silas let her go, his gaze traveling around the room as if looking for something. Or someone.

I feel you, he whispered. *Stay safe. Come home. No matter what it takes.*

Heat flushed my cheeks, and I opened my eyes, returning my awareness to Aegir's Hall.

I didn't know what to say, or even if Silas would hear me if I did, but I couldn't open up in front of everyone else. Whatever I wanted to say would be for his ears alone. Now, it was time to get to work.

"Here goes nothing." I turned my gaze to Virginia.

"I'm first?" She squeaked.

Before I could respond, her image faded. She went from being a solid figure to a hazy outline, then disappeared completely. Gabi followed suit, then Ben.

"Okay then. Bruce, you're going to be my anchor in the room, and Dion, you're going to get him inside."

"I am?"

"If you want out of Aegir's demesne, free passage to the Seen, then yeah."

Dion frowned. "You might as well try to get into a locked vault. The gods don't suffer fools—or intruders."

"Too bad. Bruce, time to get half naked. I need to study your tattoos."

The man was covered in traditional Samoan tribal tattoos from his right wrist across his shoulder, and descending down his back and right pec. I knew the geometric shapes carried meaning, but I didn't know what they meant. All I really knew was that no one else in history had this exact tattoo. It was unique to Bruce, and he'd earned the tattoos from his mother's family. It would be a perfect visual to anchor myself in the new space.

Bruce quirked an eyebrow but pulled off the Hawaiian work shirt without protest. I spun my finger in a circle, telling him to turn around. The guy was thick with muscle and a little extra around the middle, but he carried himself with surprising grace. I memorized the shape of the art in his skin, knowing if I did any more than that, his wife would take it out of my hide. She was not a woman to mess with.

I spent a few careful minutes studying a particularly intricate section that featured a stylized lizard climbing over his shoulder.

"Why is this necessary?" he asked.

"Because you're unique. Aegir and Rán won't recognize you, but I can use your tattoos to pinpoint a location in the Aether. It's the best way you can help." I swallowed and stepped back. I could do this. "Okay, I think I'm good. Just keep your shirt off."

Bruce wadded up the material and handed it over to Dion, who threw it beneath the counter with only the smallest sneer of disgust, which I ignored.

"I can't be tripping over chairs and drawing attention. So when you get inside, stack the barrels near a wall. Then Bruce can stand with his back to the barrels, like he's on guard or something, and I can jump into the gap. You'll keep me from being seen."

"Makes sense." Bruce agreed.

"While you're setting up, I'll try to get a peek into the feasting hall. The more I know before I cross, all the better."

The plan wasn't fool proof, not by a long shot, but it was going to work. I could feel it.

CHAPTER 31

I pushed my way through the crowd of souls, finding it much more difficult without Eldoris and her magic. Not that I wanted Bitch Queen Supreme anywhere near me, but it would have been helpful to have that ability given the thousands, maybe hundreds of thousands, of souls gathered in front of Aegir's doors. It reminded me a bit of an arena concert, but instead of some pop idol, everyone was waiting with bated breath for the appearance of the gods themselves. Good to avoid being noticed, bad for getting close enough to see anything useful.

At last, the front edge of the crowd was visible between souls. Red velvet ropes kept everyone back from the base of the stairs that lead up to Aegir's carved doors. Those stairs had widened and expanded, creating a stage that reminded me of a Hollywood awards show, but without the heavy curtains. They'd even installed a red carpet.

Four of Aegir's demon sons—they were too solid and too human-looking to be anything else—stood behind the ropes watching the milling crowd, guarding it from encroachment.

A portly man with a biker 'stache and a bulbous nose nudged me with his elbow. "Were you here for the last feast?"

"No," I replied. "I'm new."

I glanced around, trying to avoid engaging with the guy but he seemed determined to chat.

"You're gonna love it! Aegir's buddies are something else. Power, man. Power. You can feel it," Biker 'Stache proclaimed eyes glued to the stage. I almost wasn't sure if he was actually talking to me, except that he leaned in my direction.

"I'm sure."

"Just don't get in their way. I had a buddy with me last time. Poor guy. Accidentally stepped in front of one of the ladies and she took his head clean off. What a way to go."

"He was dead, then?"

"Nah, don't you know? We're all already dead. She took him off to her place, I guess. Claimed him, or something. Haven't seen 'im since."

"That sounds . . . horrifying."

The man shrugged. "Once you're dead, you're dead, you know?"

I shuffled away from the man, edging to the right side to keep away from the center of the stage. The last thing I needed was to be spotted by one of the guests—or worse, have my head cut off just for being in the wrong place at the wrong time. Talk about an unfortunate end. Dion hadn't been kidding.

I spotted a group of women wearing what could best be described as cruise attire: wide brimmed hats, sunglasses, and loud floral patterns. They chattered in the high-pitched whiny way of privileged ladies whose vacation had been rudely interrupted.

"Isn't there going to be any entertainment?" The darker-haired lady's thin lips curled in a sneer as she twisted and turned, gazing around the crowded space.

"I wouldn't mind seeing a few nicely muscled fire dancers, if you know what I mean," growled a rather obese woman wearing a muumuu and waving a tiny, folded fan at her sweaty face.

I winced, knowing exactly what kind of guest I was looking at. We had plenty of them come into the Trident. Tourists with attitude, they thought they were entitled to belittle the staff, just because they had paid to get in.

They were the perfect cover. Hell, their hats alone could shield me from being seen.

"How long are they expecting us to wait?" Ms. Disdain asked. "Do they even have a buffet? I don't see any food at all. I expected better service."

"Patience, Gerty." Muumuu Lady's sausage fingers squeezed her friend's shoulder. "I think they're getting started."

A rumble of thunder echoed across the ceiling drawing every eye upward. A gong the size of a small house appeared on stage. Peithon emerged from the wall on the left. He looked significantly different than the last time I'd seen him. His figure seemed more solid and settled. The flesh of his face had narrowed and been sculpted into high cheekbones and a dimpled chin. Green eyes flashed with mischief as he twirled a mallet like one of those ninja staffs. Even his clothes were more put together, his appearance more refined, if a bit anachronistic. Picture a Viking lord, with puffy pants and a sleeveless embroidered vest tunic thing that revealed tightly muscled arms and a dusting of chest hair.

"Mmm. Yummy." Muumuu lady purred.

Peithon danced a little jig as he reached the top of the stairs and waited. The crowd still chattered and laughed. He took the mallet and lifted it above his head. A few of the voices stopped. At last, with a full body swing, he slammed the mallet into the gong.

The sound reverberated in waves that vibrated through my

chest and seemed to touch my very essence. All around, people gasped and went silent.

Peithon grinned. "Welcome to Aegir's Hall. The Feast of Renewal is about to begin. Grab a drink and join the party!"

The mass of souls shifted, opening the way for a procession of Aegir's nine daughters. They strode in from the bar area, leaving their posts at the brewing vat behind. Eldoris led the way and Tempest brought up the rear, so I guessed they had lined up in order of seniority.

As soon as the women had climbed the stairs, the carved double doors to Aegir's private rooms opened in unison, pulled by some invisible force. Standing framed in the center: Aegir. He'd managed to craft his appearance in the happy middle between the casual hipster I'd first met in his office, and the terrifying sea monster with a man's face. He wore his coral crown, and his beard had been carefully oiled and braided with gold beads. His upper body was bare, revealing the broad shoulders and trim waist of a swimmer. Much like Bruce, stylized tattoos of ocean life swirled across his upper body. His legs were encased in billowy blue harem pants, tight around the ankle and calf and loose everywhere else. An enigmatic smile spread across his face. If I didn't know any better, I'd think he was a magnanimous host here to ensure a good time.

My lip curled. I'd seen the truth of what he really was. What he represented and what he wanted. And it wasn't for the benefit of the souls in this room. It wasn't for the benefit of Rán or his children. Everything he did was for his benefit and his benefit alone.

Aegir turned and extended his hand behind him. Rán stepped forward from the interior of the room. His tenth wife wore a simple floor-length gown in some kind of shiny blue material that brought to mind the deepest depths of the cold oceans; dark and forbidding, yet shimmering with life. Rather than a crown, she wore a silver circlet on her forehead, with a single large blue stone nestled between her brows. She supported Ezra on her arm and pulled him forward to face the crowd. It took something away from her regal appearance, and yet also softened her impression—she looked the doting mother.

Once again, I knew better.

Like Aegir, Ezra's upper body was bare. His skin glistened, oily, like one of those bodybuilders they showed on the cover of men's fitness magazines. His hair had been carefully combed back from his face. Even his eyebrows appeared to have been plucked and shaped.

I was never going to let him live that down—assuming I could actually figure out how to break him free of this place.

Ezra's lower body was encased in the lobster shell and wrapped in swaths of shining blue cloth that left his legs exposed. Each step looked as if it took massive effort. The motion was jerky and uncoordinated. Nothing like my athletic brother's normal movement pattern. He was forced to grip Rán's hand like a lifeline, like the crippled old man that he wasn't.

In a moment of clarity, I realized she wanted him to depend on her. She wanted someone to need her, to want her presence and her comfort. She probably hadn't had that at all since the night she tried to cut the spirit away from my body while I slept.

"She won't get away with it." I whispered to myself, more determined than ever to break Ezra free.

I tore my attention away from the individuals and peered into the room behind them. As far as I could tell, everything looked exactly as it had when Abdulbaith dropped me into Aegir's office. Same couch, same chair, same rug. But that couldn't be where the feast would be held. The gods wouldn't all fit in that space together. And besides, there was no place for food or drink. Which meant they were going somewhere else. I would just have to be patient. Not my strong suit.

A shout of "*Skål! Aegir!*" erupted from one of the balconies overhead. Another voice answered with "*Cheers!*"

Aegir flashed bright white teeth in a broad grin and regally dipped his chin toward his supplicants. A glass of mead appeared in his hand. He lifted the drink into the air for a toast. The room fell silent.

This was it.

"Welcome, guests of Aegir's Hall! I hope you are enjoying your time in my demesne."

"Huzzah!" A man yelled from the back of the room.

"Best party I've ever been to in all my life . . . and death!" Another voice added.

Aegir lifted his empty hand into the air, palm down, in a settling motion. "You honor me. And so it is time I honor you." He turned, extending his empty left hand behind him again toward Rán.

"But first, I must introduce you to the newest addition to our family. Rán's son Ezra has been raised by our combined efforts to stand at our side."

Rán pulled Ezra, stumbling, forward to stand next to Aegir. My brother stared down at the mass of souls, brow furrowed, and eyes pinched in pain. He forced a smile to his lips, but the angle of his shoulders was stiff.

Her smile wasn't forced. The joy that lit her face was completely out of touch with what was going on around her. Once Ezra was stable, she accepted Aegir's hand with the tips of her fingers and stood at his side, the consort of the king of this place.

"Welcome my wife and my son."

I couldn't tell if the last was a command, or a greeting, but the crowd of souls erupted into whistles and cheers. I brought my hands together in forced applause but couldn't bring myself to smile. They had bound my brother to the Aether, but they wouldn't get away with it.

Aegir and Rán stood together, smiling magnanimously down at the gathered masses and accepting the praise they clearly thought was their due. Ezra crossed his arms over his chest, looking uncomfortable and exposed. The daughters lined the stairs opposite Ezra. Peithon stood with the mallet in both hands, ready to ring the gong once more. The posed tableau waited for something. I just didn't know what.

The carved doors swung shut on silent hinges.

CHAPTER 32

The hair on the back of my neck lifted. Static charged the air. A bolt of lightning sizzled from ceiling to floor in the center of the crowd. The unlucky souls in the way were vaporized, their forms exploding on impact. In their place stood a man with cruel dark eyes and a beard as black as coal.

Gasps and startled shrieks carried through the space. Everyone stilled, their attention caught on the man in the middle.

"Enlil, my friend. Welcome!" Aegir's voice boomed, and his smile grew even wider. "You are the first to arrive. I am glad you could join us."

The man strode forward with purposeful, proud steps. Aegir's son unclipped the red velvet rope, allowing him to pass through the barrier between the souls and the feast. "When have I ever missed a feast thrown by Aegir?" He asked as he climbed the stairs to Aegir's side.

The men embraced with a brusque hug.

"Not once in our many thousands of years, my friend. And

today is a great celebration, for not only have I found my Rán, but she has found her children. Our hearts are full."

"And so your power grows."

Aegir didn't answer the non-question, but his eyes narrowed, and his wide grin turned into a calculating smile. "Please, enjoy the hospitality of the feast. The cups are full, the plates await your pleasure."

Enlil smirked and dipped his chin. Eldoris stepped forward. The doors opened. They no longer led into Aegir's office. Instead, a fire roared in the center of a space nearly as large as the main hall in which the souls gathered. A whole pig rotated on a spit above the flame. Delicacies of every flavor and description had been set out on the buffet tables that lined the walls: pastries, overflowing baskets of fruit, roasted vegetables, whole fish laid out on beds of rice, oysters displayed in piles of pink Himalayan salt . . . I couldn't even begin to take it all in. Long wood tables with fur and pillow covered benches had been arranged around the fire, interspersed with intricately carved columns that held up the ceiling high above. Shifting blue light trickled in from skylights set into the second story gables, as if we truly were housed underwater.

"Welcome," Eldoris chimed. She curtseyed and extended her arms toward the room, then followed Enlil as he proceeded into the hall, grabbing an apple from a basket on the nearest table and taking a bite without pausing his steps.

The doors shut behind them. I hadn't even had time to find the barrels of mead or Bruce's tattooed presence. He and Dion should have already been inside. I tried to clear my thoughts to find him in my mind's eye.

A freezing wind blasted through the hall, nearly knocking me off my feet and distracting me from my purpose. Lanterns flickered and candles sputtered. Snow swirled along the edges of the curling gusts, finally coming together and spiraling into the shape of a woman with white-blond hair and icy blue eyes who stood at least seven feet tall. Blue veins pulsed beneath the nearly translucent skin of her arms and neck, even encroaching up onto her face.

"Liluri, my dear, welcome," Aegir greeted the new arrival. At least she hadn't destroyed anyone on her entrance.

"Aegir," was the woman's icy response.

"Thank you for leaving your mountains to join us as we celebrate the Feast of Renewal."

"Yes. Well, I would not miss an opportunity to taste the latest winter mead. I do hope my bees supplied enough honey for a barrel or two."

"They did, indeed. And you shall take some home with you." Aegir waved a hand, and the doors opened. Dion and Bruce stood near the entry with a barrel between them. "Please join the feast. Enlil is waiting inside."

Aegir's second daughter stepped forward. "Welcome." Like Eldoris before her, she led Liluri into the banquet. Dion and Bruce followed behind, rolling the barrel toward the tables. I was going to have to wait to get inside. Bruce had to be stationary, his back to the wall, or I would be sure to make a scene.

The doors closed and the lights went out. Every flicker, gone. The hall descended into darkness so black, so impenetrable, I lost all sense of place. If not for the gasps and short screams of the souls around us, I would have sworn I was alone. A moment later the flames burst back to life. A woman stood on the steps directly before Aegir, close enough to strike if she had wanted to. Her head was shaved bald, her skin as dark as the night she brought with her.

"Nyx, you have arrived right on time, as always." Aegir's smile was tight, and tension radiated down his shoulders and stick-straight spine. It was a grim satisfaction to see him intimidated by someone else, even if he refused to step out of the way. "Your presence is a boon to my hall. Welcome to the Feast of Renewal."

The woman said nothing. Her lips pressed together in a subtle sneer. The doors opened and she passed Aegir without deigning to acknowledge anyone at all, not even the third daughter who raced to follow her into the room. The doors shut.

I growled deep in my throat. I hadn't had a chance to see anything. I had to get into that room, and I didn't know how many more chances I was going to get. How many gods were coming? Tempest hadn't said, but even if there were hundreds (which would take forever to arrive, at this rate) I needed to be inside before it got too crowded for me to hide.

Next to arrive was a man with the head of a ram. Horns as thick as my bicep curled back from his forehead in a spiral that ended just over his shoulder. He carried a tall, narrow pitcher with a delicate handle and elegant pouring lip. Blue and gold paint highlighted the soft curves and accentuated the crafts-manship of the piece.

"Knum! Welcome. I am so glad you could join us."

"I heard you have someone new to celebrate." He dipped his chin toward Rán. "My lady, this gift is for you. Just a small trifle of congratulations on your binding. However, should you ever require someone with more skill in his hands, you may seek me out." If a goat could flirt with a smile, this one just did.

"Thank you," Rán replied taking the beautiful pitcher even as Aegir scowled. "I appreciate the offer, but Aegir has given me my heart's desire. I want for nothing."

Knum shrugged, drawing attention to shoulders and pecs even more defined than Aegir's. He was stacked like an award-winning bodybuilder. It only took a minute to get past his head to notice. "If you find that changes in time, my offer remains open."

"Enjoy the feast," Aegir growled. "Your seat has been reserved next to Apep."

"At the farthest end of the table, then." Knum winked at

Rán. "At least I won't lack for entertainment. The snake is never short of conversation."

The doors opened, and Aegir's fourth daughter strode forward. This one was one of the oar pullers. A sultry smile played across her lips as she took in Knum's form. I had to admit, if you could ignore the animal head, the rest of him was actually rather agreeable looking if you liked hairless greased muscles. But those horns . . . I shuddered.

Quickly, before she could lead the Ram god into the banquet hall and the doors closed, I shifted my gaze inside.

There! Bruce stood with his back to a large fern-like plant in a blue pot that had to be as tall as my waist. The plant itself was bushy and added another five feet at least. The barrels had been stacked in a pyramid shape another foot or two to Bruce's left, leaving me a shadowed gap to jump into behind the big guy. Between Bruce's tattoos, the plant, and the barrels, I had my unique coordinates. I just had to envision them in the right perspective.

CHAPTER 33

Dogs barked in the distance, getting closer with every breath. Souls jumped out of the way as three giant hunting hounds bounded into the room. One of them spotted me, making eye contact and changing direction to head my way. My eyes widened when he paused right in front of me and sat, tail wagging with friendly, if persistent intent. He was a gorgeous animal, solid black except for a white starburst on his chest, sleek with muscle and shining with good health. He cocked his head to the side, his short floppy ears bouncing with the motion.

I glanced around, hoping no one noticed.

"Eww. Get that creature away from me," Ms. Disdain scuttled away from me and the dog, bumping into another group of souls behind her. "I can't stand dogs, with their slobber and incessant need for attention. Who let the dirty animals in here, anyway?"

I gingerly patted the hound on the head—which came up to my waist—and then tried to gently shoo him away. He woofed and licked my hand.

"Go on, now," I encouraged, simultaneously attempting to step back and stay in the shadow of Muumuu Lady's broad hat.

Woof.

I grimaced.

The stately clop of a horse drew all eyes to the back of the room and a whistle called the dogs to heel. A goddess in a red dress and golden knee-high boots sat astride a horse black as night. She rode without a saddle or bridle, directing the mare with just a twitch of her heels. She whistled again as the crowd parted. The dogs sprinted with gleeful lolling tongues to reach her side.

She was beautiful. Flashing green eyes dominated a heart-shaped face. Her skin was unlined and blemish free. Dark hair had been twisted up into a series of intricate multi-layered braids along the sides and back of her head.

Her gaze swept out across the gathered souls as she crossed the golden floor. Our eyes connected.

Go now. A voice commanded in my head.

With a start, I realized she was right. I was distracted. But how did she know?

Was the voice even hers? She hadn't paused her examination of the room, hadn't done anything to draw attention to me. Maybe my conscience was interrupting my awe.

Whatever. It didn't matter. I couldn't waste any time. Even if it was just the voice in my own head, I had to make my move while Aegir and everyone else was distracted.

"Welcome, Hecate!" Aegir boomed. "I see you brought your familiars. I suppose we can make space for them in the hall, so long as they refrain from putting their paws—or hooves—on the table."

"Aegir, you disappoint me. Where are the magnificent creatures you promised? All I see is a man uncomfortable in his shell and a self-conscious woman who has surrendered her own agency. Then again, you do seem to have a type."

Ten points to Hecate. Now, time to port. And do it right this time.

I closed my eyes. Stopped my thoughts. I ignored the sounds of the room around me. Ignored the banter of the gods. Ignored Muumuu's perfume. I thought about the banquet hall, what I had been able to see. I envisioned myself in the space, the plant in front of me and to my right, the barrels to the left, and Bruce's tattoo in front.

I considered the noises that I would hear in the space. Knum had placed himself next to Liluri midway down the room on the opposite side of the fire. He laughed in a bleating sheeplike manner. She looked at him askance, as if she had no idea why he was laughing or what he was laughing at.

Enlil's feet were on the table. He'd finished his apple and was starting in on some kind of hand pie. Nyx was in the far corner, near the throne-like chair that must be Aegir's seat. She'd drawn the shadows around her, isolating herself from the rest, and yet she too had a drink in her hand. I wondered if she'd loosen up once the alcohol hit her bloodstream.

With a last breath of air, I took a step and bent into a crouch. The fern fronds brushed against my face. I could hear the laughter with my physical ears, not just in my thoughts.

I opened my eyes and grinned. I'd done it. I'd stepped from one place to another in the Aether, transporting myself by thought alone. And I hadn't tripped over anything. No one paid any attention to me. One thousand points to Lil. Except, even as I mentally celebrated, I sagged on my feet. Fatigue weighed on my body and my mind.

Three jumps in the Aether, and I was wiped. My jaw cracked in a wide yawn. Remembering Grams's warning, I tried to count the number of hours I'd been awake. I honestly had no idea. It was too easy to lose track of time in this place.

I shook my head. It didn't matter. I had a job to do, and I was going to do it. I bit the inside of my cheek, the pain helping jolt my brain. I pushed myself back against the wall, sliding into the shadowed gap behind the barrels.

"Bruce," I hissed. "I'm here."

The big Samoan kept his arms crossed over his chest and gaze forward, but took one big step backward, putting him within touching distance.

"Took you long enough," he whispered out of the side of his mouth.

"Give me your hand." Time to get him back to his body and out of here.

"You can't be serious."

"You promised. You got me in here, now it's time for you to go. I can't be worried about you and everything else all at the same time." I pulled the pen I'd stolen from Gabi out of my hair and reached for his arm. "Besides, I need you to tell Silas I'll be listening for him. For his solo. Tell him I'm coming home."

Bruce shifted to glance over his shoulder. The pen slipped and the sigil smeared. I grimaced.

"Dammit, now I have to start over," I complained.

"Listening for Silas, eh? I take it the date the other night went well then."

I shook my head. "You're all a bunch of gossips, you know that?"

Bruce grinned, unrepentant. "I'll tell him, don't worry."

"And everyone else, too. I'm sure," I grumbled. Not that I'd said anything particularly incriminating, but we both knew that wasn't the point. I'd chosen Silas as my anchor, and he would bring me home.

I finished Lilith's sigil on the underside of Bruce's forearm and gave his wrist a squeeze. The design was a little wobbly, but good enough. "Thank you, my friend."

Bruce faded from sight.

CHAPTER 34

The primordial gods of the Aether were oblivious. At least, it sure seemed that way. No one had taken notice of my arrival or Bruce's departure; their attention was focused on the food and drink and one-upmanship around them. Plus, Bruce had chosen his station well. The bushy fern and stack of barrels made for a rather decent hiding spot, where I could observe without being observed.

The room was at least fifty yards long, but only about twenty yards wide, with scattered seating and tables arranged around a central fire pit. More gods had arrived while I had been sending Bruce home, and conversations had started in all corners. Only Enlil, with his feet still on the table, and Nyx, standing in a shadowed alcove, stayed apart, seemingly content to keep to themselves.

This side of the great entry doors was carved not with the image of Aegir, but with the scariest version of a leviathan I'd ever seen. Its jaws gaped wide, crossing the entire width of the two doors. Fang-like teeth extended from both the top and bottom mandible, longer than I was tall. Behind the fangs, rows of smaller teeth curved back into the gullet, emphasizing that once trapped inside that gargantuan mouth, there was no coming out.

An eye bigger than my face kept watch over the gathering, and the dragon-like head nearly touched the ceiling. The body of the carved creature curled back across the wall and around the right side of the room, passing behind my hiding spot. I reached out a hand to touch the scaled expanse behind me, marveling at the intricate detail work.

Each individual scale, about the size of my hand, had been painstakingly rendered with the ridges and texture of the real thing. Here and there, some kind of shell or stone had been inlaid into the design, making the scales appear iridescent. Combined with the dim, shifting blue light from the overhead skylights, and the flickering lamps and candles, the creature looked ready to swim out of the wood and eat the guests at the banquet.

A shadow descended over me. I yanked my hand back from the wall and tried not to breathe.

"Gorgeous, isn't she?" Hecate stood with her back to me, leaning against the barrels where Bruce had been standing just minutes before. Her whispered words were clearly meant for me, and yet she was trying not to draw attention to my position. If anything, she was trying to protect me. Why?

"She?" I asked.

"Leviathan. She was magnificent in her day. I treasured her."

"You? Treasured her?"

"Mmm." Hecate took a sip from her mead glass, using the drink to shield the movement of her lips from the rest of the room. "There was a time when Aegir and I were allies. One might even say unified. The kiddos like to believe that the first Rán was Eldoris's mother, but they would be wrong. In the early days, Aegir and I ruled the sea together. Of course, I also gained favor over the skies and the earth, and even held influence in a few of the underworld myths. I like to be diversified. Aegir, on the other hand, put all his eggs in one basket, so to speak. He gave everything he could, everything he was, to the oceans and the seas, making mortals fear his every wave. As I found I preferred the love of the mortals to their fear, I eventually left him."

"Oh. Huh." I didn't know what to say.

"Now he takes a perverse pleasure in warping my ladies to replace me."

"What are you talking about?"

"Even you must know, uneducated and untrained as you are. You called to me, and I answered."

"I did?"

"Lucky thing, too. That poor girl didn't have a chance on her own. Neither of them did."

Gabi and the biker chick at the bar. That's who she was talking about.

"When the moon is full, I am at my strongest, especially in favor of the women of the world," she continued. "So often they have no idea who it is they reach out to, but still, I hear and I answer when I can. Your voice is particularly loud, Daughter of Lilith."

I had reached out to the moon to help them, used the symbol of Lilith which contained the phases of the moon to banish the eel demon. I hadn't known who I was reaching out to. I thought it had been the symbol of Lilith, but Hecate had come to my aid?

"Are you Lilith?" It was probably a stupid question, but I had to ask.

Hecate chuckled, hiding her smile behind her drink. Knum glanced in our direction, but she shifted, further blocking me from view. She nodded her head in his direction and waved her fingers just as the doors opened again and a red-scaled serpent nearly as large as the leviathan on the wall slithered into the room.

"Ah. Apep is here. That should keep things entertaining," she echoed Knum's words before taking another sip.

Unfortunately, the snake headed straight for us. I slid farther back into the shadows, keeping my head and body tucked as tightly against the wall as I could. A small triangle-shaped gap between the top barrel and the two supporting it was my only view of what was happening.

"Apep! How goes the devouring?" Hecate asked, intercepting the snake before he got too close.

"Modern mortals have no ressspect, no fear of the abyssss. It is dissssapointing." The snake's sibilant response sent shudders down my spine. "Aegir's feassst is much needed this cycle."

"Indeed." Hecate's voice caught, as if holding back a laugh.

Apep's head rose to Hecate's eye level and the muscular frill around his neck spread wide. "I hear you have already renewed yourself in the modern world. Perhapsss we may discussss your efforts?"

"It is the Feast of Renewal," Hecate replied, noncommittally. "But first, let us enjoy ourselves. The mead is top notch, yet again. A good omen, I think."

Hecate patted the topmost barrel and I ducked back farther from the snake's questing tail. Without moving his head or turning his lidless gaze from Hecate's face, Apep pulled it from the stack with one thick coil and popped the cork with the more dexterous prehensile tip. The serpent lifted the entire barrel above his head, opened his mouth wide, and poured the golden liquid down his gullet.

In all honesty, I was rather impressed. For a creature without hands, he managed to manipulate the process without spilling a drop.

"I am the great devourer!" He shouted when he was done.

I rolled my eyes.

"*Bibe multis annis!*" Knum shouted from across the room. "Come, Apep! I was promised your good company. Grab another barrel and join me in toasting our many lives."

Apep dipped his nose in what I assumed was the equivalent of a nod. "We will sssspeak again later, Hecate."

The serpent lowered his head, snaked another barrel with his tail, and slithered around the fire to Knum's side. The ram god greeted him with another loud cheer.

When Apep was gone, Hecate leaned back to peer around the now only two-high stack of barrels.

"Are you still there, Daughter of Lilith?"

"You can just call me Lil," I whispered.

"Well done, then. Not many can face the abyss snake without losing all sense. However, now that he's gone, I can answer your question: no, I am not Lilith. Lilith was human, first woman to be precise."

"So I've been told, but apparently some of the stories are wrong."

"Truth can be a tricky thing." Hecate paused, as if she would say more, but then shook her head as if she thought better of it. "In any case, Lilith was blessed by Gaia to be able to see the Unseen. She was a radiant creature, fully independent. She never worshipped any of us. I admired her. I dare say, we might even have been friends. After her death, I promised to watch out for her daughters as best I was able."

The olive-skinned woman tilted her head to the side, scanning the room which had begun to fill ever more quickly as the gods arrived, some with servants and familiars. Hecate's horse munched on some hay in the corner closest to the doors, and her dogs wandered around the room, sniffing at the other elementals and begging for scraps or a scratch behind the ear.

Seemingly satisfied no one was watching, Hecate bent at the waist and retrieved something from her boot, palming it in her hand. She straightened, scanned the room again, and moved her hand behind her back. In it, a knife pointed downward.

"Take it. You'll need it."

"A knife?"

"An athame. It is not a weapon, but a tool. Use it to sever the connections between Seen and Unseen, Earth and Aether."

"How?" I asked as I gingerly took the knife from her fingers.

Hecate shrugged. "I am no Daughter of Lilith to answer that. As I understand it, each of you must find your own way."

"Hecate! Why do you act the wallflower?" a male voice called from the gathering around Apep and Knum. "Join us and let's drink to new beginnings."

"Come now, Opochtli, cast your line elsewhere. I prefer a bit more meat on the hook." Despite the heckle, Hecate lifted her glass in the air for a toast and winked at the thin man wearing a cape over one shoulder and a green feather headdress.

She rose from her seat, still not turning around, and held the glass to her lips as if about to take a sip. "Use it well, Daughter of Lilith."

CHAPTER 35

The knife lay in my hand, somehow scary and unfamiliar. It wasn't like I'd never used a knife before. I wasn't five. Sharp steak knives, big chef's knives, short paring knives, serrated bread knives . . . everyday use knives.

This wasn't any of those.

The handle was black, made out of some kind of ebony wood or something. I could just barely see the grain within whatever varnish had been used in the finishing. Not that it felt like wood. It was too heavy, too smooth, too hard. Inlaid into the handle was a delicate filigree of some kind of whitish-blue stone shaped into the symbol for Lilith that Grams had drawn on the napkin.

The blade itself was dual-edged, like a dagger more than a kitchen knife, and sharp. Maybe four inches long, it was nicely balanced by the handle, which fit perfectly in my hand.

I hadn't moved from my crouched hiding spot, and my knees were starting to hurt. Glancing around the barrels and through the fern leaves, I could see Hecate leaning against a short, thick man with a heavy beard. She had her elbow resting on his shoulder as if he were a bar counter rather than a person. He glanced at her boobs—which were almost directly at eye-level—every so often, as if he couldn't help himself. Needless to say, he didn't seem to mind the positioning.

The rest of the gods had gathered in cliques around the room, some reclining on fur-draped couches or sitting on wooden benches, others standing in conversation. They all had drinks in their hands, and all seemed to be having a good time. They paid very little attention to Aegir's daughters as they passed with pitchers and trays, not even pausing their conversation as they pulled one-bite delicacies from the platters.

I glanced down at my clothes. I wished I'd worn something that would let me fit in with the daughters and the servants a little better, but the black on black was going to have to do. At least I wasn't wearing the loud Hawaiian shirt. Black was neutral, and there were enough shadows around the room that I might be able to fade into the background. Or at least, be as ignored as Aegir's daughters.

I waited for a distraction. That was all I needed. Something to draw focus so my movements wouldn't be noticed.

At last, the doors opened. Aegir entered with Rán at his side. Three steps later, Abdulbaith appeared, levitating on his tentacles while also supporting Ezra, who clumsily stumbled in on his many new legs.

My stomach lurched. I hated to see my brother so weak and helpless, changed against his will and in pain. I wanted to rush to his side, but that would ruin everything. I had to do this right.

The quartet paraded around the tables, moving to stand in front of the wider than average chair, what I had correctly assumed was Aegir's throne. With a genteel turn of his wrist, he moved Rán into position at her own slightly smaller throne. Abdulbaith and Ezra remained standing to either side of the couple, not warranting thrones but each having their own stool to rest on. I wasn't sure how Ezra was expected to sit on any kind of stool or chair given the lobster tail bottom, but at least he was given the courtesy of having a seat at the table.

The rest of the feasting elementals paused their conversations and turned to their host. Some wore expressions of expectant anticipation. Some were more hostile, looking on him with disdain, or even malice. Still others seemed neutral or actually happy to be in the room.

Surprisingly, Hecate was one of the latter. Of all the gods present—except maybe Enlil, who still had his feet on the table—she seemed the most at ease, the most unfazed by the feast and its host. Even Aegir seemed less comfortable than she, or at least, more formal.

"Now that we're all settled in," Aegir began, pointedly looking at Enlil, "I would like to make a toast."

He paused and grinned when one of the gods shouted, "*Salud!*"

Aegir lifted his glass in acknowledgment and then continued, "We, the primordial gods, who were there at the beginning of everything and have remained through the rise and fall of the lesser pantheons—"

"Misfits and troublemakers!"

"Upstarts!"

"You're the upstart, so shut it!"

"As I was saying," Aegir tried again with a scowl, "We gather now to celebrate the renewal of our longstanding alliances, and the enrichment of our immortal pneuma."

"*Skål!* Enough with the platitudes. Let's drink and make merry!" Hecate heckled.

"*Sláinte!* Agreed! Where's the music?"

Aegir lifted his hands in that placating manner he was so fond of. "Come now, this is the Feast of Renewal. We must celebrate what has begun."

"So let's *begin* drinking!" Knum lifted a cup that looked remarkably like a ram's horn. Perhaps he was going for irony.

"I don't know about you lot, but I've *been* drinking!" Enlil growled. "You all had better catch up."

"Huzzah!"

"Ninatta! Kulitta! Strike up the band!" Hecate commanded.

The gathering quickly devolved into chaos as the elementals ignored Aegir in favor of their own pursuit of pleasure.

The god of the ocean scowled, as two women—I assumed Ninatta and Kulitta—began playing a flute and a fiddle. Moments later, an entire band appeared behind them, faceless creatures that strummed and banged and blew on all manner of instruments in a rollicking tune that begged the listeners to get up and dance. Several of the gods obliged. Even taciturn Enlil tapped his foot to the rhythm, causing the table to vibrate and the dishes to rattle.

Now was my chance.

Tempest stood by the rotating boar, sharpening a long kitchen knife against a honing rod. She whipped the steel back and forth like a pro chef, preparing to slice and serve the meat onto platters carried by her sisters.

I lifted an empty silver platter from a nearby table and crept into line. No one appeared to notice my presence, they were all too distracted by the dancing and music.

At last, my turn. Tempest looked up. Her eyes widened and she quickly glanced around the room.

"What are you doing?" Tempest hissed as she loaded my tray with meat.

"Getting close to Ezra. Are you ready? Where's Dion?"

"He's bringing in more mead, which, given the rate Apep is sucking down the stuff, will be needed soon."

"Good." I took a deep breath and blew it out as if it was my birthday. Except, I was never this nervous on my birthday.

"What's the plan?"

"I get Rán to reverse the change on Ezra and we leave."

"That's not a plan. It's a wish."

"Well, I wish I had something better, but . . ." I shrugged, awkwardly holding the now-heavy platter. "It's what I got."

Tempest continued to stack meat on the tray until the pile was bigger than my basket on laundry day. "Go around the far side, then. Aegir's too busy trying to make Hecate and Enlil jealous to pay attention."

"Hecate and Enlil?"

"His ex and his former best friend. It's all posturing. Don't worry about it. Just don't get caught until after you have Rán on your side. She's the only one who can defy him in his own demesne."

CHAPTER 36

I kept the platter high against my chest, hoping to hide myself at least a little behind the stack of sliced meat, and made my way toward my brother at the head of the table. One of Hecate's hounds followed at my heel. I couldn't say why.

I passed half a dozen of the gods, weaving between their laughing figures and flailing gestures. A few stopped me along the way, taking meat from the platter without pausing their conversations or noticing a thing about me. As far as they were concerned, I was a ghost walking through their midst, invisible but for the delicacies I carried.

As I walked farther from the fire, I was forced on a path near Knum and the abyss snake. I kept the platter high, blocking their view of my face while I watched each step, carefully avoiding Apep's red scaled tail which slithered restlessly across the ground. The serpent had already gone through at least three additional barrels of mead, as evidenced by the precariously stacked containers at his side.

A fourth barrel slammed onto the stack to another set of boisterous cheers. Apep's tail unexpectedly shifted the wrong direction. I missed my step. Tripped. Careening sideways, I slipped on a puddle of mead that had missed its mark in the great devourer's gullet. Or perhaps one of the other gods had spilled. In any case, I was too far off balance to correct myself, and too close to the snake to avoid him. I crashed into his length. The platter and athame crashed to the ground with a clang of metal on metal. Meat spilled across the golden floor.

"What is thisssss?" Apep asked, his voice lowering to a hiss. His tongue flicked out and tasted the air around me. His head snapped up, rearing back and expanding like a cobra about to strike. A cobra that stood twenty feet high. "Another Daughter of Lilith?"

His eyes bored into mine, examining me from the inside out. I froze. Couldn't breathe, couldn't think, couldn't react. Terror washed through my system as scarlet red iridescent scales twisted and coiled around me. "She is unbound, unattached."

My brain screamed at me to move, to do something, but my body refused to respond. I was stuck, feet rooted in place, as the serpent took his time winding around me like thread around a spool.

This was what Hecate had meant. I had been protected from the force of his gaze by the barrels and my hiding spot. Now that I faced him directly, I was paralyzed with primal fear.

The giant Great Dane that had trotted at my heels started barking. Apep ignored it. His tongue flicked out again as his serpentine body lifted me into the air.

"Aegir, my friend," Knum bellowed, mimicking the host's first greeting while shouting over the dog. "Have you been holding out on us?" The ram-headed god peered at me with disconcerting rectangular pupils. His lips pulled back in an awkward grin. "Hello there, girl. Why do you not spirit yourself away, like all your forebears?"

"I'm here for my brother," I wheezed, finding my voice too late. Apep's coils held me tight. No matter how hard I pushed against the scaled strength, I couldn't budge an inch. I was the prey caught by the boa constrictor, having the life squeezed out of me.

A second dog joined the first, leaping over the end of Apep's tail to stand in a hunting challenge.

"Brother?" Knum turned to face our hosts. Ezra was there, his eyes wide. "Ah! I see the family resemblance now."

"Let her go!" My mother shouted, but I could hardly believe it was actually her. After all, she had been the one to want us all here together in the first place. Even now, she stood at Aegir's side, taking no action. Her hands twitched toward me, but she didn't pull on her abilities to stop them.

No one moved. Aegir's daughters were scattered about the room, alternately gaping at the commotion and carefully not meeting my gaze. Even Tempest, still at the roasting spit, continued slicing the meat from the carcass, turning a hunched and defeated shoulder toward my predicament.

Ezra's legs tapped an irregular syncopated rhythm. I could see the shock and indecision written on his expression, but in his current state, he wasn't strong enough to do anything against a snake ten times his size.

The elementals, meanwhile, watched with rapt expressions. Even Hecate smirked at me while taking a sip from her mead glass. Enlil hadn't taken his feet off the table. He lounged, as comfortable as if he were watching a movie on his own couch at home.

I wasn't going to get any help. None of them cared a whit for me. I was going to have to rescue myself.

"I told you if she didn't stay in the room, I would end them both. Now I don't have to. Take it as a lesson, children. The elementals are not to be trifled with."

My heart pounded. The dogs growled.

"Hecate, get your houndsss under control," Apep hissed. One of the dogs lunged forward, snapping its teeth near the base of the snake's coils. I felt the shifting motion as he slid his length out of the way of their teeth.

I wheezed in a pained half-breath. I couldn't concentrate. Couldn't move. Couldn't speak.

"They're just excited at the commotion," Hecate replied. "Calm down and they will, too."

My ribs ached and my vision started going black around the edges. I was lifted higher in the air. Apep's diamond shaped head and arm-length fangs came into view. His tongue flicked out. Light bulbs flashed in my peripheral vision. "I am the great devourer. I will consume her and gain her power for my own."

The dog's growl turned into a snarl. The third hound joined in. The gods watched on, entertained. The daughters and servants turned away.

"Aegir, stop this!" Rán cried. "Stop him!"

"If she dies, her soul will remain here forever. Is that not what you wanted?" he asked.

All three dogs barked frantically. My guardian dog, the one that was all black except a starburst of white on his chest, snarled and lunged at the snake. Apep slid back toward the wall, out of his way without loosening his grip.

Apep's black throat opened, and I stared into the cosmic abyss. He could swallow me whole without a hiccup. There was nothing I could do.

This was not how I had imagined this would go. Granted, I hadn't had a great plan to begin with, but I'd thought . . . well, I didn't really know what I'd thought. I thought I was sneakier than I actually was. Or something.

"Ow! It bit me!" Apep screamed. His tail flicked. The coil loosened. I heard a canine yelp. I fell. The ground rushed up to meet my face.

"How dare you touch my dogs!" Hecate screamed, her voice low and filled with fury.

Blood filled my mouth. My ribs ached. I didn't want to move. Didn't think I *could* move.

Get the athame, girl! the goddess's thoughts spoke in my head.

"Leave off, Hecate," a male voice I didn't recognize growled. "Your hounds are out of control."

I cracked open an eyelid. My whole body throbbed from the fall, but the athame was only a few feet away. The black handle beckoned. It wouldn't take much to reach it, but everything hurt.

"And what are you going to do about it, Utu? Give me a sunburn?"

"She is mine! I am the devourer! I will devour her!" Apep had a one-track mind. A bit like Peithon. Was he regressed? Not enough power to sustain his brain? Or was it just because he was a snake?

I didn't know and didn't really care. My thoughts were bouncing around with no real purpose. I needed to focus, but everything hurt.

I could hear Apep slithering along behind my head. I couldn't afford to wait any longer. The dogs had kept him back, but it wouldn't last. It was now or never.

I clenched my hand, surprised when it responded. I pushed my elbow into the ground and managed to move a few inches closer to the ceremonial knife. Apep lunged for me, but one of the hounds got in the way. With a vicious snarl, it tore another chunk out of the snake's tail. Apep screeched.

"Call off the beasts, Hecate," Aegir commanded. "She is not yours to protect."

"You think I protect her? Hah! She has no need of my protection. She is a creature of the wilds, a true Daughter of Lilith, unlike that witch at your side. She has already declared her truth. If the dogs choose to protect her, that's their business."

The dogs were barking as if someone had just rung the doorbell.

"Lil!" Ezra's voice cut through the tumult. The clack of claws on tile spurred me on. I pushed myself forward a few more inches. I was almost there. My ribs ached. I panted, unable to take a deep breath. So close.

"No, Ezra! Stay back," Rán urged.

"Get off me, Rán," Ezra growled.

A storm built into a rage, the sound of thunder and lashing rain pounded against the walls and ceiling. The racket made me want to cover my ears and curl into a ball with the blankets over my head. I couldn't succumb.

I pulled myself forward. Stretched out my arm. My ribs protested. My fingers brushed against the black wood.

Apep's tail curled around my calf.

"She is mine," he hissed.

I clenched the athame in my hand, not a second too soon. Like lightning, the snake flipped me over and wrapped me up once more. But this time, I had something to use against him.

Apep's coils squeezed around my middle. I gasped as I turned to face him. The frill of his neck expanded as he loomed over me. Beady black eyes glared at me with emotionless menace, my own face mirrored in their depths. His mouth opened, once more ready to swallow me down to the bottom of the cosmic abyss.

No.

I lifted the athame in the air. The blade seemed to glow from within as the handle warmed in my grip. I concentrated on the image of Lilith's sigil emblazoned there. Traced the shape with my mind. Used it as the focal point for my thoughts and energy.

"I am no one's plaything," I paused, forced to suck in tiny breaths of air, all that Apep's strength would allow. "I am a

Daughter of Lilith, and I will not be tamed nor contained. You will release me."

The blade exploded into flame. Surprised, I almost dropped it, but caught myself just in time to turn the knife's fall into a slash toward Apep's face.

The snake's head reared back, and he hissed, the sound something between nails on a chalkboard and the screech of an owl. His coil loosened. Luckily, this time I was closer to the ground, and slightly more conscious of what was happening. I managed to land feet first, but crumpled to the ground in a heap, gratefully pulling air into my poor abused lungs.

The athame, still in my hand, had not lessened its strength. If anything, the flames grew taller. I held it aloft like a torch in the old Indiana Jones movies. Given that I faced off against a giant snake, I thought that was rather appropriate. If my ribs didn't hurt so much, I might have laughed at the image.

Instead, I forced myself to stand and face the serpent. I took a step forward, pushing Apep back toward the wall. He hissed again and recoiled, rearing back away from the fire in my hand.

"Go back to where you came from, abyss snake." The words burned as they left my throat. I slashed the athame through the air, diagonally, as if drawing a line from the creature's head to the tip of its tail.

With a squeal, Apep disappeared.

I turned to face the room. "Who's next?"

CHAPTER 37

The room fell silent. The dogs sat in a rough semi-circle around me, tongues lolling, goofy grins on their faces. Beyond them, the central fire burned. Hecate and Knum stood off to the left, she with a smirk on her face while his mouth gaped open in surprise. Aegir stood near his throne with his arms crossed, eyebrows furrowed in a glower, while Rán held on to Ezra's arm so tightly his skin was turning white where her fingers gripped his forearm. On the other side of the fire, Enlil still sat with his feet propped on the table. I don't think he'd moved at all. He stared at me with eerie contemplation.

The flames on the knife faded, as if the gas had just been turned off.

Just then, the doors opened. Dion pushed a barrel through the mouth of the leviathan. Everyone turned to look. As if hearing the silence, Dion paused. Looked up.

"Anyone order more mead?"

Ezra started laughing. A soft chuckle at first, then a deep belly guffaw. I felt like I'd been hit by a bus, so I didn't find it amusing. I ignored Dion and limped my way toward Ezra and my mother, still gripping the athame in one hand, while the other tried to hold my ribs together.

"Stay right there," Aegir ordered. "Come any closer, and I will end your brother's life."

"Pfft," I replied. Each step jarred my ribs, and one foot dragged a little as I struggled to keep moving. If I stopped, I wasn't sure I'd be able to start again. Besides, it wasn't like I could do any harm to Aegir. I couldn't send him home. He already was home. I *could* escape myself, but not without Ezra. And I'd promised Tempest and Dion to get them out of here as well.

No, I had to keep moving. I had to stick with the plan, as formless as it was. I needed to remind my mother of who she was and what she really wanted. She might not deserve my forgiveness, but I could use her misguided maternal instincts to my advantage.

"You dare disrespect me in my own demesne?" Aegir's voice roared through the hall.

Under other circumstances, I would have been terrified, but all the fear had bled out of me after facing Apep's fangs. This place was the worst. Sure, the drinking hall had been fun at first—Mr. Navy had been a good dancer—and the feast looked tasty. If I'd been invited as a guest, I'm sure I would have enjoyed myself. As a prisoner who'd been nearly crushed to death by a giant snake and whose brother had been transformed into a lobster-man, I would rather go to actual hell.

"Honestly, I'm too tired to play nice," I replied, dragging myself another step. "You stole my mother, kidnapped my brother, morphed him into some kind of strange chimera, imprisoned me in a room without doors or windows, tried to get me drunk so I'd feed your power, and after all that, you want me to be *polite*? Pfft."

"Oh, this really is going to be good," Enlil mock whispered

as he took another loud sip from his mead glass. "I'm so glad I decided to attend."

"And here I thought *I* was going to be the one to irritate Aegir to a temper," Knum replied. "I had it all planned out and everything. Seduce the new lady, convince her to leave with me, rub the victory in Aegir's beard . . ."

"Why is it that you bovidae creatures are always so randy?" Hecate asked.

"Have you never watched the sheep in the field in the spring?"

"Meh. Livestock never interested me."

"Nor me," Liluri said from her seat at the end of the table. "As dramatic as all this is, I have no desire to remain for the fireworks. I shall take my mead and go. Farewell." She waved a hand and the barrel of mead in front of Dion disappeared in a swirl of snow, along with the ice queen.

Several of the other gods seemed to agree, popping out of existence as if they'd never been present in the first place.

I kept walking, ignoring as much of the gods' banter as I could. I'd covered about half the distance from where Apep had disappeared to where my brother stood, still in Rán's grip.

Thunder rumbled in the distance. Waves crashed against distant cliffs I'd yet to see, a storm brewing outside Aegir's Hall. The man with the coral crown shifted forward, moving to stand between me and my family.

"Daughter of Lilith, you have desecrated the sacred Feast of Renewal. You have defied my orders not once, not twice, but three times," his voice rose in a wild crescendo. "You. Will. Stop." The floor shook with what could have been an earthquake, except each rumble was so perfectly timed with Aegir's words.

"No." I replied. Simple. To the point. No use arguing. Years at the institute had taught me one thing, and one thing well. There was no arguing with crazy.

In a flash, Aegir transformed. His face elongated and hinged wide at the jaw, revealing the rows of sharp pointed teeth of his water-based form. His body expanded and grew, reminding me of the scene in *Aladdin* when Jafar turns into a genie. His head nearly touched the beams overhead. A hand swept down, fingers reaching out to grasp me.

"No." I said again. I wasn't about to let my ribs get even more bruised. I lifted my puny little knife between us, once more thinking of the Lilith sigil and drawing it with my mind. The silver blade lit from within, a light so bright it was blinding.

Aegir flinched back. "You will stop, or I will take your brother to his final death."

"No!" This time, it was Rán who stepped up. Finally, her protective instinct kicked in. "That is enough. You will not harm a hair on my children's heads!"

Aegir spun on her, towering over her in a menacing hunch. "How dare you defy me? I have given you everything! A second life, a crown, the power of creation, and the return of your children. I have fixed your son and built him a new body out of the Aether. I have drawn your daughter here to your side, where, at last, you can teach her the ways of her ancestors."

"You will not touch my children. Their souls are their own."

Aegir scowled at the lot of us. Still in his genie-ish form, he stretched himself to his full height, at least two stories over our heads. He extended an arm. A gold trident appeared in his hand, crackling with energy.

With a flamboyant twirl, Aegir pointed the trident at Ezra. The middle prong sizzled, gathering and focusing the energy from the other two points. "I am ruler here. I will decide the fate of the souls in my demesne. The living and the dead."

"I said, no!" Rán physically placed herself in front of Ezra. She lifted her chin and squared her shoulders. She stretched her arms wide, palms flat and facing Aegir. The air in front of her rippled in a heat haze.

A bolt of energy released from the trident and slammed against Rán's shield. Her body jerked as if she had taken the blow to the stomach, but she remained standing.

"Try that again and you will face *my* wrath, Aegir," she grunted.

Surprisingly, the woman moved up a few notches in my eyes. I had hoped she would step up, but I hadn't expected her to do it quite so dramatically. Maybe she was stronger than I realized.

"You are *mine*. All of you are mine! I found you; I shaped and protected you. You cannot turn on me now. I will not allow it!" Aegir launched another bolt of energy, and a third.

Rán took the impacts, absorbing the energy into the shield. Sweat dotted her brow. Her face scrunched in a pained grimace. By the fifth bolt, Rán was bent at the waist, hands still in the air, like Atlas holding the world. But with each bolt, Aegir shrank in size. By the seventh, he was almost back to human size. He was expending too much energy too fast.

Transferring the trident to his left hand, Aegir reached out with his right toward the fire. At first, I thought he was going to somehow take energy from the flame. I glanced where he was pointing. Tempest and Dion stood together near the spit, along with two other daughters. All four watched us with wide eyes and horrified expressions.

Dion's body spasmed. His skin rippled. Tempest clutched at him, holding him up as she tried to place herself between her father and her brother. She took a blow to the back, and her face slackened.

Aegir was stealing their essence.

"No!" It was my turn to yell. I lunged forward, ignoring my injuries and throwing my hands out. I gripped the athame in my fingers. The light that glowed within the blade extended out like a whip, severing Aegir's connection to his children.

I scrambled to put myself between Tempest and Dion and extended my hands. I had no clue what I was doing, but figured if I just mimicked Rán, maybe it would work. That's how kids learn to walk, right?

"Fire opposes water," Rán said. "It is the wild to liquid's order. You must channel heat to counter Aegir's spirit!"

I had no idea what she was talking about with the wild and the order, but the fire part made sense. With the athame in my right hand, I drew a line from the fire at the center of the room across my body. I circled my arm around, pretending like I was creating a vortex of flame in front of my face. The athame seemed to understand what I wanted, because it pulled the heat out in front of me. Soon, I was as parched and sweaty as if I were doing hot yoga in a steam sauna.

Aegir screamed his frustration as his connection to his younger children failed.

"Abdulbaith, end her," he ordered. "Take her spirit and drain her. Send her soul to me."

"With pleasure, father," the Sharktopus-man replied.

CHAPTER 38

Sweat beaded my brow and my arms shook. The shield was holding, but it took every ounce of concentration I had in me. Even on a good day, I wasn't great at multitasking, and this was not a good day. My ribs ached, my face throbbed, I could still taste blood in my mouth, sweat stung my eyes, and I'd been awake for . . . I couldn't even tell you how long.

Abdulbaith approached, riding on his tentacles like a spider instead of the sea creature that inspired his form. His mouth split open in a grin that literally spread from ear to ear, leaving his shark teeth on full display.

"I can see the family resemblance now," I quipped. "Daddy's favorite little boy, eh?"

"I am the eldest son of the elemental of the sea."

"Don't care much for your siblings, then?"

"They are of weaker stock. Diluted. Unable to claim their heritage."

"Unable? Or just unwilling to turn into a deranged monster? I mean, you have to admit, your look is pretty creepy. Even at the Trident the girls kept their distance."

"Your friend Gabi didn't seem to mind. She would have given herself to me if not for your interference." Abdulbaith was close now, just a few feet away. I stepped back, closer to Tempest and Dion, still hunched together next to the roasting spit. I wasn't going to be able to fight him. Even if I knew how, I couldn't stop him and keep up the shield that prevented Aegir from regaining his power from Dion.

"To you? I thought you worked for Aegir."

"Of course. I am a harvester."

"Then why doesn't Aegir harvest from you? You should give yourself to him, as loyal as you are. Right?"

"I am no longer a peon. I am self-sufficient."

"And yet you still do his bidding."

"I am loyal."

I pressed my lips together in a disbelieving frown. "If you say so."

"You will say so when I siphon your soul to Aegir's feast, then eat your heart."

Well, that was graphic. I glanced around the room. "I'm already at Aegir's feast. Honestly, underwhelmed."

Abdulbaith lunged. I closed my eyes and braced myself for the impact. Something swept by my shoulder. I flinched away and the impact I expected never came.

I peeked an eye open.

Tempest stood to my left, holding the iron skewer from the spit like a spear. The remains of the whole roasted boar were still impaled on the stake but had slid to the bottom end and helped prop the spear at an angle, right into Abdulbaith's chest.

How had he failed to avoid it? He frowned, looking down at his chest and touching the entry point with his fingers, as if he couldn't believe he was bleeding. To be fair, neither could I. His tentacles flailed against the ground, trying to push his body up and off the makeshift spear. He managed to rise a few inches, but slipped on his own blood, instead managing to fall even farther down the metal.

"Father?" he whispered, his voice weak.

Aegir spun to face his son, turning away from Rán and Ezra who he continued to batter with energy blasts. His eyes widened, taking in all that had happened. In an instant, he shoved power into Abdulbaith with one hand, extending his other toward the only remaining available source of power in the room, Eldoris.

Bitch Queen groaned and fell to her knees but did nothing to stop the drain. Her face slackened, and eyes dulled. She slid to the floor and lay on her side in a fetal position, while her mouth gaped open like a fish pulled from the water. I would have felt sorry for her, except that even in her diminishing state she glared at me with hate in her eyes, as if I were the one causing her pain.

Still, Aegir couldn't feed Abdulbaith enough energy to keep pace with his death. As Sharktopus-man's tentacles slowly drooped toward the ground, Aegir also weakened and shrank, prolonging Abdulbaith's life for mere moments with the loss of his own power. With a final gasp of air, the eldest son and greatest minion of Aegir died a final death.

Aegir fell to his knees with a sob. Returned to his fully humanoid form, he crawled to the mangled corpse as a frail old man. Despite his weakened state, I kept my distance as he approached, pushing Tempest and Dion behind me. I didn't trust that he was truly as weak and enfeebled as he seemed.

"My son," Aegir groaned. He lifted a limp tentacle in his hands. The body hung from the spear, caught between the weight of the half-carved boar and his own feet. Aegir wrapped his arms around the corpse and pulled, trying to dislodge it from the makeshift weapon.

"Help me," he commanded no one in particular.

Tears streamed from Eldoris's eyes, but her body remained

prone on the floor. Her appearance had shrunk in on itself, looking more like a desiccated mummy than a living, breathing person. I couldn't say how much of her identity remained, but it wasn't enough to understand or aid her father.

My mother and Ezra stayed back, her arm outstretched to keep my brother in place, not that I thought he would or even could help the sea god. One of the smaller claws tapped a mindless syncopated rhythm on the floor, drumming his anxiety into the still room.

The other elementals had fallen silent at last, their quips and heckles no longer appropriate in Aegir's fall. Most had returned to wherever they came from, leaving only Hecate, Knum, and Enlil to witness Aegir's sorrow. However, they, too, seemed unwilling to interfere, even in the care of the body.

Rán Número Uno rushed in, limp hair streaming around her face along with her tears. She stopped short of Abdulbaith's body, her hands reaching up to cover her mouth. She shook her head, slowly at first and then faster, until, at last, broken sobs erupted from between her fingers.

"Nooooo," she moaned and fell to her knees. Her hands stretched toward her motionless son as Aegir struggled to bring him down on his own. "How could you do this? How could you let this happen? He was the best, the strongest of all your progeny. He was our finest creation. *How could you*?" She buried her face in Abdulbaith's blood-drenched shirt, effectively thwarting Aegir's efforts. The pair collapsed at the feet of their lifeless son.

A hand grasped my shoulder and I nearly jumped out of my skin. I'd been so preoccupied with the scene in front of me, I hadn't been paying attention to what was happening behind me.

Tempest stood with Dion and her sisters, gazing at me with sad eyes.

"You have to go. Quickly. While he is still weak. Once you are home, he won't be able to hurt you directly."

"I'm not leaving without Ezra, or the two of you." They had helped me. I would keep my promise and protect those who had protected me.

Tempest smiled sadly. "It won't work. Dion can't go. Aegir took too much from him already to allow for the crossing."

Dion leaned against his sister with a vacant expression. Like Peithon when I first met him, his skin was sallow and lax, the circles under his eyes pronounced. Even his hair seemed duller and drained of life.

I glanced back at Ezra. His brow furrowed in resigned anguish as he took a few uncoordinated steps toward me.

"You can't stay, Lil."

"I'm not leaving without you."

"Good!" Rán clapped her hands together in childish glee. "Then it's settled. You'll all stay, and we'll all be a family together."

"Are you fucking kidding me?" Ezra swung around to face her, fists clenched. Tension radiated across his shoulders. "After all this, you think we're a family?"

His words were icily furious, so cold they stung.

Rán flinched back. "I don't know what you mean."

"You left us for a megalomaniacal fish-man, kidnapped us, turned me into a monster, put your daughter in danger, and stole our lives, and you think we're going to be a family?" Ezra stepped forward, his eight legs clacking ominously on the golden tile floor. His shoulders pushed back, and he towered over the woman who had once been called mother.

"I was only trying to help. To take care of you." The sound of waves crashing against distant cliffs echoed around us, louder than before.

"I'm thirty-fucking-two years old. I don't need you to take care of me. You don't know me. Not anymore. You forced this on me, gave me no choice, and now you act like the savior. You're mad!"

Rán's lip trembled. "You don't appreciate my sacrifices."

"You've sacrificed nothing. You've done nothing but serve your own interests and those of your new benefactor. I may be forced to stay here, but you are not my mother. Not anymore."

With visible effort, Rán pressed her lips together and straightened her spine. "Well. If that's how you feel."

"How I feel? You've never cared how I feel. You've never cared about anything outside your own head."

Thunder rumbled overhead. The floor began to shake. Dust rained down from the rafters.

"That's enough. You've made your point. You don't want to be here." She pointedly sniffed and refused to look at any of us.

"Of course not." Ezra stamped one of his legs. "This isn't my life. It's worse than actual death."

"This death is too good for you." The words grated and crunched, like stones on the beach. A shudder wracked Aegir's body and a crack radiated across the floor. His head lifted just enough to watch us from the dark recesses of shadowed eye sockets.

Fear coursed through my body, and I squeezed the handle of the athame, ready to defend myself with whatever ability I retained.

"There's no time for this." Tempest pushed at my shoulder, urging me away from my brother and toward the leviathan doors. "You have to go. Already Aegir is retaking his power, shrinking the demesne into himself."

One of the columns split in two. A wicked smile lifted Aegir's lips. Tempest shoved me again as her sisters sprinted for exit, Knum, the ram-headed god, close on their heels. Dion still clung to Tempest's shoulder, but even in his witless state he seemed to be leaning toward the doors.

"Trust me, you don't want to be present in the coming storm."

"She's right," Hecate's gaze was trained up at the ceiling, which continued to shower us with a steady trickle of dust. "You can't stay here."

"Come," Rán interrupted "This way. All of you." She waved a hand toward the corner of the room behind Aegir's throne, opposite the front doors.

I hesitated, glancing toward the leviathan's maw and possible escape. I didn't trust Rán, didn't know where she wanted to take us, but I couldn't leave Ezra.

The rafters above us groaned. I took a step toward the leviathan doors.

"To be unbound, Ezra must go to the primordial waters. If you want any hope of returning to Earth, we have to reach them before Aegir shuts the way," Rán shouted over the growing noise.

I narrowed my eyes, suspecting a trick, but the ground rolled beneath my feet, and I stumbled in her direction. More cracks appeared in the floor and walls. One of the leviathan's inlaid shell scales launched across the room. Pressurized water sprayed through the gap it left behind to soak the last remaining barrels of mead.

Rán waved her hand, impatiently urging us all toward the back.

"You would release him?" Tempest shouted, hope lacing the words. She didn't know my mother.

Rán's lips puckered in a sour frown. "I won't keep him against his will."

The building gave another ominous rumble. Aegir stood, shoulders hunched and knees bent, skin hanging loose from his bones in the wrinkles and folds of the extremely elderly. The eerie thump of a heartbeat vibrated beneath my feet. Aegir's body pulsed. The golden tile beneath his feet shattered.

"No one leaves," Aegir growled.

"Go. Follow Rán," Hecate shouted as the floor shuddered again. She whistled and her familiars trotted obediently to her side. She mounted smoothly, before the horse had even stopped moving, and patted the animal on the neck in reassurance. "Her intentions are honorable."

The cracked column crumbled like dry rot infested wood and the pile sent up a plume of moldy-smelling splinters. The black mare danced sideways, the whites showing around her dark eyes.

I stared at the goddess in red, thoughts whirling. Could I trust her? She was of the Aether, too. Hecate smiled. "I will see you soon, I'm sure. Now go."

Enlil, the brooding elemental who'd been first to arrive, flicked a hand and a gust of wind slammed into me, forcing me toward the woman who had once been my mother. Tempest and Dion stumbled at my side, all of us unable withstand the gale.

"I have waited for this opportunity for eons," the dark-haired, dark-eyed god twisted his lips in a wicked smirk. "I will contain him while you escape. I look forward to meeting you again someday, Daughter of Lilith."

CHAPTER 39

With a crack that nearly blew out my eardrums, a bolt of lightning arced from ceiling to floor. The smell of ozone and burned hair whipped toward us on a wind of Enlil's making.

I sprinted for the nondescript door at the back of the room. Rán had a white-knuckled grip on the handle, using her weight to hold it open. Ezra had already gone through. I pushed Tempest and Dion ahead of me, into the dark and damp of the primordial cavern.

I took one last look behind me as I crossed the threshold. Enlil stood in a vortex of spinning debris; his hands stretched wide toward the floor. Lightning sparked within the cloud. As I watched, a bolt arced out and zapped Aegir, who grunted and fell to one knee.

Meanwhile, Hecate rode in a circle around Aegir, chanting words I could feel but couldn't hear over the raging storm. A ring of light glowed on the ground, connecting each hoofprint as her horse beat a rhythm on the floor. When the circle closed, the light expanded upward, arching over Aegir's head in a dome, hiding him from view.

Rán slammed the door shut and whispered a word. The door and its frame disappeared, leaving nothing but a blank stone wall.

"We'll be safe here. Aegir won't diminish the primordial waters. He can't. But I don't know how long the others can hold him." Rán whispered, but the words echoed with eerie clarity.

"Why are you doing this?" I blurted. I didn't mean to look a gift horse in the mouth, but I didn't understand what had changed. She'd been so determined to keep us here, to make us a 'family' again, it didn't make sense.

Rán's shoulders slumped, and she pressed her back into the wall behind her. The corner of her lip trembled in defeat.

"I can't let him take you. I wanted my family back, but not like this. I never meant to hurt you or Ezra, and I certainly don't want you to hate me. I just wanted to make it all better."

"So you give up? Just like that?"

Teary eyes searched my face. "I was hoping—am hoping—that this isn't the end. I'm not giving up, just looking for a new way forward, to become the woman I want to be, rather than the woman I've become."

"You want forgiveness?"

"If you can, but I'll take acceptance if that's all you have to offer."

"Only if you're offering the same."

"I'm trying."

"Then unbind Ezra. Accept that he is satisfied with his situation, that he excels at what he does. Let us go home and live our lives the way *we* see fit. Don't let Aegir or any of the so-called gods control us."

"For the first, that's why we're here. But that last bit is more complicated than you think." Rán paused, taking a deep breath before ushering us toward the eerily motionless underground lake. "Aegir is the guardian of the primordial oceans. As his wife, I am now bound to his cause. My fate is tied to his."

"But you're also a Daughter of Lilith. You can't be tamed."

Rán's tilted to the side. She swallowed and her eyes flicked toward the ground. Tear tracks still glistened on her cheeks. "But I have been. I can't escape now. But I can—and will—help you escape."

"Awesome, let's go." Ezra interrupted. "I don't want to stay in this underwater hellhole a second longer than I have to."

Rán sighed, motioning toward the water. "Very well. Dion will take the place of Aegir in the water, and you must be on the island for this to work. Can you swim there on your own?"

Ezra gave our mother an incredulous look. "Even without a lobster tail I could swim at least that far."

"So long as Aegir doesn't increase the distance without warning," I muttered.

"Yes, we must hurry." Rán's eyes drifted out of focus, as if she were looking at something inside her head. "He is still weak, but the other elementals are expending more energy than they can recoup outside their own demesnes. They will have to release him soon."

Tempest led her brother with a hand on his arm, guiding him toward the edge of the softly glowing water as Ezra began the swim toward the island.

"May I see your athame?" Rán asked as we waited for Ezra to reach the far shore. She bit her lip, face pinched as if expecting a rejection.

I hesitated, but she was finally helping us, and I needed all the help I could get. Maybe she could tell me something useful.

I held it out without a word, and Rán's expression cleared with relief. She took it gently from my hand and held it up to the flickering lantern.

"This is goddess made. Finely crafted and powerful. It's no wonder you were able to channel and absorb so much power so quickly, with so little training." She paused, flipping it over and examining the inlay in more detail. "My mother once told me that a goddess-made blade was a blessing and a curse, powerful and dangerous. Be careful with this." She handed it back to me.

"You had an athame. Before . . ." I let my words trail off, giving us both time to remember that night and the blade that had nearly ended my life and Ezra's, and the events that had led to her presence here.

"It was my mother's, passed down from my grandmother. It was lost after . . ." she cleared her throat. "Anyway, it's gone. But I don't really need it here."

"Why didn't you teach me any of this? Why hide so much from me?"

"I read the myths to you. Gave you the legends of the gods. But you were so young, so innocent. My mother trained me almost from the day I was born. I never had a childhood, never experienced life without seeing the spirits of the Aether or the fear of being obtained and controlled. I thought if I could take that burden from you when you were young, let you grow up a bit first, that you might be more balanced than I was. I thought I had more time. But I will teach you as much as I can, now."

Rán gazed out over the water, watching Ezra as he climbed out onto the rock of the central island.

"He's strong," I told her. "Stronger than I am."

Rán shook her head. "That's not true. He takes his strength from you. You cut away his fear, and later his depression. You made room for him to experience joy, even in his pain, and see himself as a whole person. You're a good sister."

"He was never not whole."

Rán dipped her chin. "You are better than I."

My throat tightened. I didn't know what to say.

Ezra cupped his hands around his mouth. "I'm ready!" he shouted. "Let's get this done and get home already!"

"Will you be alright?" I asked my mother. I was taking everything from her, everything she had worked for in the last fifteen years and leaving her to face an ocean god that would most certainly want vengeance.

Bittersweet sadness etched her face as she turned toward me. "I'll be fine. Will you come visit now and then?"

"Will Aegir let me, after all this?"

"He will, or he'll face my wrath. Again."

I chuckled. "I guess that's enough. Tell him I'm sorry about Abdulbaith. I never meant for anyone to die . . . or I guess, end their existence . . . over this. I only wanted Ezra to be able to come home. To live his life."

"Like I said. You're a good sister." Rán smiled sadly and turned back toward the water. She lifted her hands. The water began to churn, the waves spiraling around the island, but clockwise this time.

"There are five elements that make the world," Rán murmured as the waters spun faster and faster. "Earth, Air, Water, Fire, and Spirit. Each has an opposing force and combines with two others. As daughters of Lilith, we work primarily with fire and spirit. Those are our elements to control. Some daughters have gained strength in other elements, I'm told, though I never learned it." Rán grimaced in shame. "Truth is, I wasn't much of a student. I wanted to be normal."

"Whatever that means," I replied.

Rán chuckled. "I wish I'd had you for a sister. In any case, fire will split the spirit from Ezra's body, water will wash him clean. That will be Dion's job."

"Does he know that? He's a little . . . vacant."

Rán shrugged. "I'm hoping it will be instinctual since he is Aegir's son. Because he is in a weakened state, he should call the spirit back into himself."

"Will he be the same after? I mean, still the same Dion?"

"I don't know. I hope so. I assume so. Aegir animates the spirits in his demesne. Without him, none would exist. The daughters and sons are semi-independent because they are half human. He can take from them, but they can also gain their own power."

"Like Abdulbaith."

"Right. But the spirit attached to Ezra was intentionally left mindless. It was a just a container to hold a piece of Aegir's energy, enough to give Ezra the ability to walk again."

"Then why the lobster form?"

Rán shrugged. "Aegir is an ocean elemental. The creatures of the sea are all he knows. He couldn't directly fix Ezra's spine, only support it."

"So the lobster is what? A prosthetic?"

"Essentially."

The water was spinning in a vortex by now. Dion sat on the edge of the drop off, Tempest still at his side.

"It's time," Rán announced. "Tempest you must get out of the water, and Dion must be fully submerged."

"He'll drown!" Tempest protested.

"He won't. The current will lift him."

"Are you certain this will work? Are you certain he'll still be my brother?"

"Yes," Rán lied. I glanced at her out of the corner of my eye, trying not to give anything away. She lied to save Ezra. To bring him back to himself so we could go home. I hoped we didn't regret it.

Tempest nodded, though her expression still looked uncertain. She guided Dion the rest of the way into the water. The current caught him and tore him from her grasp, sending him whirling around in the water. He grinned like a child on a rollercoaster. I almost expected him to shout "whee!"

As soon as he was in the deepest section of the torrent, Rán pointed the first and second fingers of her right hand toward Ezra like a pretend gun. The muscles of her jaw clenched and unclenched as she stretched toward the rocky island. Ezra's back arched. With a resounding crack, the lobster legs split down the middle. He screamed.

"Ezra!" I shouted, unable to stop myself.

"Stay there," Rán warned.

I struggled to do as she said, watching in horror as the process that bound my brother to the Aether was reversed. The spirit peeled away from Ezra's human body. His legs collapsed beneath him. Primordial water washed over the stone, taking the demon back into the liquid where it had been birthed.

The current caught it, pulling it in toward the deepest water where Dion floated and spun. At first, it looked like the two would miss each other entirely, spinning at the same speed on opposite sides of the circle, but then Dion slowed, or maybe the spirit sped up. Dion reached out his hands as if to catch the creature for a bear hug. As soon as the two touched, the spirit wrapped itself around Dion and sank into his skin, leaving behind a soft blue glow, like the bioluminescent waves I'd watched with Silas.

Silas. I hadn't thought about him almost since I'd left, but now I could hear the call of his trombone. I could almost see him in my mind's eye. My eyes closed. I was so tired.

"No!" Rán shouted. "Not yet. Hold on Lil. You must wait for Ezra."

My eyes snapped open. She'd caught me just in time.

"I'll get him," Dion called. He swam with sure strokes toward the island, pulling my brother into the water in a lifeguard's hold. The distance between the island and the shore seemed to shrink as Dion approached. Tempest helped pull Ezra out of the water, the two carrying my unconscious brother between them.

My eyelids were heavy, so heavy. I swayed on my feet.

"She's nearly spent," I heard Rán say. "She's being called home, but I don't know how. She doesn't have an anchor."

"Yes, she does," Tempest replied, curtly. "Here. Take Ezra, Lil. You have to get him home."

I staggered under my brother's weight as she draped him over my back and gently tugged his arms into place over my shoulders. I'd never given my big brother a piggy back ride before. Now I knew why. He was *heavy*.

"I promised I'd take you, too," I grunted. "Both of you. Dion, you good?"

The bartender nodded. "Better than good. I've never felt so full of energy."

"Don't rub it in." My eyes drooped, but I wasn't about to let go. Not yet. "We're all going back."

"You don't have the strength," Rán replied. "You'll never make it."

I swallowed, stiffened my spine, and slapped myself across the face to wake myself up. "I keep my promises." I held out my left hand.

Tempest's gaze searched my face, but Dion just twisted his lips in the wry half smile he gave to all his customers and grabbed my forearm. At last Tempest followed suit.

CHAPTER 40

We made it. I crashed to the floor, Ezra on top of me. Something wet and sticky squelched beneath my cheek. Tempest groaned at my side, Dion echoing her from a little farther away.

A guitar squealed and the trombone melody that had called me home fell silent. Gasps ricocheted around me.

"What the hell?" a man's voice shouted. I recognized that voice. Who's voice was it? I couldn't remember, but I knew it was supposed to mean something. Knew that whoever it was, I was in trouble.

"Help," I gasped. Ezra's weight pressed into my back, making it hard to breathe. I couldn't do anything about anything until someone got him off me.

"Lil?" Silas's words carried over the silence of the room. A crash of metal on metal, running footsteps. All I could see was the dirty wood plank floor. I blinked and the next thing I knew, Ezra was being pushed off me. My brother groaned. His eyelids fluttered but remained closed.

I sucked in a grateful breath and tried to push myself upright, but I was too tired. My arms and legs didn't want to move. Honestly, if it hadn't been for the fact that the floor clearly hadn't been mopped recently, I might have curled up and taken a nap.

At last, I managed to get upright. Sort of. Mostly. My head weighed ten tons. Every breath hurt. My eyelids drooped. I blinked again and my head jerked me awake.

Silas was there. He gathered me into his lap. My head rolled back so I could see his face. Dark stubble lined his jaw and his battered old fedora had been knocked askew. Concern pinched the corners of his eyes. I reached up to awkwardly pat his cheek and smiled drunkenly. Though I wasn't drunk. I didn't think.

"Missed you." The words cracked. My throat was dry. I licked my lips and swallowed, tasting blood.

Silas lifted an eyebrow. "You look awful."

He tried to brush a hair off my face, but it stuck to my skin. I must have looked like hell. I sure felt like it.

"Lil, what the hell? You're late." I finally recognized the voice. It was Chaz, the owner. He stomped into view, hands on his rather robust Hawaiian shirt clad waist. "Two *days* late."

"'M sorry." I mumbled. "Couldn't be helped. Had to get Ezra."

My eyelids dropped again.

"Can't you see she's injured and exhausted?" Silas demanded.

"How'd she even get in here? How did any of them get in here? Where'd they come from?" Chaz asked. "And why in god's name is he wearing a loin-cloth?"

"Does it matter? She's back, thank god."

"Which one?" I muttered. "Too many." No one heard me. Or at least, they didn't respond. My eyes were still closed, so I couldn't be sure either way.

"Out of my way!" Grams's voice carried over the mumbling, milling crowd, and startling me enough to lift my eyelids. She came in like a storm, the force of her will cutting through the lookie-loos and moving them out of her way. She peered over Silas's shoulder, bright eyes taking in everything. A purple haze gathered in a cloud over her shoulder, not touching her, but hovering like a nosy neighbor.

"You sure had an adventure, didn't you?" Her tone was reproachful, but the grin belied the reprimand. "But you survived and held your own. Good girl. Sadly, you forgot one very important rule: take a nap!"

"'M trying," I blearily blinked up at her. "They're all very loud."

"Yes. Well." She placed a hand on Silas's shoulder, opposite where I still rested my head. I just couldn't drum up the strength to move. "Silas, you're taking her back to my house. Her brother and her guests, too. They can rest up there while we figure out what happens next."

"No." Chaz shoved a finger toward Silas. "You're finishing your set." He jerked his hand toward me. "She's fired."

"You fire her and I quit," Silas replied. "The band won't play another minute. Ever."

A few voices protested from somewhere behind my head, but no one outright disagreed.

"You'll have to fire me, too." Bruce's deep voice reverberated from farther away to my left.

"And me. She saved my life," Virginia declared.

"You can't seriously try to tell me you're sticking with that ridiculous story. Amphibious monsters with octopus legs—"

"Tentacles!" Surfer Jeff loudly interjected.

"—and shark teeth don't exist. She didn't show up for work, went on a bender, and now she's fired."

"An ice pick couldn't make a dent in that thing!" Ty proclaimed.

"Because it wasn't real! It was rubber or foam or something. Ya'll are nuts if you think otherwise."

"Then why did Carlos quit? And Ferghus?" Gabi demanded

with a snap of her gum. As annoying as it was, I'd missed that sound. "Even if it was just a guy in cosplay, like you say, it was still a traumatic event. I almost didn't come back either, except I have student debt up the ass and can't afford to quit."

"This can all be decided some other time," Grams interrupted. "Right now, she needs rest. Probably a few days of it. And you're going to give it to her."

There was an unmistakable sound of command in her voice. Chaz made a strangled gurgling sound, like he'd swallowed something the wrong way before acquiescing. "Fine. But if she wants to keep her job, she'd better be back here to open on Tuesday."

Arms lifted me into the air, but I reached for Ezra. My eyelids fluttered open. "He needs his chair."

"I'll carry him," Dion picked Ezra up as if he weighed little more than a big dog—which I knew was absolutely not true—and gently maneuvered him into position over his shoulder. I was grateful for the extra care. The last thing Ezra needed was to wake up with bruised ribs or a banged-up head.

Like me.

My fingers drifted to my face, and I winced, finally recognizing the throbbing pain across my right cheek and nose, where I'd connected with the floor in Aegir's Hall. Apparently, what happened in the Aether didn't stay there.

"Does it hurt?" Silas asked. "It looks like it hurts."

"Of course it hurts, Silas. She needs rest, and time to recover. All you lot, follow me." Grams declared. "Everyone else, back to it. Nothing to see here. Nothing to notice or remember. Have a wonderful evening." She waved her hands and the hovering purple cloud spread out across the crowd. Wisps of violet air surrounded heads and reached into noses and ears. Everyone returned to their conversations as if they had never been interrupted in the first place. Even Chaz turned away without another word, distracted by a customer's order and ignoring everything else.

The last thing I remember was the sound of the band—minus their trombone—and a gentle rocking as Silas carried me out of the Trident.

CHAPTER 41

S mell reached me first. Coffee and sugar and spice. The scents of a baker's kitchen.

Then sound. Whispers in the distance, trying to be quiet but arguing over something.

I was in a big bed with a heavy blue and gold comforter. The memories wafted into my brain. It took a few minutes, but finally I placed it. I was in Grams's house, in her guest bedroom. Silas had brought me here from the Trident.

At last feeling somewhat centered, I slipped out of the sheets. Almost as soon as my feet hit the floor, the voices stopped. I wiggled my toes in the stiff nap of the oriental rug, a little apprehensive about what I would find in the other room.

Would Silas be here? Was Ezra okay? Did Bruce and Gabi and Ben remember Aegir's Hall? Would they think I was crazy?

And what about Tempest and Dion? What were they going to do now that they were outside the Aether? I imagined, even as half-humans, they would need food and shelter, which meant a place to stay and a job to afford it. Or something.

Still sitting on the bed, I dropped my forehead into my hands. I'd gone from zero responsibility except for myself, to worrying about everyone around me. I didn't want any of this, and yet I couldn't go back to sticking my head in the sand and ignoring the demons that swirled around humanity. Now that I knew what they could do, what they really were, I couldn't just forget about it.

I rubbed the heels of my hands into my eyeballs, trying to dislodge the headache that perched at the back of my brain. I squeezed my eyes closed, then opened them again. Pressed my hands onto my knees.

I was still wearing my work uniform, the now-disgusting black pants and tank top I'd been wearing since Abdulbaith attacked the Trident.

When was that? How long had it been?

I sniffed my armpit and grimaced. It had definitely been a while since I'd had a shower, that much was certain.

A soft knock on the doorframe drew my attention.

"Hey, sis." Tension radiated in tight lines from the corners of Ezra's eyes as he poked his head around the door.

"Ezra!" I jumped up to greet him, but a head rush had me sitting back down quick before I blacked out.

"It's okay, don't get up." My brother wheeled himself into the room. "How are you feeling?"

I smiled at the nimble twisting of his chair as he maneuvered himself into position. Much better than the awkward lobster legs Rán and Aegir had given him. "You got your chair back."

Ezra shrugged. "It's my old one. From a few years ago. Dad brought it over. He's in the other room."

Shit. I kept myself from saying it out loud, but barely, and Ezra must have read it on my face anyway.

"I know, but he wants to see you. He wants to check on you."

"As if he cares what happened. What really happened . . ." My words trailed off. Ezra might not remember things the way I did. He might think it was all a terrible dream, or a nightmare. But then, how would he explain being here in Grams's house?

"You've been asleep for about twenty hours. Moaning about bitch queens and sharktopus-men. It's five o'clock on Sunday. Just in time for dinner with Dad."

I shook my head. "Nope. Not going."

It was one thing to accept my mother's actions. Her attack had been an accident. She was trying to help, trying to make things better. Dad hadn't wanted to deal with me, had never believed in nor supported me, and instead had locked me away with the cutters and the rich kids with drug addictions.

"He just wants to check on you. He's been worried."

Because I had called him to find Ezra.

"What did you tell him?" It was as much as question about what he said, as about what he was willing to remember.

"I covered as best I could. I said I'd been out on the boat with Tempest without cell reception, and you lost your phone and had been visiting out here for a few days. It's not too hard to believe."

My lips twisted to the side. "Right."

"He wanted to talk to you, and I kept putting him off, but eventually I had to tell him something."

"And now he's here."

"Lil, you can't tell him what really happened."

I lifted an eyebrow.

Ezra rolled his chair forward so we were knee to knee and leaned in. "I remember everything. No one else does—I mean, Tempest and Dion do, but they hardly count. Your boyfriend—"

"He's not my boyfriend."

"He wants to be. Anyway, the guy out there that's been waiting for you and watching out for you, that guy knows you disappeared. He knows you have an ability, but he doesn't know exactly what that is. He doesn't seem to care. Then again, he grew up with Grams, and that lady makes you look downright normal."

"What precisely do you remember?" I had to be sure we were on the same page, remembering things the same way. If not . . . well, I hated keeping secrets from my brother, but I would if it meant saving his sanity.

"You don't have to hide from me, Lil. I know our mother is bound in another dimension. I know you can travel between the realms as easily as walking through a doorway."

"It's not that easy."

Ezra's mouth pulled to the side in a half smile. "Yeah, well I guess that's why you've been asleep for an entire day."

"And I still feel like shit."

"You look like it."

"Thanks so much."

"Grams is out there arguing that you need your rest. She's somehow managed to hold Dad off—quite an impressive feat actually. She's an interesting old lady."

"I'm aware."

"Anyway, she kept him from barging in here, but now that you're awake you have to go talk to him. He won't leave until he sees you."

"Fine. But I can't go out there looking like this."

"Fair enough. Grams put stuff for you in the bathroom. I'll tell them you'll be out in a few minutes."

"Wait! What about Tempest and Dion? Where are they?"

"Silas drove them to the marina. Tempest's boat is there, and she and Dion can live on it until they find someplace better."

"Grams wouldn't let them stay?"

Ezra shook his head. "They insisted on leaving. Dion seemed a little . . ." Ezra's gaze drifted to the ceiling as he considered his words. "Overwhelmed, I guess."

"Makes sense."

"But you'd better get going and get out there before Grams eats Dad for dinner."

I chuckled. Given what I now knew of Grams and the Aether and the Daughters of Lilith, I could almost imagine her shifting into a dragon to bite off his head.

CHAPTER 42

T he mirror did not reveal a pretty picture. My face was puffy and bruised. Dark blue-black circles hung beneath my eyes and greenish-blue splotches spread down my right cheek. If I said I'd been in a barroom brawl, no one would question it.

It wouldn't even be too far from the truth. After all, what was Aegir's Hall if not an underworld bar? And Apep had certainly put up a fight.

A glint of silver caught my eye, and I turned to find a stack of clothes and a towel on a stool behind me. On top, the goddess-given athame gleamed in the bright white vanity lights.

I touched the blade with a single finger and traced the Lilith sigil in the handle. It was real. It was solid. I hadn't imagined it, or anything else. If I had needed proof—which I didn't, not really—but if I had, I held it in my hand. I had brought Hecate's blade home with me. It was mine.

Carefully setting the blade on the bathroom counter on a spot where it wouldn't get wet, I sorted through the clothes. I found a clean pair of jean shorts and my favorite blue three-quarter sleeve henley top folded neatly on top of a plush white towel. Someone had raided my apartment for clothes. I hoped it had been Ezra and not Silas, given the bra and undies discreetly hidden between shirt and shorts. Regardless, it was a thoughtful touch.

After a quick shower I felt infinitely better, even if I didn't look it. Without a sheath or anywhere to stash it, I gripped the athame in my hand and prepared to enter the fray.

Grams faced off against my father, he on the couch, she on a stool at the kitchen pass-through. Ezra had rolled himself next to Silas, who sat in an overstuffed easy chair in the corner, out of firing range. No one spoke.

"Well, this looks cozy and warm," I quipped.

All eyes snapped toward me. Silas grinned and jumped up, but Dad was closer. The man who claimed to be my father rushed forward as if to give me a hug.

I stepped back and lifted my empty left hand, stopping him before he could touch me. I didn't need that man's approval, and I didn't need his pity. "I'm fine."

"Clearly, that's not true."

"Actually, for the first time in a long time—maybe ever—it's precisely true."

Dad frowned and his jaw clenched. "You disappeared for two days, off on a bender, just like your mother." Disgust dripped from every word, but it was fear that I saw in his eyes. "I knew you'd hit bottom eventually. You need help, Lil. You always have."

Grams, spry old lady that she was, was off her stool with a finger jammed into Dad's shoulder in an instant. "Now listen here—"

"It's okay, Grams. Let him get it off his chest." As much as my dad's words hurt, they weren't unexpected. In fact, I would have been more shocked if he'd said something loving and supportive. That would have been a first. This was old news and old pain.

I lifted my chin and stared into my father's eyes as he pressed into my personal space.

"Is that who you want to be? How you want to live? Never to be able to have a normal life?" He demanded. "Like this old hermit, completely off the grid with no family to speak of?"

"She has me," Silas interrupted.

"As if some twenty-something *musician* is capable of being anything but a freeloader himself."

I tilted my head to the side and squinted, as if seeing my father for the first time. A pale gray demon, thin and hazy to my sight and less formed than the typical lust or party demons I encountered in the bar, rode on my father's shoulders. It had poured itself over my father's figure like a second skin. Maybe that's why I'd never seen it before. It was so thin and unfocused it was almost undetectable.

My athame warmed in my hand, reminding me of the power I held. I could free my father from the demon's influence. I could sever its connection to his spirit and give him back his free will.

"I'm not normal. I'm not even sure what that means. And this life that Grams has built might seem isolated, but it's filled with purpose." I lifted the blade, pointed it at the demon feeding off his insecurity. It drove him to control everything and everyone around him, even at the expense of driving away those he loved.

Dad's eyes narrowed, but he lifted both hands and stepped back. "Are you threatening me?" His voice was low and tight, scared and commanding, furious and fearful.

"No. I'm freeing you."

I rubbed my thumb across Lilith's sigil and focused on the sickened creature that haunted my father. With a slice of my goddess-forged blade, I severed the demon siphoning his spirit and sent it back to where it came from.

I grinned. I was getting better at this. "You're welcome."

My father gaped at me, his expression frozen. I wondered briefly what it would feel like to have your sense of self returned. Would it be a relief? Or would it feel like something was missing? That demon could have been riding him for years. Probably had been.

"And now you can go," Grams put a hand on my father's shoulder and guided him toward the door. "You should really say thank you. I know some who charge thousands of dollars for that kind of spiritual cleansing."

"Thank you?"

"See? That wasn't so hard now, was it." Grams patted him on the back. "I suggest a hot shower and a stiff drink while you reevaluate your relationship with your daughter. Self-reflection can be painful." She opened the door and pushed him out onto the porch. "Have a lovely day."

$$)O($$

As soon as the door shut, I sagged onto Grams's evacuated stool. Whatever energy I had restored with my "nap" was gone. A headache pounded behind my eyes. My stomach rolled. I put a hand to my mouth, hoping I wasn't about to barf all over Grams's antique oriental rug . . . right in front of Silas.

"What were you thinking?" Grams stood in front of me, hands on her hips. "You haven't rested nearly long enough to refuel your spirit from your walk through the Between, and now you go expending your energy for a man who clearly has no respect for you or your talents."

My stomach heaved. I lurched toward the bathroom. Luckily, nothing came up but a bit of stomach acid. There probably wasn't anything else in there.

I lay my cheek on the cool tile floor.

"Here. Swallow this." Grams held a spoon within my eye-line. "Honey and ginger. You've overexerted yourself. Spent too much energy and now you're paying the price. I warned you to take a nap."

"Nobody likes to hear 'I told you so,'" I replied after swallowing down my medicine.

"Yes, well, all the same, I told you so."

"Thanks."

"For what, dear? You did all the work. Too much work, I'll grant, but I did nothing."

"You watched for me. You brought everyone home."

Grams rubbed a circle on my back. "No, dear. You did that. You did it all. I only made sure the idiots didn't interfere by giving Mnemosyne a bite of their memories."

"Mnemosyne?"

"Yes, dear. Goddess of Memories. I called on her to hide you from the children of Eve. No one at the Trident quite remembers what happened the night you were taken or the night you returned. Except Silas, of course. He can be trusted to keep your secret."

"But my friends . . . they were in Aegir's Hall. You called them back with the sigils—"

"That you drew and fueled. And good work, too. All I did was guide the soul to its body at the right time to prevent true death. In all honesty, between that and the Aether jumps, and walking the Between, I expected you to sleep for at least another twelve hours. As it is, we need to get you back to bed."

Grams put her hands beneath my armpits and heaved me upward. For an elderly woman, she was strong. Pulling my arm over her shoulders, she walked us toward the guest bedroom.

"But won't they remember the journey? What do they think of me now?"

"Mnemosyne is the goddess of memory for a reason, dear. She records and remembers the histories of the world, but she loves a good plot twist now and then." Grams shifted sideways so we could pass through the doorway. "You know, it's nice to have someone else in the house again. I didn't think I wanted an apprentice, but I hadn't realized how isolated I'd actually become. Your father wasn't wrong about that." She pulled the covers over me, lightly tucking them in. "With all this activity, I almost feel young again."

"You're the youngest Grams I've ever met," I mumbled. I meant it as a compliment but wasn't sure it came out quite right.

Grams chuckled. "Yes, well. Enjoy your rest. I'll have something ready for you to eat when you wake."

"Is Silas . . ." I trailed off.

"I'll send him in."

My eyes drifted closed, but a few moments later, Silas opened the door. "Lil?" He whispered. "You wanted me?"

He had no idea.

I scooched over to make room and patted the top of the coverlet. Silas sat down gingerly. His hands twitched, moving from his knees to the covers and back as he tried to figure out where they would be safe.

I put him out of his misery, covering his hand with my own when it was in range. "I want to thank you." I paused, trying to figure out the right words.

"I didn't do anything."

I gripped his hand a little harder and gave him full eye contact. As always, the warm brown depths drew me in, and my stomach fluttered. "You believed in me. You've never made me feel like a crazy person."

He shook his head before I'd finished the sentence. "You're not crazy."

"Maybe. Maybe not."

"You're different. Unique. And that's a good thing. A great thing."

I had to swallow the lump in my throat before I could say another word. "Not everyone sees that. Thinks that. Most—"

"Your dad's an ass, but Ezra's a good guy."

"Until now, he's the only one I could trust. Which is why, again, I'm saying thank you. I don't think I would have made it back without you." My smile was a little wobbly, but I hoped he understood what I was trying to say.

My brother had been the only person in my life I felt connected to. When my mother stole Ezra from this world, she thought it would force me to come to her, that we would have no choice but to join her in Aegir's Hall and be the 'happy family' she thought she wanted. Silas had given me options. He'd been the anchor that bound me to this world. The bond might be tenuous and fragile, but it was there. And it had been enough.

Silas brought my hand to his lips and kissed my knuckles. For such an outdated, awkward gesture, it felt oddly natural. Tingles swept up my arm from the warmth of his breath. "Any time." He smiled. "But I'd better let you sleep before Grams comes in and yanks me out of here by one ear."

My eyelids were drooping. "See you when I wake?"

"I won't go far. Sleep tight."

I felt Silas's weight disappear and heard the door snick shut, but I was already asleep.

CHAPTER 43

It was a Tuesday. Slowsville. Thank the gods.

Even after thirty-six hours asleep and another full day in bed resting, I didn't need any more excitement. Silas had driven me to work straight from Grams's house, only stopping at my apartment to grab my last clean Hawaiian shirt. My other one was lost to the Aether, but Grams had helpfully washed my black pants, tank, and other unmentionables. No need for Silas to see that. At least, not yet.

I smiled, thinking of the man who had hardly left my side since I'd stumbled back into the Trident. He hadn't hovered, hadn't pushed. He'd just been there when I needed him. Grams and I had listened to him practice in the canyon while she baked muffins and I drank my coffee. He'd eaten lunch with us and then waited while I got ready for work. I'd always valued my independence, but being out there with them, in the hidden wilderness . . . it just felt natural. Easy. No expectations. No demands. He dropped me off with a wink and another quick kiss to my knuckles and left to rehearse with the band in Ben's garage.

Chaz was in his office when I arrived, still grumpy about my bike in his space and my unexplained absence. Well, I explained it—sort of—but he didn't believe me. That was okay. With everyone else backing me he didn't have to believe me. He just had to let me keep my job.

So I would be perfect tonight. No broken glasses, no messes, no bar fights, and most of all, nothing strange happening at the Trident. I prepped the garnish, wiped down the counter, set up the glasses and bottles at my station just how I liked them. Nothing to distract me, nothing to stumble over. Easy.

My hand drifted to the athame on my hip. Grams had given me a black leather sheath with a belt attachment that I could wear over my pants. It was black, my pants were black, and the knife handle was black, so it almost blended in. Chaz hadn't noticed it at any rate. After what had happened with my dad, I felt better keeping it with me.

The front door opened. Virginia skipped inside, Gabi close on her heels.

"I'm so glad you're back!" Virginia practically launched herself over the counter to give me a hug. I smiled, unable to help myself.

"I'm glad to be back." I still didn't know what she remembered of our adventure in Aegir's Hall, but I didn't know how to ask. "But what are you doing here? You're not on tonight."

Virginia let go and slid back until she was just leaning on the counter. "No, but I had to check on you. Silas sent an update, said you slept for nearly two days! I had to see you with my own eyes. After that bar fight, I'm shocked you're not taking the whole week off."

I glanced at Gabi, who was wrapping a half apron around her waist. "Bar fight? What happened?"

"You tell us! That guy in the octopus costume grabbed you and left. Where'd you go? What happened? How'd you get away? Who was he?"

I held up a hand to stop Virginia's endless questions. "It's a long story, and I'd rather not relive it if I'm being honest."

Besides which, I had no idea what they remembered or how they remembered it. Grams had said Mnemosyne had "eaten" their memories, but I didn't know exactly what that meant. I'd rather avoid saying anything until I was certain I was saying the right thing.

"Don't suppress the trauma," Gabi urged. "If you need someone unbiased to talk to, I can ask my professor for a referral. PTSD is a real thing."

"I know. I'll think on it." I wouldn't. I'd had enough of therapists for three lifetimes. No one ever believed me anyway. "So you guys are okay?"

"Thanks to you," Virginia replied. "I'm just thankful he didn't have a gun. It was bad enough that he knocked out Bruce. He was a big dude."

"Evil," Gabi added as she took the chairs down off the tables.

Virginia visibly shuddered. "For sure."

The door opened to the sound of laughter. I was saved from responding by our first customers of the day.

Gabi greeted the new arrivals as I finished setting up the garnish. Virginia leaned in close over the counter. "So Silas stayed with you all weekend . . ." she let the sentence trail off, clearly searching for information.

I laughed. "At his Grams's house. It was definitely not romantic." Sweet, but not romantic. Or at least, not sexy times romantic. Maybe we'd get there, but I'd give it at least a few dates first.

Still, it was good to know some things—like Virginia's proclivity toward gossip—hadn't changed.

L ater that night, when the crowd had grown to just over a handful, Surfer Jeff slid onto a bar stool. "Crazy night last week."

My hand paused its wipe down as I glanced up at him. "I'd forgotten you were there."

He'd been in the corner, hiding under a table. Abdulbaith either hadn't seen him or hadn't cared. "The craziest part about it was how little I actually remember."

"Right? It was all such a blur. I think I've already suppressed the memories." I chuckled, but it sounded nervous, even to my own ears. Luckily, Surfer Jeff didn't seem to notice. At least, he moved onto another topic.

"Did you know, there's a theory that zombies are real, but they're not dead?"

I frowned, confused. "Really?"

Where was this going? Surfer Jeff liked his fun facts of the day, but they usually had a point.

"Mm-hmm. See, there's a drug called burundanga. It's used legitimately in anesthesia, but crime syndicates have figured out how to use it to control people. Cancels their free will and makes them pliable."

"And they think this is what creates zombies?"

"Maybe. Some of its major side-effects are memory loss and confusion. Combined with other things, it causes twilight sleep and hallucinations."

"Crazy."

"All it takes is someone blowing it in the air or dropping some in a drink."

"Yikes." I didn't know what else to say. "Do you think that's what happened? What the cosplay guy did?"

Surfer Jeff shrugged. "Who knows? We live in crazy times, my friend."

I lifted an eyebrow and nodded. "Crazy times."

Surfer Jeff lifted his empty glass into the air. "So here's to the zombie, back from the dead." He grinned. "And speaking of which, can I get another?"

I laughed. "One Zombie, coming right up."

THANK YOU FOR READING

Thank you so much for reading *Aether Bound*. I hope you enjoyed the story as much as I enjoyed writing it!

Want even more? **Join Haskell's Heroes**, my approximately bi-weekly email newsletter where I share progress updates, short stories, current inspirations, reading recommendations, and anything else I think of.

Plus, just for signing up, you'll receive *Ezra's Story*, the subscriber exclusive epilogue to *Aether Bound*, where Ezra tells Lil what happened in Aegir's Hall while she was gone.

www.MeganHaskell.com/SubscribeEzra

In addition, if you're up for it, I could use your help. Independent authors like myself are at a huge disadvantage because we don't have a big publisher pushing our books out to their networks. We rely on readers like you to share our books and spread the word. So if you have a moment, could you leave an honest review on any sites where you purchase or find the books you want to read? Even a star rating and a few words about what you liked or didn't like could make all the difference.

The more you talk about a book, the more you share, the more successful a book will be. It all depends on you!

About the Author

Escape into Myth, Magic, and Mayhem

I've been a fantasy reader for as long as I can remember. I've always loved joining extraordinary adventures in the written word, imagining myself alongside heroic men and women, fighters and warriors who strive to improve the world, or at least kill the bad guy. Ensconced in the safety of my bedroom, I explored strange lands with dangerous creatures. It was an addiction I was happy to accommodate, especially when my mom wanted me to do my chores.

A West Coast native, I'm living the dream of writing while raising two daughters in Orange County, CA with my husband and our ridiculously energetic dog.

Join me, and let's fight some bad guys together.

Shop my store for signed paperbacks and swag! https://www.MeganHaskell.com/shop

ACKNOWLEDGMENTS

A book may be written in isolation, but it takes a team to publish something worth reading. At least, it does for me. Even the first draft often requires a sounding board to bounce ideas and work through the rough spots in the plot. Which is why I'm so honored to have a robust group of people to help with *Aether Bound*. Endless thanks are owed, but here at least are a few of them.

First, I have to thank my husband. Without him, I'm not sure I would have ever started writing. He has encouraged me every step of the way, despite the fact that he doesn't read fantasy (he's a sci-fi, space opera, kinda guy.) He patiently listens to me prattle on about the book industry, and gives great advice on plot fixes, cover critiques, and every step in between.

As always, my sister, Kim Peticolas, editor extraordinaire, has been a phenomenal resource. She has helped me work through writers block, critiqued my early drafts for story problems, and fixed my typos. If you need an editor or author consultant, she's a fantastic choice, and I'm not just saying that because she's my sister. (www.kimpeticolas.com)

In addition to letting me grow up in a household that encouraged reading and introducing me to Tolkien at an impressionable age, my mom and dad have both been a supportive foundation for my writing efforts. They are early beta readers and proofers, going through the books in detail to help make sure they're the best they can be. I would get a lot more things wrong if it weren't for their help.

Aether Bound is set in a tropical beach bar, a location I enjoy visiting but an industry I have never had the opportunity to work in. Since Lil is a bartender, I leaned heavily on my good friend Scott Cushman (www.cushtender.com) to fill in the gaps of my knowledge. As a bartender and cocktail historian, he's been an invaluable resource. He's also a really funny guy. You should go check out his YouTube channel to see what I mean. Thank you Scott, for all your help, and please forgive any remaining mistakes. They are one hundred percent my own.

Many individuals have given input into *Aether Bound* as early beta readers, advanced reviewers, typo hunters, and cheerleaders. I couldn't produce at the quality I strive for without them. Specific thanks to M'lissa, Stacey, RQ, Katie, Natalie, Tonya, and Jen for their first draft feedback. And to Carmen, Lisa, and Tom for their eagle-eyed proofing!

To my writer friends around the globe, thank you for always being there to discuss books and plots and stories and process and goals and achievements. The writing community never ceases to amaze me.

An extra special mention must go out to my partner in crime at The Author Wheel, Greta Boris. I can't wait to see what we do together.

Last, to all my fans who have encouraged and supported my efforts over the years, I wouldn't be doing this if it weren't for you. Thank you from the bottom of my heart!

ALSO BY MEGAN HASKELL

THE SANYARE CHRONICLES

The Last Descendant

The Heir Apparent

The Rebel Apprentice

Guardian: A Companion Novella to The Sanyare Chronicles

The Winter Warrior

THE WAR OF THE NINE FAERIE REALMS

Forged in Shadow (Book 1)

Quenched in Secrets (Book 2) - Coming Soon!

THE AUTHOR WHEEL

(NON-FICTION FOR WRITERS BY G.C. BORIS AND M. HASKELL)

Publish: Take Charge of Your Author Career (Second Edition)

The Author Wheel Quick Guide to Productive Writing Habits: How to
Set Goals You'll Keep and Make the Most of Your Writing Time

Made in the USA
Columbia, SC
19 February 2023

12527856R00193